The El Paso Summer Series - Book 3

Dave Owen

Ash Grove House Press™
Dallas

Published by Ash Grove House Press

For more information contact the publisher at

Ash Grove House Press

PO Box 830973

Richardson, TX 75083

www.AshGroveHousePress.com

The Ash Grove House Press logo is a registered trademark of Ash Grove House Press

Cover art and book design by Chris Owen and Plaid Bison

Summer Camp Danger: An El Paso Summer Series novel by Dave Owen

First United States edition, Dallas, Texas

Ash Grove House Press 2024

ISBN: 978-0-9996453-6-9 (Soft Cover)

ISBN: 978-0-9996453–7-6 (Hard Cover)

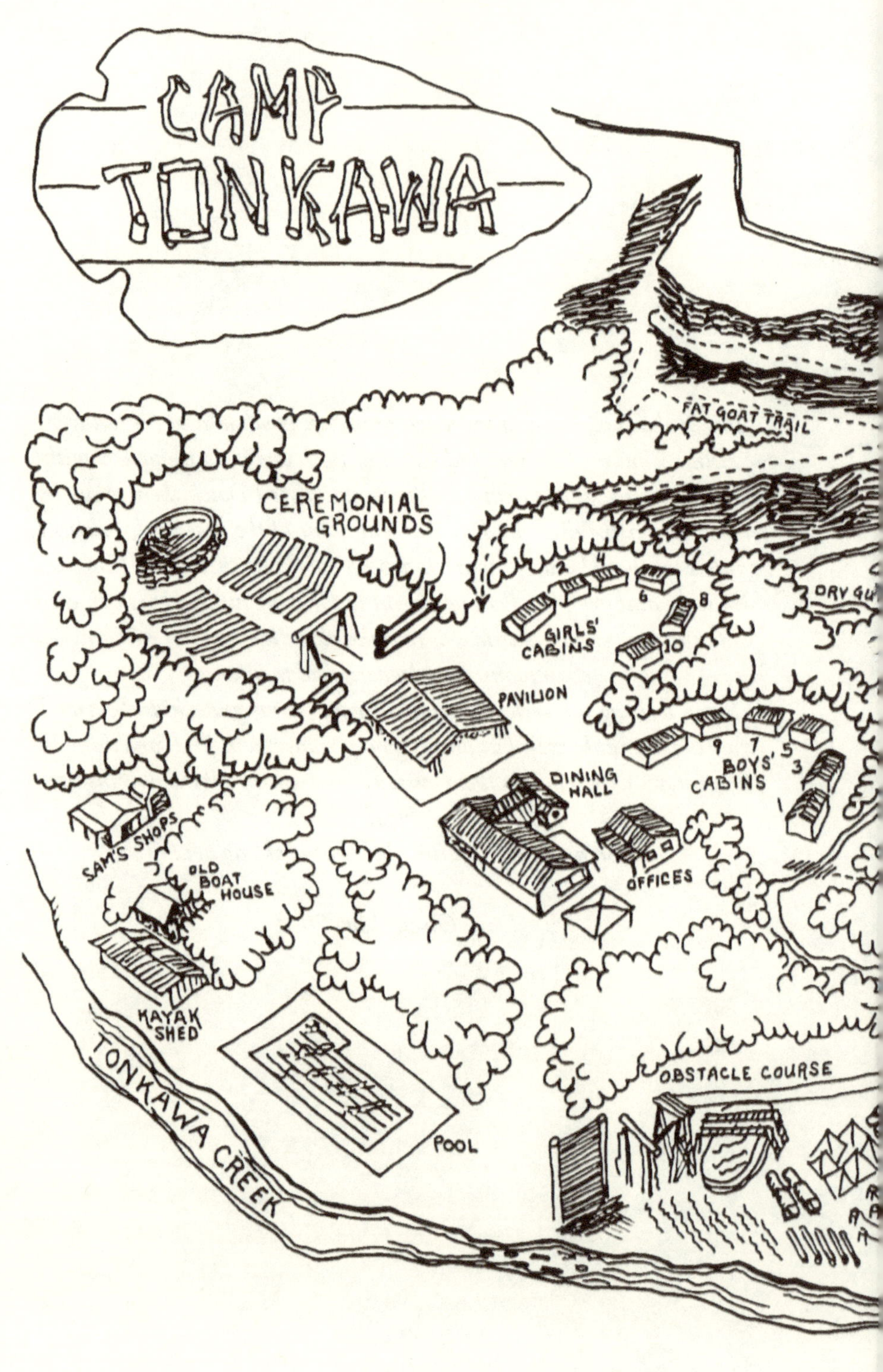

CAMP TONKAWA
FAT GOAT TRAIL
CEREMONIAL GROUNDS
GIRLS' CABINS
2
4
6
8
10
DRY GU
PAVILION
BOYS' CABINS
9
7
5
3
DINING HALL
SAM'S SHOPS
OLD BOAT HOUSE
OFFICES
KAYAK SHED
OBSTACLE COURSE
POOL
TONKAWA CREEK

OLD UPPER PASTURE
FARM-TO-MARKET ROAD
BRIDGE
GHOST RIDGE
GHOST RIDGE TRAIL
LOW WATER CROSSING
TRAILS
BUZZARD'S PEAK
COLORADO RIVER

1

———

"I'M SINKING!"

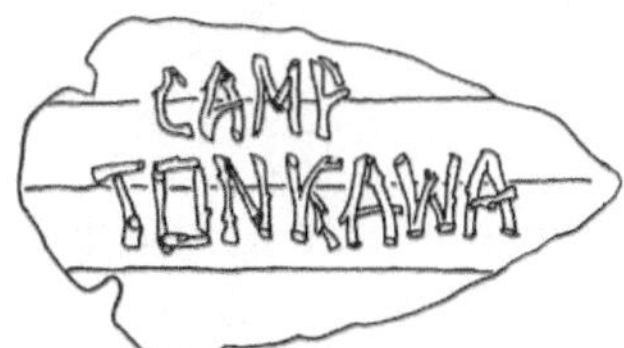

Mackenzie shoved the left end of her paddle deep into the water and tightened her grip to give the kayak a powerful starting stroke. She immediately shifted her focus to the blade on the opposite end of the paddle and repeated a firm, long stroke on the right. She could feel the water moving behind her as she got off to an early lead in the championship race to decide the best kayaker for the girls' cabins at Camp Tonkawa.

Close beside—yet slightly behind her—was Cassie, the racer for Cabin 10. Cassie had handily won against two other girls yesterday afternoon to make it to the final. Mac had only just managed to win her final race yesterday at the last moment, winning by about two strokes and eighteen inches to qualify as the other semifinalist. Tomorrow, the boys would have their turn.

She dug her paddle in again, determined to beat Cassie to the colorful string of flags strung across the river ahead of them. The race was downstream with the current but that didn't matter. The only way to win was to have the fastest and the deepest strokes. From the shore, she could hear the campers from Cabin 8, her cabin, cheering for her, calling out her name and chanting, "Go, Mac, go! Go, Mac, go!"

She glanced sideways and saw this was going to be very close all

I

the way, so she tried to get everything she could out of each stroke. But as she was changing from her left to the right, Mac noticed water in the bottom of her kayak. Not just a little bit—like the drips that drain off as you paddle left and right—no, she was actually sitting in water! She struggled to push through another full stroke but could hardly move the little boat forward as it became heavy and filled with water.

Cassie pulled ahead and Mac tried again to inch her boat forward, but it was pointless—she was sinking . . . right in the middle of the river where the water was the deepest. *This isn't supposed to happen!* she told herself. KAYAKS DON'T SINK!

But the lightweight yellow craft was no longer floating swiftly on top of the river. Instead, it was now like a log drifting with the current. Mac had no real control of where it was going and watched helplessly as the river spun her around backwards. She knew she needed to get out and swim to shore but she felt stuck and was struggling to get her legs out. As the kayak spun around again, she saw Cassie, now several lengths ahead, cross under the flags and heard her cabinmates cheer for her victory. But the cheering lasted for only a moment, because now everyone could see what was really happening. They were all yelling and pointing and shouting advice as Mac continued to sink.

As she floated under the flags—faster now that the river was narrowing and the current was picking up speed—she felt her boat scrape some rocks and spin around again. The next thing she remembered was a hard, jarring shove to her gut. She had struck a large pecan tree that had fallen across part of the river during the spring storms. Now it was creating a trap, a whirlpool current, for anything that floated under it. After the thud of her kayak wedging under the fallen tree, the current immediately flipped her over and plunged her head into the water.

Mac fought to free herself from the water trap. For a brief moment she felt helpless and disoriented—upside down under water, in spite of her life jacket. In her panic she was finally able to kick her legs free of the little yellow boat and bob up to the surface. She gasped a lungful of air, coughed, and then screamed, still totally disoriented and confused, bobbing in her lifejacket. But before she could figure out where the bank was, the fast current grabbed her and pushed her further down the river, banging her quickly through the big rocks of the Devil's Rapid. After the rapids, the current popped her free of the rocks and into a wide, deep pool of water. She finally felt her panic subside. As she drifted more slowly, now in calmer water, she turned onto her back to float and begin to swim toward the river's edge.

"Hang on, Mac!" she heard a voice call from somewhere behind her. She spotted Cassie in her red kayak coming up alongside her. "Grab ahold of my paddle!" she shouted. Mac did and suddenly she felt the worst was over.

"Can you grab onto the strap on the back of my kayak? If you can, I'll paddle us to shore."

Mac held onto the strap and drifted behind as Cassie's boat pulled her into the shallow water near the bank. The kayak beached on the rocks at the edge of the shore. "You okay, Mac?" Cassie asked as she tossed her paddle onto the shore and quickly climbed out to check on the girl from Cabin 8 who had almost drowned.

"Yeah. Yeah, I think I'm okay," Mac said, sitting in the shallow water. "Just confused. How does a kayak sink?" Mac shook her head and looked back up river, then smiled at Cassie. "Thanks! Thanks for getting down here to me." She wiped her wet face with her hand and looked upstream again, at the rocks and beyond.

"Sure," Cassie said. "Sorry I couldn't get to you before the rapids."

"Probably just as well—we'd both have ended up in the water, right?"

"I imagine so." Cassie glanced up along the shore. "Looks like the counselors and the camp nurse are just about here." She pointed to a group of adults running along the riverbank trail. She shook her head and looked back at Mac, then smiled. "I guess we'll need a rematch tomorrow, huh?"

Mac laughed as she pulled her wet hair out of her eyes. "Yeah. You're on. Assuming my kayak doesn't sink again." They both laughed and stood up to greet their rescue party, each of whom was carefully making their way down the side of the muddy riverbank to the gravel shoreline. *What just happened?* she asked herself. *Kayaks don't sink!*

______

WHAT JUST HAPPENED?

Big Mike had been leaning back in his chair with his feet on his desk, staring out his window when the door to his office opened. He quickly changed positions and stood to meet Mac, Cassie, and their two cabin counselors as well as Chuck, the resident director of Camp Tonkawa. "Hi, everybody. C'mon in and have a seat," Mike said. He pointed them toward steel folding chairs that looked like they'd been in his tiny office for several decades as Chuck moved behind Big Mike's desk to lean against the wall in the corner.

Mac looked around nervously and slid her feet out of her lime green flip-flops. The bare concrete was cool to her feet, which was a good thing since it was approaching 102 degrees. She almost wished she was back in the river to cool off.

"So, first of all, Mac, let me say how sorry we are for what happened out on the river this morning." Mike looked behind him at his boss who nodded his head enthusiastically as if their apology might somehow help avoid their being named in a lawsuit. He looked at Cassie and added, "And thank you, Cassie, for being such a heads-up camper and going after Mac when she tumbled out of her kayak out there."

Tumbled out?! Mac winced as she heard her near-drowning now described as a "tumble" into the river, but she didn't say anything.

Mike Murkowski was the sports director and camp manager—basically Mr. Chuck's number one guy. All the camp counselors reported to him, but the only time he wanted to talk to a camper was usually if they were in serious trouble. Or if someone had called from home with bad news.

Mac and Cassie nodded their heads and looked at each other, then grinned when they figured out they weren't in any trouble. The incident on the river had been scary this morning, but by lunchtime the two of them were already becoming legends among their fellow campers. But it was still intimidating that she and Cassie had been summoned to meet with Big Mike, Mr. Chuck, and their counselors.

Big Mike leaned forward with the stubby fingers of his hands laced together and his elbows on the desk. "Mac," he said, slowly now, "did you notice anything strange about your kayak this morning?"

"No," she said, "except that it sank—and kayaks don't sink." She glanced at her counselor, Leslie, who grinned back.

"True enough." Mike nodded in agreement. "But, I mean, was there anything unusual about the way your kayak *looked* when you got it from the shed this morning? Anything at all?"

"Not really," Mac began, and then she paused, recalling the frustration she'd felt when she saw how muddy the kayak was when she pulled it off the rack. "Actually, I was kind of upset," she said, changing her tone to curious. "Somebody hadn't bothered to wash it down yesterday before they stowed it. The bottom of it was covered in dried, caked-on mud. I was running late from breakfast so I just figured it would come off in the water anyway. All the same, somebody was lazy and didn't wash it down like they were supposed to when they put it away."

A knowing look spread across Mike's face as if Mac had somehow answered a very important question. He nodded his head and glanced quickly at Mr. Chuck. "That would explain why you didn't see the holes someone had drilled in a couple of spots along the bottom of your kayak and into both ends," he announced, glancing again at his boss.

"Holes?" Mac asked, confused.

"Yup, holes. We asked Kelley and Leslie try to locate your kayak from the bottom of the river since it's only about ten feet deep there at the bend. They found it and when they pulled it back to shore, we discovered someone had tampered with it. There were five or six half-inch holes drilled in the bottom."

"And the foam flotation blocks in the both ends had been removed," Kelley added.

Mike paused for everyone to register what that really meant. "Whoever did that must have covered up the holes with mud so no one would notice them. As soon as you climbed into the kayak, the mud would have gotten soggy and the water would have pushed it free, opening up those holes. Wouldn't have taken long for it to start filling with water and with no foam—well, you know what happened next."

"Who'd want to do something like that?" Mac asked, now frightened that someone had deliberately messed with her boat before the race.

"Well," Mr. Chuck said, finally getting involved in the conversation, "That's what we were hoping you two could help us with."

"Us, two?" Cassie asked, confused about where she fit into the question.

"Both of you," Mike agreed. "Cassie, was there anyone in your cabin who was so set on your cabin winning the race that they might have sabotaged Mac's kayak?"

"What?" Cassie asked, angrily jumping up from her seat. "No one in Cabin 10 would have tried to throw the race! I wouldn't even know how to do what you said they did. You'd have to have a drill or something—and I forgot to pack mine this year!" she announced sarcastically.

"C'mon, Cassie, calm down and have a seat. Mike's not saying you or someone in your cabin did it." Kelley said. Her cabin counselor put a hand on her shoulder to reassure her. "They just need to ask the question in case someone in our cabin *was* involved, or might have acted like they wanted to interfere with the race somehow. That's all."

"Well, that's just stupid," Cassie said and glanced over at Mac. "We don't cheat. I didn't cheat. It was a race. What would it prove if you didn't win it fair and square?"

"Right. We all like a fair race," Mike said, his voice sounding a little more sympathetic. "What about you, Mac?" he asked, changing his approach. "Can you think of anyone who may have wanted to embarrass you or your cabin? I'm not accusing anyone; we just need to know where to start to figure this out."

"No, no idea," Mac replied. "Like Cassie says, a good race is a fair one. I don't know anyone out to get me, either."

"Who's going to want to hurt Mac?" Cassie added, asking the obvious. "Everybody likes Mac."

Mackenzie blushed and glanced out the window, not anxious to have people talk about her that way. It was embarrassing. "So who would do something like this?" she finally asked. "Has something like this happened before?"

Chuck and Big Mike exchanged a brief glance before Mike answered. "No," he said, shaking his head but looking frustrated for a moment. "No, we've never had anyone try to sabotage a kayak to win a race here at Camp Tonkawa. Ever."

3

1938

Major Hoffmeier turned off the gravel road then carefully eased the shiny green International Harvester pickup truck into first gear before slowly trundling over the steel bars of the cattle guard. He followed the two parallel tire tracks worn into the field which led across his upper pasture. At the far edge of the field he stopped the truck and turned it off, setting the parking brake. Below him, from this ridge line, he could see for miles out across the Colorado River valley. Away, over to the east in the direction of Austin, the sun was climbing into the morning sky. He loved this view. It was his favorite spot on the entire 6500 acre Bar H ranch. Spotting his thermos bottle on the truck seat beside him, he opened the door, picked it up, and climbed out. He held the door open for Duke, his Australian cattle dog, to join him on the ridge.

As Duke wandered off to patrol their favorite spot, the major uncorked the thermos and poured himself a cup of hot coffee. But before he could take a sip, he felt one of his coughing attacks coming on. He quickly set the thermos cup on the truck's hood before doubling over in a series of violent coughs. They'd become increasingly frequent these last few days and would sometimes go on for so long that his stomach muscles would start to cramp. As the episode subsided, he spit out some of the nasty mucus he'd coughed up then and took as deep a breath as he could manage.

He took a quick, short swig of coffee and swished it in his mouth to get rid of the awful aftertaste before spitting it out. *Tuberculosis isn't for sissies* he reminded himself, shaking his head. He took a longer and more enjoyable gulp of the coffee and this time he savored the flavor. *At least living on his own on his ranch meant he wasn't holed up in a TB sanitarium,* he realized once again.

The long rays of the early sun were clearing the trees on the eastern edge of the pasture and starting to paint the tall grass with a magnificent yellow-green color. "He-yaw, Duke!" he called and his dog came bounding back to the truck for his morning treat. He scruffled Duke's head and thought about the TB that was slowly sucking away his life. *What will happen to Duke when I'm gone?*

The dog crunched his hard biscuit then ambled off to sit and watch the perimeter he'd set for himself. Hoffmeier reached into his pocket and pulled out an old arrowhead. He gently rubbed its carefully hewn ridges between his fingers. He'd found it on the ranch one afternoon when he was ten and had managed to hang onto it for sixty years, now.

"Tonkawa." his dad had told him that afternoon when he'd shown it to him. "This was all theirs back in the day," he'd said, looking around. "As far as the eye can see and more."

His younger self had been amazed at that description.

"But that was before my great-grandpa Franz settled here, before the Apache followed the buffalo herds to this part of Texas and made trouble with 'em, and before the Comanches arrived with their horses and drove the Tonkawa further east, out of this valley."

After fingering the arrowhead one last time his father had handed it back to him. "Land belongs to God, son; but if he sees fit to give you a chance to work it, then you take good care of it and do what's right. But don't you ever forget this, Simeon: the Tonkawa were here first."

Hoffmeier held the arrowhead up to the sun and then put it back in his trouser pocket with his pennies, dimes, and two quarters. He patted his field jacket and located the legal document and pulled it out. It was double-folded and bound in a blue legal cover. He opened it and read through it one last time.

His lawyer, Tom Collier, had done a good job. Tom had made it clear that no one would understand what he'd done and everyone would think *he must have lost his mind before he'd kicked off,* but it was the right thing to do. Keep 2500 acres of the ranch for his "project" and sell the rest to fund a family inheritance. He knew his wife—*"God rest her soul"*—would've approved. *But his three children?* Well, he could only hope the cash share he was leaving to each of them would allow his new will and his bold plan for the remaining ranch land to go unchallenged.

Regardless, he was going to do the right thing before he died. He'd remember the Tonkawa Tribe and their people, just like his dad had told him that day. Simeon refolded the document and tucked it back into his field jacket then watched his dog.

The only real question left—and his biggest concern since that day he'd received the TB diagnosis was still, *Who was going to take care of Duke when I'm gone?*

He finished his coffee and recorked the thermos before opening the truck door and tossing it onto the seat. "He-yaw, Duke!" he called out. The dog looked over towards him then sprung up and bounded over to the truck before hopping in to take his regular place on the bench seat.

"Good boy!" he smiled and climbed in himself. He gave Duke's head another scruffle then started up his truck. "What you say we drive over to Burnet this morning?" The dog panted and blinked, his eyes loyally focused on him. *You don't really have an opinion on that, do you? So long as the window's rolled down and your favorite driver is behind the wheel, right?* Duke was along for the ride, anywhere Simeon felt like heading on any given day of any given week.

Hoffmeier smiled and then, after admiring the view once again, he shifted the truck into reverse and backed up to leave. Someday—hopefully—there would be young people enjoying this view as much as he had enjoyed it. More important, they'd be having the best adventure of their lives at a place called Camp Tonkawa.

4

DANGEROUS TRADITIONS

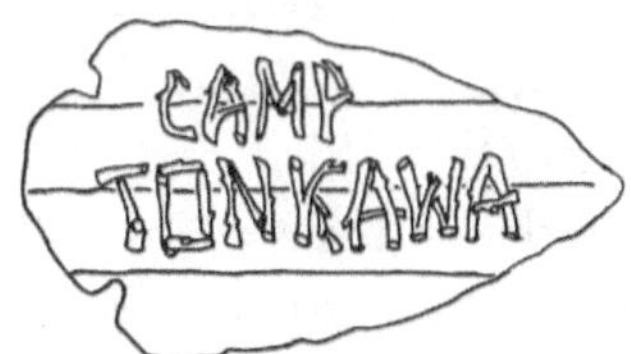

"**M**an, I thought you were a goner when your kayak flipped under that tree!" Tyler said. Mac and her cousin Tyler were sitting at a picnic table with Alex and Monica under the open-air pavilion, working on today's arts and crafts project. They were each decorating their hiking sticks with strings of leather and creative combinations of beads and trinkets.

They'd quickly figured out that Camp Tonkawa was brutally hot by two o'clock every day, so craft time under the shade of the pavilion was a welcome break each afternoon. It was also one of the few "free-time" co-ed activities the campers had each day, and that meant a chance for Mac to catch up with Tyler and their best friend, Alex. She was excited that Tyler and Alex had ended up as cabin mates for the next three weeks.

"Okay, Alex, that looks plain dumb," Monica said as she watched Alex add a sixth strand of silver beads that looked exactly the same as the other five he'd already attached to his walking stick.

"Monochromatic," he corrected her. "Good art can be monochromatic, and that's the look I'm going for. You can do happy-unicorn-rainbows all day; I'm going with a wizard staff."

Monica shook her head and quickly decided it was best to change

II

the subject before Alex started teasing her more about her choice of bead work. She turned to ask Mac about how she and her friends were able to get into camp at the last minute. "So, did that Morrison-Parker lady *really* pay for *all* of you to come to Camp Tonkawa this year?" Monica asked.

"Yeah. I guess she's on the board of directors or something," Mac nodded. "She thought we might like to have a break from El Paso for a few weeks."

"Pretty amazing break!" added Tyler.

"But just as hot as home, if you ask me," Alex noted.

Earlier in the summer, Tyler, Mac, and Alex had been involved in an incident at what they thought was a "lost" silver mine in the desert mountains southeast of El Paso. After discovering a break-in at her Uncle Eric's desert trailer, Mac and Tyler found a map with a riddle left behind by whoever had broken in. Alex had figured out how to decode the riddle and that led them, along with Mac's dad, plus Eric, and Eric's girlfriend to check out an abandoned mine in the desert mountains southeast of El Paso.

The map turned out to be very real and they'd made a surprising discovery in the old mine. But after their discovery the expedition had turned very dangerous. Everyone involved *did* eventually make it home but it turned out that what they'd found in the mine legally belonged to the owners of the old mine: a family foundation that was run by a wealthy philanthropist in El Paso named Sandra Morrison-Parker.

As it turned out, Sandra was a very generous person who took a serious interest in their desert adventure and their story. She'd called last month to invite the three of them to attend the August session of Camp Tonkawa as her guests.

She'd explained to them and their parents that the sprawling, rustic summer camp had been built in the late 1930s above the Colorado River, about fifty miles west of Austin. It had been a cattle ranch for five generations, dating back to the 1840s. "That made it almost as old as the early Texas Republic itself!" she'd noted proudly.

The land had been gifted to be used as a summer camp by Major Simeon Hoffmeier who'd loved the beautiful, rugged setting of his ranch among the limestone ledges of the Balcones. He'd insisted in his will that it should become a living legacy to honor the Tonkawa tribe who originally called the lands of central Texas and beyond, their home.

Over the years the camp had become increasingly exclusive, and Sandra Morrison-Parker freely admitted that was her only real disappointment with the camp. It was very hard to get a spot these days and expensive if you did get in. All the same, those who did come always learned the history of the Tonkawa people, and *that,* she insisted, was an appropriate and lasting tribute to Major Hoffmeier's vision.

Mac had been anxious to tell her best friend, Monica, the news and was surprised—and very excited, to find out Monica was already enrolled for the August session herself! That meant she'd know at least one other girl at camp, which made it less intimidating. Monica said her mom and her two uncles had attended Camp Tonkawa back when they were kids too, so she was considered a "legacy camper." Mac had needed to ask Monica to explain what a "legacy camper" was and found out it just meant that family members of previous campers had first priority for getting in.

Mac suddenly realized she'd been daydreaming and took a quick look around the table to see if anyone had noticed. They hadn't. Bored with the temporary silence, Mac set her craftwork aside and asked a question to no one and everyone. "So, I guess we get to have a do-over on the kayak race tomorrow, right?"

"Sounds like it," Monica answered, looking up from her work. "Ya think you can beat Cassie this time?"

"Only if Mac's kayak doesn't sink on her!" Tyler laughed. He got glaring looks from Monica, Alex, and Mac, and suddenly realized it was still a sore topic. "Sorry. Just thought it sounded funny," he apologized.

"Well, I guess there's no worry about *you* going under," Monica said to him. "That Liam kid from Cabin 7 won both of his races this morning so you'll just be watching the boys' finals tomorrow from the riverbank."

"Yeah, whatever."

Alex was satisfied with his finished work and set his "wizard staff" on the table. "So, what did Big Mike have to say?" he asked, turning his attention to Mac. "We saw that you and Cassie got called into his office just before lunch."

"I'm not supposed to talk about it," Mackenzie said, then added, "so if I tell you, you've got to keep it a secret just between us." She looked around quickly to be sure everyone agreed, because actually, she was dying to tell them what she'd found out.

"The yellow kayak had been messed with on purpose!" she announced with the excitement of a good mystery. "Someone had drilled holes in it. They'd covered the holes up with mud and also pulled out the foam flotation blocks. It was a setup. They intended to drown me."

"Wow," Alex said, his imagination suddenly intrigued. "Sabotage, huh?"

"Yup. Sabotaged!" She paused for effect. "Big Mike wanted to know if I knew of anyone who might've wanted me out of the race or anything. I mean, like—it was totally deliberate."

Monica nodded her head and kept threading another string of beads. "You do know that Cabin 10 wins the kayak race almost every year, right?"

Alex, Mac, and Tyler didn't say anything; they just stared at her. Monica finally looked up. "Well, it's true," she announced like it was a well-known fact. "All the regular campers for the August session eventually figure it out. The best legacy campers always end up in Cabin 10—kind of like a sorority. Big Mike knows their parents expect them to win the race, so the only person who isn't a legacy is usually a new girl, someone who does competitive rowing for their school. They go into that race every year pretty much guaranteed to win."

It took Mac a minute to process what Monica had said. "So, like, Cassie is a plant? She's like some big-time rowing athlete and I didn't have a chance?"

"Well, Mac, I didn't say it always goes their way." Monica said, shaking her head. "Last year Cabin 6 won and everyone in Cabin 10 was really mad. They'd come into camp with this five-year streak going, and it was this *really big* upset to them. Go look at the winner's board and you'll see what I mean."

"That sounds like a lot of trouble to just win a silly kayak race," Tyler said. He wasn't convinced it had anything to do with Cabin 10's history.

"I'm not so sure that's what this was about, either," Alex said, shaking his head. "I smell something more sinister than winning a kayak race. Something as intentional as sabotaging a boat is pretty dangerous. You know, I thought Mac wasn't coming up when I saw her go under. That's a pretty dangerous stunt just to win a race."

Mac stared at Monica, then at Alex and finally at Tyler. Up until a minute ago she'd felt like she was getting over the whole thing. Now that Alex had said how worried he'd been, she suddenly wasn't so sure. *Was someone really out to get me?* she asked herself. She was feeling goosebumps all over again!

5

———————

CAMPFIRE

Mac and Monica were standing in a long, single-file line of girls, waiting for the signal to begin the procession into the campfire circle. While they were waiting, they were trying to decide who was going to be selected as the "feather keeper" for their cabin.

"So, tell me again what the feather keeper does?" Mac asked, still finding it kind of funny to get used to so many camp traditions—but glad to have Monica to explain things to her.

"Kind of like the junior counselor for the cabin. She's the one who'll be in charge of things when the counselor's not around, and all the feather keepers get invited to a special meeting every day after supper to find out what the staff has planned for the next day. Kind of like the queen bee for our tribe." Monica glanced over Mac's shoulder at a girl standing further down the row—there were three girls between them and it was noisy but still she lowered her voice, "Let's just hope they haven't picked Dory," she whispered.

"Really!" Mac agreed. Dory had already started acting like she was the *Most Important Camper* in their cabin and seemed clueless as to how irritating she was getting to be.

"I'm hoping they pick Kaitlyn. I've known her for the past two

16

years and she just barely got beat out by Addie last year. But since Addie couldn't come this year, I think they'll give it to Kaitlyn."

Mac nodded, deferring to Monica's insider knowledge of how things worked. She'd be fine with Kaitlyn, who seemed pretty nice and had been really concerned about her yesterday after the kayak incident. She glanced around at the two long rows of kids, from youngest to oldest, girls' cabins on the left and boys' cabins on their right.

There was a lot of pushing, shoving, and teasing going on in the boys' line, just like when they were in elementary school—and she figured if they didn't go in soon a real fight might break out. "How much longer are they going to keep us waiting to go in?" she finally asked Monica.

"It's always like this," Monica laughed. "But it'll be fun when it starts—just wait and see. It's especially fun to watch the younger campers once it gets dark and the stories start and all the smoke comes out. It gets really spooky for them."

"Hmm," Mac murmured. "I've never gotten into campfire ghost stories; they all seem kind of dumb."

"Yeah, but when it gets dark and there's so many campers and with all the tricks, it gets kind of fun. You'll see." Monica looked back behind them, beyond the campers from the cabin that was a year older than her and Mac's tribe. "There!" she whispered loudly to Mac. "They're coming. The Elders."

Mac looked around and saw four of the counselors dressed in shirts and pants of cream-colored deerskin and long, hairy, bearskin vests, and lots of beads. Three wore a headdress of a deer's head with short antlers. Mac recognized the fourth Elder as Kelley, the counselor for Cassie's cabin. She wore a small, buffalo-looking head with two short white horns and was leading the other three Elders.

"I think that's Charlie from Tyler's cabin carrying the ceremonial torch behind Kelley," Monica said. Since it was late dusk and the sky was starting to get dim, it was getting harder to make out faces.

"I think you're right," Mac said. "And I think the third person is Zoe from the Cardinals' tribe. Who's the fourth guy?"

"Dunno. The face paint makes it pretty hard to tell."

Mac stared and tried to figure out who it was, but half his face was painted blue and half was yellow. He looked like one of those crazy football fans on TV. She thought it might be Carson, but gave up. "Hard to make out," she finally said.

The procession of the Elders had passed beside them and then made their way along the entire line. When they reached the front where the youngest campers were waiting, they paused. They seemed to stand at the entrance to the fire-ground forever with everyone watching in silence.

Suddenly, a flame could be seen dashing along a channel set into the ground that Mac hadn't noticed before. It quickly arrived at the tall stack of firewood in the center of the clearing. As the flame lit the kindling, the campfire erupted in a bright yellow and orange fireball as the bonfire, which had been well-soaked with flammable liquids, burst into flames.

A collective gasp of surprise could be heard, especially from some of the younger tribes. This was followed by plenty of comments of "cool!" and "awesome!" from the campers. Then the four Elders shouted in unison, "Come and follow," and proceeded to walk toward the blazing campfire.

When they arrived at the giant fire pit, the two senior Elders turned to face the tribes while the remaining female Elder led the girls to benches facing the fire on the left side and the male Elder led the boys to their benches on the right. Everyone had a great view of the fire and also of the four Elders who were running the show.

This was a little more exciting than I expected it to be! Mac thought as she and Monica took a seat on the wooden benches assigned to their cabin. They were on the back row beside the girls from Cabin 10. In the flickering firelight she looked across to try to pick out Tyler and Alex, who were sitting with their cabin's tribe on the back row of the boys.

The head Elder held her walking stick in two hands above her head and called out loudly, "We come to the tribal fire tonight as many tribes and yet as one. The Tonkawa people were known as The Ones Who Stay Together! We honor them tonight with our time around the fire and repeat as one: 'We stay together!'"

All the legacy campers knew to shout back in unison, "We stay together!" ten times. By the third time, every one of the campers around the fire—new and old—were on the same page. The unison sound of over one hundred voices chanting "We stay together!" over and over was pretty amazing!

Even if the stories turn out to be silly, this is still pretty cool, Mac thought, totally immersed in the moment.

6

STORIES AND A VISITOR

I t turned out that Dory, not Kaitlyn, was picked to be feather keeper for the Cabin 8 "Road Runners"—which was disappointing to both Mac and Monica. Monica shook her head and sighed as Dory stood to make her way to stand with the other new feather keepers gathering around the council fire. "Just what we *don't* need!" she whispered to Mac. "This is not going to be good."

Mac agreed but then heard Alex's name called to be feather keeper for the Grumpy Bears of Boys' Cabin 9. "Well, at least we know *one* of the keepers," she said and gave Monica a nudge. When all ten keepers had been announced, they were each given a white-tipped black feather as a symbol of their responsibility to their tribe and the council. This was followed by their taking a solemn oath before being sent back to sit with their tribes.

Dory was grinning ear-to-ear with excitement as she returned to their row. "Whatever," Monica muttered in a whisper to Mac. "Okay, now we get into story time," she said, continuing to serve as the play-by-play guide to the evening's fireside events.

Kelley, the senior elder, had made her way to the front of the fire and announced that it was now time for stories to be told. But there was an important catch: the stories had to be impressive because the

20

"Great Buck" would be listening. "If the Great Buck is pleased, he will appear and let us know he is pleased with the quality of the stories. If he is—" and she emphasized *if*— "then he may decide to leave a gift."

She announced all of this with a solemn voice which seemed to imply there might be some unspoken consequence if, on the other hand, the stories *failed* to please the Great Buck.

"The Great Buck?" Mac whispered to Monica in a quizzical voice.

"Yeah. You'll see. Typical camp stories. But honestly, I don't think the stories have ever let the old buck down!" Monica said with a wink.

One of the other Elders—Charlie she figured, now stood and in a loud voice invited Bubba, counselor from the Elks' cabin to come to the fire and tell his best story. Everyone in the camp had already gotten acquainted with Bubba and the Elks of Cabin 5. He played guitar after supper in the dining hall each night and he and his campers had entertained everyone by leading silly songs and tribal competitions. Monica had mentioned she thought Bubba was kind of cute. Mac just thought he was goofy.

When Bubba got to the fire, Kelley, the senior-elder gave him a brightly colored wool blanket to put around his shoulders to create the impression of something important about to happen. Once he got started, Mac recognized the story of "The Hand" that she'd heard at other campouts and sleepovers over the years. It was guaranteed scary the first two times you heard it in the third or fourth grade— but not so much anymore. On the other hand, though, she had to admit that Bubba did a really good job of making it extra creepy and surprising his listeners with new details he'd added. As he came to the climax of the story you could hear gasps of surprise and even a few squeals from some of the younger campers who'd never heard the tale before. *That was worth the whole thing,* Mac thought with a smile.

Next up was Zoe, the counselor for the Cardinals of Cabin 6. After donning the story blanket, she told the story of a deep sea diver who was trying to recover priceless artifacts from a boat that had sunk in the Second World War. On his way out of the wreck—after locating what he'd been sent to find, he got distracted when he noticed a hatchway door along the sunken corridor he was leaving. He paused and opened the door to look around and suddenly, the beam of his light spotted twelve floating bodies that had never decomposed!

Twelve dead men were staring at him with a smile on their faces—just as the steel door swung shut and trapped him!

Once again, squeals and gasps, and even some of the sixth grade boys were surprised by Zoe's story in the darkness around the campfire. "This is really great fun!" Mac whispered to Monica.

Last up was the counselor for Cabin 1—the Bobcats. No one outside his cabin really knew this counselor yet. His name was Trevor and he was kind of short and wore glasses that seemed to keep slipping down his nose. Mac wasn't too sure how this last story would play out. But once Trevor put the story blanket on his shoulders and started spinning his tale, everyone was listening intently.

Bubba and Zoe had been good; but Trevor was amazing. When he got to the climax of his story, Mac jumped and grabbed Monica's arm who also jumped before looking over at Mac. Then they both laughed to break the tension.

"He's really good at this," Monica said. It was a sincere compliment that Mac rarely saw from her friend.

"Totally. I sure didn't see that coming!"

"Sounds like the plot for a good Halloween movie."

"Absolutely."

They started to discuss the best parts of the story but stopped when they noticed a plume of smoke rising near the edge of the woods, just beyond the campfire. A beam of light had appeared, pointing up to the sky to fully illuminate the smoke. Suddenly there was a loud series of explosions like M-80 firecrackers, which was followed by a second, much larger billow of white smoke.

As everyone stared to see what was going on, the smoke cleared and in the dim light, they could see a giant deer head with big antlers floating about eight feet high above an old fence. Draping down from around the neck of the head was a long white robe! Slowly, the eerie-looking head and robe rose higher and higher into the air, still illuminated by a powerful flashlight. Suddenly it stopped and paused to look left and then right in the darkness. Without warning a loud, deep voice spoke from beyond the fire: "We are pleased!" and the eerie shape began to nod its head as it looked around. Then it laughed with creepy, hollow sound that made the hairs on Mac's arm stand on end.

"Woah," she whispered to Monica, staring at the head.

It spoke again: "You have fed our hearts and our ears rejoice and so we commend you. You have done well. So go now, and find a small token of our appreciation in your cabins. Good night!"

And as the Great Buck said good night, the light illuminating him went out and he disappeared in the darkness of the night sky. Another long round of loud firecrackers went off to close the encounter with the creature. After a moment of awkward silence the older campers started clapping and soon everyone joined in the raucous applause whistling and cheering.

"That was pretty cool!" Mac said nodding, a smile filling her face.

"Told you it wasn't so bad," Monica replied with a grin. "When we get back, there'll probably be a candy bar on each of our beds. Not sure who goes in and does it while we're down here at the campfire but it kinda feels like Santa Claus has come through your cabin when you get back."

"Nice. So I guess we head back now?"

"Yeah," Monica replied, "except now we Road Runners have to follow Dory back to our cabin, since she's got the feather. Kind of like kindergarten line leaders all over again."

Mac grinned. "I can think of worse things."

LITHIUM GREASE

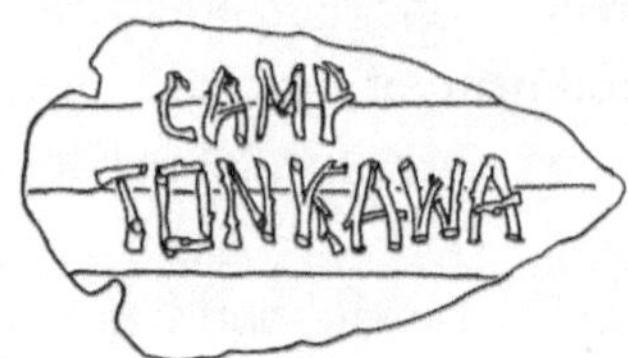

It was dark at Camp Tonkawa. Lights-out was at 11:01 p.m. on campfire evenings and was marked by the big bell above the dining hall clanging eleven times. When it tolled the eleventh time, something like a choreographed light show began to take place across the camp as the lights in all ten cabins went out.

And, since Tonkawa was a "dark skies" camp, the only lights after eleven were tiny, dim LEDs illuminating the cabin steps and the eerie, red-glowing exit signs that could be seen through the window screens of each cabin.

A figure in a dark hoodie and jogging shorts leaned against the wall of the dining hall watching it all with fascination, chewing loudly on a big wad of pink bubble gum. Even with the lights finally out, the figure wanted to delay a couple of moments to make sure nothing extraordinary happened; nothing that might interfere with the plan. Checking the clock on their flip phone the figure decided it was time. No last minute stragglers, *Time to get to work!*

Tomorrow was the big obstacle course competition, the highlight of the first full week of camp. But if things went according to the person in the hoodie's plan, it would be a gooey mess and another camp accident just waiting to happen! Smiling at the thought, the figure climbed on their bike to ride the wide path out to the clearing where the towering climbing walls and the rest of the ropes course equipment had been installed.

Slowly, the figure ascended the thirty-foot high climbing wall. Having climbed it so many times in the past, it was easy for them to get to the top, even in the dark and without a harness or a safety belay rope as a backup. Once at the top the dark figure took a tube of lithium lubricant from their hoodie pocket. The sticky, white grease was usually used to make sure garage doors and other mechanical contraptions roll freely without squealing or squeaking. *But tomorrow, this grease would play a very different role!* Quickly, each of the handholds along the top row got a generous smear of grease. The odd shapes now promised frustration to the fingers of tomorrow morning's climbers, just as they each were making it to the top of the wall!

Satisfied with the job they'd done, the dark figure put the cap back on the tube and stuck it back in a pocket. The starry night invited a pause to enjoy the view from atop the big wall. A chance to blow one more giant bubble before sucking it in with a loud, smacking POP! Then the dark shape made its way back down the wall, careful to avoid the booby-trapped hand holds. At the bottom, the figure stood looking up to cast one last admiring glance at the wall and once again imagined tomorrow's chaos! And then, with a sinister grin, got back on the bike and disappeared into the dark night.

Tomorrow was going to be so much fun!

8

OBSTACLES

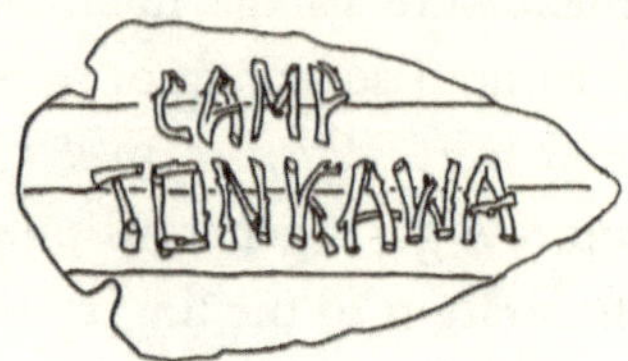

Wednesday was not a normal day at camp . . . it was actually one of the more exciting days of Week One. Every cabin was represented by a camper who'd been picked to race the obstacle course. After several days of practice, most groups knew who was fastest and now were anxious to prove their cabin was best. Each group was chanting their own "tribal song" at the top of their voices, each tribe trying to be louder than any of the others.

The girls had gone first for the kayak races, so this morning the boy's cabins were competing first. The four boys representing the older cabins were already in their safety gear and each had clipped the carabiner of their recovery ropes to their harness.

From their carabiner clip, each climber's bright blue safety rope ran across the ground to the base of the wall where each line then went straight up in the air to the overhead pulleys high above the top of the wall and then fed back down the face of it and into the hands of their cabin counselors. Each counselor would "belay" the slack in the rope for their camper, ready to hold onto it just in case anyone slipped.

Carson—Liam's counselor—had a big grin on his face as he did some friendly trash talking with his buddy Charlie, who was the

26

counselor for Jonathan, Tyler, and Alex's cabin. Charlie and Carson had worked with each other for three summers at Camp Tonkawa and this was one of their favorite events. Of course, both of them knew that Liam was the favorite to make it to the top first. After watching the practices since Saturday, it was pretty obvious he had the speed and agility to scramble up the wall faster than anyone else.

In spite of Liam's speed, Tyler and Alex were cheering as loud as they could for their new friend Jonathan, whose nickname was "Mr. J." But, as hard as they tried to be loud, the Cabin 9 Grumpy Bears tribe were no match for the noise being made by Cabin 7, Liam's Silly Beavers.

The Grumpy Bears had been talking about all the race details that morning at breakfast. And while everyone knew Liam was going to be the fastest in the first leg, their big chance was the second leg. After the wall climb, the competitors faced the hand-over-hand challenge. A pair of 20-foot aluminum ladders hung parallel above a big blue swimming pool full of inflatable alligators, just for added fun. If you got going too fast it was easy to lose your grip and "splash." And, a splash meant you were out! So, even if Liam won the wall, Jonathan had proven he was always the fastest across the alligator pond. A fast start didn't guarantee a win.

Jonathan had been totally upbeat after scarfing down his chocolate chip pancakes at breakfast. "No sweat!" he'd proclaimed with a smug confidence. "Liam may be faster up that wall, but I can catch up on the alligator pond and I *know* I can beat him through the stink tunnels!"

"Yeah, but what you've really gotta do to win," Alex had told Jonathan, "is get the biggest jump at the end of the rope swing!" Everyone else at their table, nodded. They all knew the stink tunnels could make you puke if you didn't hold your breath—all the more reason to cut through them as fast as possible.

Then their new friend, Kyle, weighed in. "That jump helps," he'd agreed with a nod, "but the course is always won at the end." Kyle had been coming to the camp every summer since he was eight and seemed to know everything about everything, so everyone else simply murmured a collective "hmmm," as they considered his observation.

With their close attention focused on him, he'd added, "Whoever can keep their footing across that final 50-yard mud dash is the winner. Period. And the whole race is always pretty close." He'd paused before adding one last thought: "If you ask me, it's that Eldon kid with the Elks you'd better keep your eye on." He spoke like he was some kind of a TV commentator preparing the audience for an unexpected spoiler.

So did the Grumpy Bears really have a chance to win the prized maple hunting spear back—or not? The old, ugly, but beloved spear shaft was the camp's traveling trophy given to the winning cabin after each event. Camp legend had it that the old relic—the broken shaft of a Tonkawa hunting spear, had been found up on the ridge by one of the original Hoffmeier settlers in the 1840s. The family thought it special, so they'd kept it in the family even though it was broken.

It had been given to the camp when it opened in the 1930s. Legacy campers would tell stories about their mom or their dad or some great-uncle winning it in some competition years and years ago. During their orientation, Mr. Chuck had said the camp had offered to return it to the Tonkawa tribe in the 1980s but the president of the tribe had told them they had better examples of hunting spears in their collection and suggested the camp simply hang on to it and keep telling its story. Alex still wasn't too sure if the spear shaft was really *that* old, but he knew it was *THE* traveling trophy that every team was determined to win. The Bears had lost it to the Beavers when Liam had beaten everyone in the finals for the boys' kayak race. The Bears wanted it back!

Tyler had sensed the mood shifting at breakfast, so he'd finally spoken up. "C'mon guys, we're going to win this!" he'd said confidently. Then he'd turned to Jonathan. "You got this—you can do this—right, Mr. J?"

"No question," Jonathan had said with a mischievous grin and nodding his head as he'd looked over at the table where Liam and the Beavers were finishing their breakfast. "We're going to win that stick back from Cabin 7 and I'm going to show 'em how it's done!"

Tyler had breathed a sigh of relief, and after that, everyone from Cabin 9 was pumped up and ready to win.

9

———

CHAOS

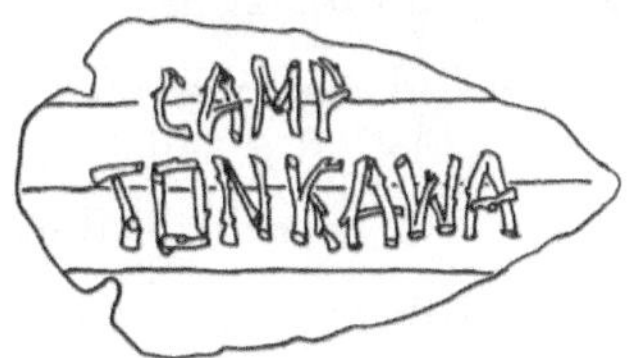

Now, the moment of truth had arrived.

Liam, Jonathan, Eldon, and a boy representing Cabin 3 named Louie were all lined up behind the white paint of the starting line, waiting for the whistle. Standing ten yards away from thirty-foot high wall, they each knew the winning strategy: race to it as fast as they could, leap as high as possible, grab a handhold and immediately plant a toehold, so they could start scrambling up the wall! They were all sizing it up one last time as they waited, getting a visual fix on the handhold they were going to go for first.

The noise of the cheering campers got even louder as Big Mike stepped onto the field. He was a very big man, a former NFL tight end who was both impressive and intimidating at the same time. With his clipboard in his one hand and his yellow starter whistle in the other, he looked over to the counselors and bellowed, "Safety team, are you ready?"

"Yes, sir!" the four counselors shouted in unison from their places along the wall, ready to take up the slack in their contestant's rope as soon as they hit the wall.

"Alright then!" he said before turning to the four boys. "Ready, Bears?"

"Yes, sir—ready!" yelled Jonathan; Alex and Tyler joined the rest of their cabin, roaring like a bear as loud as they could.

"Ready for the Beavers?"

"Yes, sir!" Liam yelled back. His cabin got louder with excitement.

"Ready, Elks?"

"Yes, sir! The Agile Elks are ready to go!" replied Eldon as his cabin chanted, "Elks do it best!" over and over.

"Ready, Coyotes?"

"Yes, sir!" replied Louie, grinning at his tribe as they noisily made a howl of "ow-ooo!!" like a pack of whining coyotes.

"Okay then. On my whistle!" Big Mike stepped back to the side. "On your mark . . . get set . . ." then his yellow whistle shrieked, and the four boys took off in a sprint.

Liam and Jonathan hit the wall first and began their scramble. Eldon and Louie weren't far behind, but Tyler could see they were just a little slower as they started the climb. Every one watching was cheering for someone and making tons of noise that got louder as Liam and Jonathan neared the final handholds just above their heads.

Suddenly, Liam's hand slipped! And before anyone could tell what was happening his second hand—which was grasping to compensate for the lost balance, slipped off a handhold too and he fell backwards. His counselor quickly tightened his belay rope but not before he'd fallen about six feet and swung into the wall with a noisy thud.

Beside him and only a hand grab behind, Jonathan wasn't sure what he'd seen out of the corner of his eye, but Liam suddenly yelled and started falling. Confused in the instant of the moment, J instinctively reached for his last handhold as he turned his head and watched Liam fall to the end of his safety rope's slack. But before any of that could register, his own hand slipped off the top handhold— and as he tried to grab another one, his other hand slipped off the second one just as quickly—and then the foot he'd just started to move missed its next toehold and he could feel himself falling sideways. It was like he was watching a video in slow motion. Down below, Jonathan's counselor had been distracted as soon as he saw Liam start to fall and hadn't yet taken up all the slack from Jonathan's last step. Jonathan fell almost ten feet before his rope suddenly tightened . . . which sent him banging into the wall chin first.

Recognizing that this wasn't simply a miss by the first climber, the cheering suddenly changed to a collective gasp just as the third climber made it to the top. And just like the other two, Eldon couldn't get a grip on his holds, either! He came off the wall swinging awkwardly before dangling upside down from his rope, totally disoriented. Louis had been just far enough behind the other three climbers that he froze in place and watched everything unfold before looking down to his counselor and yelling "Get me down!"

After the falling stopped and everyone caught their breath, each counselor worked to carefully—but quickly—get their campers lowered back to the ground. Big Mike could be heard on his walkie-talkie calling loudly for the office to "get the camp nurse over to the games field ASAP!"

Liam was complaining about his shoulder, which had taken a pretty hard hit when he swung into the wall. His counselor helped him take off his helmet to check for any other obvious injuries. When Jonathan made it to the ground, his chin was bleeding and looked like something from a bad horror movie with lots of blood. His counselor, Charlie, helped him get his climbing helmet off then pulled off his own tee shirt and after quickly folding it a few times used it to cover Jonathan's chin to help stop the bleeding.

Eldon had only one hand slip so his second hand had slowed his fall. He'd banged his head into the wall pretty good, but the helmet had done its job and he was fine when he made it down to the ground. After a few panicked moments of yelling to get down, Louie caught his breath and was able "walk down the wall" as his counselor lowered him to safety.

"What happened, Liam?" Carson was giving him a look-over to make sure there wasn't anything wrong besides the shoulder injury.

Liam caught his breath and looked over at Jonathan who was sitting on the ground, leaning against the wall. "What do you think, J? Grease or something?" he asked.

"I don't know, man. I was about to reach for the next hold— almost at the top, when I saw you fade left and then the next thing I knew . . . BAM, I was right behind you! Had to be grease or something up there. Felt like the white shortening stuff my mom uses when she's making pies."

Big Mike had been on his walkie-talkie, but now assured that the camp nurse and her assistant were on their way in the "camp medic" red golf cart, he turned his attention to the boys. "Charlie, I want you to ride back with Jonathan when the cart gets here," he said quickly before addressing Jonathan directly. "Son, you've split your chin open, not as bad as it sounds but you're probably going to need to head over to Johnson Regional to get that patched up. Charlie will go with you. I'll give your parents a call here in a few minutes to let them know and give them Charlie's cell number so they can call him for an update."

Jonathan looked at Big Mike and nodded. "It's starting to hurt," he mumbled through the pressure his counselor was still applying to his chin.

"No doubt. That was some smack you took. The nurse will have something to help with that. Liam, how's that shoulder?"

"Pretty tender, sir."

"I can imagine. We'll see what Connie has to say after she looks at it, she might end up sending you over with Jonathan to have it checked out." He paused and looked up the wall. "Lemme see your hand, Liam," he said, curious now about the incident itself. Liam held out his hand and Big Mike touched some of the grease residue still on his fingers and then rubbed his own fingers together and sniffed them. "Donnie," he said, turning to one of the other counselors, "scramble up there and have a look at what you can see. Bubba, you can belay him, right?"

Donnie slipped into Eldon's harness and when Bubba was ready, he started to climb the wall, careful to stop a row short of the top hand holds. Every camper was watching him on the wall and Big Mike knew it was time to change everyone else's focus. "Okay, team!" he said loudly, looking out over 120 campers. "Obviously we're cancelling today's race. Counselors, let's get everyone back to the cabins and change into swim gear and head for the pool." When there was a momentary pause with no one moving, Big Mike added in his commanding voice, "NOW."

Big Mike started to look back at the wall but paused, providing one additional instruction to the group. "And you feather keepers, if your counselor is tied up helping me, then you take over and get your crew back to your cabin. Make sure everyone's ready to go when they do get there." He smiled, glad that the keepers had already been selected. "Now, let's move out and give Nurse Connie some room. We'll update everyone at lunch."

The medical golf cart pulled into the clearing and the counselors and feather keepers started organizing their tribes to head back to their cabins. Big Mike turned his attention back to Donnie who was now at the top of the wall. "Whatever it is up there, get a big swipe of it on one of your fingers and bring it down with you," he said.

A few minutes later Donnie carefully, but quickly, rappelled back down the wall to the ground. He stuck his finger out for Big Mike to look at. "Looks like that kind of grease you use on garage doors," he told Mike. "And there's quite a bit of it up there on the whole top row of hand grabs. A guaranteed mess!"

"Okay. We'll talk about this back at my office after we get these boys checked out." Eldon, Louis, I want you to let the nurse have a look at you two just to be safe, then go join your cabins."

The boys nodded and Big Mike stepped back from the group gathered around the medical cart so he could have another look at the wall. *What exactly is going on around here?* he wondered aloud—but quietly enough that no one else heard his question.

10

STRANGE THINGS GOING ON

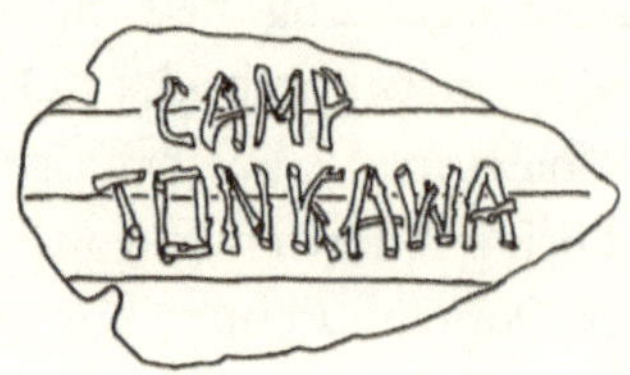

Alex was sitting in one of the deck chairs beside the huge, Olympic-sized pool that dominated the part of Camp Tonkawa between the dining hall and the riverbank. He'd only seen a pool this big when he'd visited his brother at Texas A&M two years ago. He *got it* that an NCAA Division One school would have a primo pool for swimming competitions —but a summer camp? This was amazing!

"Not going in this afternoon?" Charlie asked him. Charlie was sitting in the deck chair beside Alex, keeping an eye on the rest of the boys from their cabin. There were two paid lifeguards in the tall chairs who were in charge of the swimmers, so he was mainly making sure the horseplay didn't get dangerous.

Alex had already figured out that Charlie and Carson were going to have their hands full for the next two and a half weeks. It was pretty clear that the thirteen- and fourteen-year-old Beavers and Bears of Cabins 7 and 9 were going to be very competitive every day until camp was over. Charlie shouted out to Micah to quit dunking Liam and find something else to do. *As if that's going to stop anything!* Alex thought and then grinned.

"Sorry," Charlie said, looking back at Alex. "So, you're not swimming today?"

"Yeah, I'll probably get in, but first I just wanted stop and enjoy the downtime for a few minutes. It's really a pretty cool location for a camp if you stop to think about it."

Charlie looked at his newly appointed "keeper" and nodded. "It's an amazing place to spend a summer," he agreed. "By the way, thanks for getting all the guys back from the obstacle course today and covering while I took Jonathan over to the ER. You handled that pretty well for a newbie."

"No problemo, boss. Everyone was pretty concerned about J and nobody wanted to rock the boat. Might not work out so well next time but, you know, we'll see."

Charlie laughed at Alex's response then asked, "Okay, so tell me what your dad and mom do, Alex. You're like a seasoned old shaman masquerading as a kid. Where does that come from?"

"Hmm. Well, my mom's a customer service rep for an IT company. She was a coder after college and my dad was a coder, too. They met at their first job after college and got married; had me and my big brother and then split up. My dad moved back to Brazil but still helps my mom out with child support for me and pays for Antonio's tuition at Texas A&M. That's about it. Just me and my mom these days." He stopped to consider things more and then added some additional detail. "But I will say that this summer has been pretty exciting. Tyler—he's Mac's cousin, he moved in with her family right after school let out, so the three of us hang out a lot. They're both pretty cool. I'm a nerd, they're fun, so we do stuff and it's good."

"Got it. A nerd with a social side. Perfect combo to rule the world. Am I right?"

"Yeah, maybe." Alex grinned. He was pleased that Charlie kind of "got him." Since he was being social, he decided maybe it was safe to ask a few questions of his own. *After all, fair's fair . . . right?* "What about you, Mr. C.? You and Carson seem pretty tight. I'm guessing this isn't your first summer as a camp counselor."

"Nope, you're correct, my man. Year Three, actually. I go to a college up near the Oklahoma border in Sherman, Texas. Just a small school called Austin College. We like to say it's a little school with big ideas. After my first summer here I helped Carson get on last year. He's a math nerd, Alex. He likes to solve equations in his head for the fun of it," he laughed.

Alex hadn't heard of Austin College but he was enjoying having a real conversation with Charlie. "My brother's an accounting major at A&M," he volunteered. "What are you studying?"

Charlie had a quick glance at the pool before answering. "I'm studying anthropology. In fact, that's why I ended up working here in the summers."

"What's anthropology?" Alex asked, searching his vocabulary for a word he wasn't sure about. "Is that like studying people's brains or something?"

Charlie laughed again. "No," he said, shaking his head, "anthropologists are the National Geographic types. We study people and culture and history and civilizations and geography and how all those kinds of inputs create or shape people groups."

"Oh, okay. I know what you're talking about. You guys do all those documentaries on TV and dig up old bones and artifacts and stuff."

"No, those are archeologists," Charles said with a grin. "But if you find an archeologist at work, you'll probably find an anthropologist not too far behind!"

"So you, like, study Indians and stuff?"

"Yeah, but in my world, we're trying to use different language than simply referring to them as 'Indians.' You do know that calling the Indigenous Peoples 'Indians' or 'Indios' was a naming error made by Columbus when he arrived in the Caribbean islands, right? The dude was certain he'd actually sailed all the way around the world from Spain and had arrived in India."

"Hmm, I think I knew something like that."

"In any case, Columbus's mistake has stuck for over five hundred years now."

"Right . . ." Alex said slowly, but not so sure. "So what would *you* call them?"

"So, most of the people we're talking about would self-identify as either Native Americans or American Indians to keep things simple, but both of those terms carry the idea that they're connected with 'America' even though they were here for centuries before the idea of *America* even existed for Europeans."

"Hmm," Alex nodded, starting to feel like he was back in Mr. Johnson's social studies class.

"My preference is 'first peoples' or 'indigenous peoples,'" Charlie said, "but the best reference is to simply use their tribal name . . . like Cherokee or Sioux."

"Or Tonkawa?" Alex interrupted.

"Yeah, or Tonkawa." Charlie agreed with a grin.

"Okay. So if you know so much about Indians . . . I mean—first peoples, who were the Tonkawa people that this camp was named for?" Alex slouched a little lower in his chair and stared up into the sky. He was glad he'd brought his sunglasses for "history class."

"That's a long story, Alex. Maybe I'll share it at campfire one night instead of telling a scary story. But the short version is that they were one of the major buffalo tribes back before the Apache and then the Comanche arrived in Texas. The Comanche—and to a slightly lesser degree the Apache—they both became the big players here in Texas and as they grew more powerful, the Tonkawa were pushed into a shrinking share of central Texas. Like I said, it's a long story but this part of Texas was one of the places the Tonkawa tribes still hunted in —up to around the time the Texas settlers arrived."

"So, I guess that means you're here because that Colonel Hoppenmeir guy and his ranch got your attention?"

"Major Simeon Hoffmeier," Charlie corrected him. "But yeah, the camp's board has a scholarship for students who want to major in anthropology with a focus on the first peoples of Texas. I applied and got a scholarship. And along with the scholarship came a guaranteed summer job every year so I can do a little research in my time off."

"Nice," Alex concluded, deciding Charlie was a little more cool now than when he'd first met him. He studied the clouds for a minute or more before changing the subject. "Any ideas on what was going on at the climbing wall this morning? Do ya think it was related to Mac's kayak?"

"Actually, I'm not supposed to talk about it." Charlie replied. But after thinking about it, he decided maybe he could work around the rules if he didn't go into too much detail. "Well, actually Big Mike and Mr. Chuck are looking into that possibility, but as far as my opinion—yeah, I do think they're related. Big Mike's pretty concerned, that's for sure."

"Concerned that there's been two major acts of sabotage at the camp in four days?"

Charlie looked intently at Alex for a moment, trying to decide whether he could trust this kid. He seemed to have a pretty good head on his shoulders, but should he give him a little more detail?

After a thoughtful pause he made up his mind. "There weren't any incidents here in session one, that was the first three weeks of camp. Well, except for one thing that happened on the last day of camp—on Parents' Day. But at the time, we all assumed it was just a camper prank. Anyway, session two had three incidents. None of them biggies, really. More like—you know, just nuisances because again, all three things just looked more like pranks. No one got hurt and we just figured an ambitious camper was trying to show off to his friends." Charlie paused and glanced back over to Alex before continuing. "The two incidents this week were both pretty dangerous. Honestly, someone could have gotten hurt."

"J had his chin split open," Alex protested, "so *someone did* get hurt."

"No, you're right, someone *did* get hurt. I just mean it could have been a whole lot worse than it was. But that also suggests that the stuff that happened in session two probably wasn't done by a camper. Couldn't be. If you figure the kayak and climbing wall weren't done by a camper and they're connected, then session two wasn't a camper either." Charlie paused and glanced again at the swimming pool. "In fact, I think maybe the Parents' Day thing was connected as well, now. And, if that's the case, then we've got a pattern across all three sessions."

Alex took this all in and then took his sunglasses off to look directly at his counselor. "Charlie," he said, pointing the earpiece of his sunglasses at his counselor, "you've got a lot more than a pattern. You've got someone messing with Camp Tonkawa's reputation." Alex made his point bluntly and matter-of-factly—as though it was obvious.

Charlie looked puzzled for a moment and then nodded. He hadn't really assigned a motive to it all yet, he'd mostly been thinking out loud. But he knew Alex was right. The longer it went on and the more dangerous the incidents got, the more likely that someone might actually get seriously hurt.

"Yup, Alex," he finally said, glancing out to look at the kids playing in the pool once again. "I think you're right. Someone is out to mess with the camp's good reputation."

"That could be dangerous stuff." Alex nodded, satisfied to have made his point. Taking that as a cue, he stood up to get in the pool but paused to add, "Somebody must have a super-big grudge of some sort to plan something like sabotaging the kayak and greasing the climbing wall." He set his sunglasses in the chair with his towel. "See you in a bit, Big Guy. But you might want to chew on that some." Alex stepped out of his new sliders and headed over to the pool.

Charlie watched Alex jump in and thought again about all the stuff that had gone on so far this summer. "Dang," he finally muttered to himself. "The kid's right. We've got a real problem. *But who's doing this and why?*"

11

THE HIKE

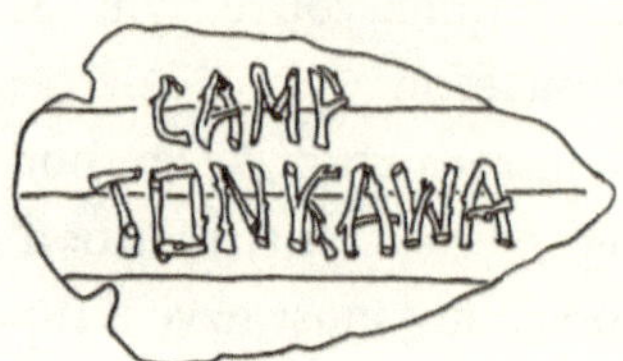

Sunday after lunch was the first of the many hikes that were built into the second and third weeks of the Camp Tonkawa schedule. The camp, which had once been part of a very large Hill Country ranch, was situated on 2500 acres of hills, ridge lines, creeks, river frontage, ponds, and open fields for grazing cattle. That was just short of four square miles of land. At the end of breakfast, all campers had been told to hang out in the dining hall to be briefed on rules and safety procedures that everyone had to follow when hiking in this rugged part of Texas.

"Snakes," said Monica, getting straight to the point. She'd just returned from her assignment to clear the breakfast dishes for their table. She was just in time to add her short version of the rules, and since most of the girls at the Cabin 8 table were return campers, they all nodded in agreement and laughed about the coming speech.

"Hang on," Dory said with her newfound sense of authority. "There's more than snakes involved in the briefing about our hikes. And besides, not everyone's heard *The List* before, so let's not scare anyone."

"Um, Dory . . . I think Mac here is the only one at the table who hasn't heard The List at least twice," Monica countered. "And besides,

40

she's hung out in the desert more than once already . . . so I think I'm fine cutting to the chase: *it's all about snakes.*"

Monica was still bristling at Dory's take-charge voice. Her attitude had notably changed since she'd been named the feather keeper for their tribe. Since Wednesday night she'd made it abundantly clear to everyone in the cabin multiple times that she was Leslie's assistant and had the feather to prove it. *Whatever!*

Mac just grinned. She wasn't a fan of Dory, either, but since she didn't have the history Monica did, it was fun to watch her friend push back a little. "Okay," Mac suddenly volunteered, glancing over at Monica and then at the rest of the campers at their table, "I've got a snake story."

Everyone, except Dory, said "Oooo" and looked excited to hear a good story.

"So, last month, my uncle and me and his girlfriend—and Tyler from Cabin 9, we were all out in the mountains near El Paso, and—well, I had to go get my uncle's Land Cruiser and bring it back to where they were trapped—but that's another story. Okay, so anyway, just as I was getting to my uncle's old truck, I spotted a six-foot rattler in my way. It was all coiled up between me and the truck!"

All the girls at the table were now totally locked-in on her story. "What did you do?" Kaitlyn asked, terrified at what she was imagining in her head.

"Well, when I saw him, I remembered what my uncle had told me about being in the desert: "Watch for snakes, 'cause they're watching you! And if you DO see one, carefully and QUICKLY step backward —but always keep your eye on the snake."

"Oooh, I don't think I could do that." Dory said, now interested.

"Well, I guess I figured I'd better do it anyway. So I stopped just as soon as I saw him and started moving backwards really careful and I just kept staring him right in the eyes. He was all coiled up and had that rattle on his tail wiggling and making noise . . . but by then I was far enough back that he couldn't strike me, and after he saw I wasn't going to run or budge he figured it was time to leave, so he uncoiled and slithered off."

"Wow! That was close!" Kaitlyn said.

"Yup, but that wasn't the end of it," Mac said, stringing the story out. "When that snake took off, he went straight under the truck! Right below the driver's door!"

"Yikes . . . that's not good! What'd you do then?" Kaitlyn asked nervously.

"I waited and thought about it and then I realized I could make a lot of noise with the horn on the ATV I'd been riding on, so first I made a lot of noise with that horn and then I noticed the running board on the side of the Land Cruiser and realized that was my lifeline! I looked as best as I could into the shadows under the truck, couldn't actually see him so I ran as fast as I could—with huge steps, jumped onto the running board, opened the door without pause, dropped into the seat and slammed the door before he could get in with me."

"That's amazing," Kaitlyn said. "Were you like, you know—scared anyway? I think I'd have headed off in a different direction."

"I was totally freaking out, yeah! But there really wasn't anywhere else to go. Besides, at the time, my uncle's girlfriend was really counting on me to get back with truck to help rescue her." Mac paused. "So, anyway, I *had* to make a run for it. But I won't lie, it *was* really scary, that's for sure!"

Before any more questions could be asked, Big Mike approached the microphone and tapped it to make sure it was on. The loud thumping heard banging out over the speakers was his answer: YES! It was on and working! "Okay, campers," he began, "Today is hike number one. For Cabins One and Two, you'll be doing the short, one-mile round-trip route around Buzzard's Peak and back. Have fun and remember: This is camp not home . . . so no whining!" The rest of the campers snickered out loud.

Then he continued: "The rest of ya'll will continue on from Buzzard's Peak and take the full three-mile Ghost Ridge trail that takes you over the hanging bridge across Dry Branch and then you'll make your way back to camp by way of the Fat Goat trail down from the ridge and back around and through the Post Oak Forest. For those of you who are repeat campers, you'll recall that's a total of five miles. It'll be well after two o'clock by the time you older campers make it back so stay hydrated out there!" There was an audible groan from the campers who'd hiked those three trails before.

"You'll all have a daypack and four bottles of water, wet-wipes, two candy bars, a sack lunch, an apple, and an orange. You'll also find a loaner-phone in each of your packs so you can take pics. Remember, no SIM card, but take all the pics you want and we'll upload them to your photo-file account this evening."

Monica leaned over to Mac. "That's new. Ever since they went no-phone we've been stuck either using those old digital cameras or no pics at all. Getting a camera phone, even if it's 'SIM-dead' will be cool!" Mac nodded her head with approval.

"Now," Big Mike said, looking around the room to make sure he had everyone's attention. "Camp Tonkawa Trail Rules Protocol." He paused to make certain the little whispered conversations ceased, then continued. "Now, listen up. This is no picnic by the lake. This is real wilderness hiking and you've got to take it seriously or someone could get hurt." He paused again and immediately it was silent in the dining hall.

"Number one: if your counselor or an adult tells you to stop, you STOP! They may have spotted a snake or a problem. In the wilderness, we don't always have time to explain. So, 'Stop!' means STOP!" He looked around again then continued.

"Two: if you see a snake, stop and quickly back up. DO NOT TURN AROUND AND RUN. I'll say it again: Stop and quickly back up. If you are 'point' for your tribe and others are following you, say it out loud to those following you: STOP! Then, immediately back up. Snakes don't like people, but even though they know they can't swallow you, they will attack you if they feel cornered or threatened. So . . . you know, just give 'em the room they need to make their own exit . . . okay?" There were murmured conversations starting again so he thumped the mic. "They don't like you any more than you like them so just give 'em room to leave. Any questions about Item 2?"

No one spoke up so he went on to Rule Number 3. "Three: drink lots of water. I don't want to see anyone coming back to camp with two or more water bottles still full." He grinned, then said, "Well, except for our younger campers who have a short trail today. The rest of you need to drink your water. Your counselors will be packing extra water so if you use yours up, ask for more."

"Rule Number 4: Stay on the trail unless your counselor has invited you to see something off the trail. DO NOT WANDER OFF." Big Mike grinned and then decided to tell them a story to make his point. "Two years ago we had to call out the county sheriff's helicopter to help us find two kids who decided they could ignore rule number four. Trying to create their own rules didn't work out so well for them. One ended up with a broken leg and a broken arm. Always stay on the trail with your tribe."

"Rule 5: Do not pick plants or eat anything that looks curious. I know you're not kindergartners, but I have to say the obvious anyway 'cause every year we have to take one or more campers over to Johnson Regional to get treated for accidental poisoning." He shook his head as if he would never understand how campers could ignore Rule 5. "Look, campers, nature creates plenty of poisonous plants and since most of you are not a Tonkawa medicine shaman, please don't do something you'll wish you hadn't."

"Okay. Rule Number 6: We've positioned plenty of porta-potties along all our trails in case you should need one. Please, do not under any circumstances go wandering off on your own to 'take care of business.' Always talk to your counselor if you have a personal issue and they can help you decide what to do." There were a few snickers, but everyone understood.

"Finally, Rule 7: Don't do anything dumb." he said, looking up from his list. "Seriously, think before you do something and ask yourself if you're about to become one of our favorite new warning stories for future campers. Do not become a *#FAIL! on the trail.*" Big Mike looked around one last time then finished by reminding each camper to have a great time, take lots of pictures, and to be sure and talk to their counselor if they had any questions.

Monica turned to Mac and cocked her head as if to say *I told you so.* "Snakes," she said to Mac.

"Yup. Snakes and water and don't be dumb. That just about sums it up," she replied. This was going to be challenging this afternoon but hopefully a lot of fun. And as for the snakes . . . well, she hoped she'd already had her one and only encounter with a snake!

THE "GRUMBLER"

Big Mike liked to have the windows open in his office for fresh air, even in the heat of summer. He always had a couple of fans aimed at his desk plus the big overhead ceiling fan so there was always a lot of air moving and with it plenty of fan noise, but there was no getting around the fact that it was always uncomfortable and warm when Mr. Chuck visited Mike's office.

"It's just all those summers of hot football training camp and then playing out your career for a northern NFL team," he'd announced to Mr. C his first year on the job. "When you've played December football in the snow and it's twenty-two degrees on the field at game time, you come to appreciate the nice feel of summer. Why ruin it with freezing cold AC? After all, it's a 'summer camp,' right?"

Mr. Chuck did not personally agree, but he understood Big Mike's personal preference and tried his best to ignore it. All the same, he preferred meetings in his office instead of Mike's for that very reason. This afternoon, though, he'd found himself in one of those spur-of-the-moment doorway conversations with Mike that had turned into a sit-down meeting—much to Mr. Chuck's growing irritation. He was already starting to feel beads of sweat form above his bushy eyebrows as he and Mike talked.

"Charlie from Cabin 9 was in earlier today about our little problem," Mike was saying.

"Yeah? And how's his camper—that Jonathan kid—doing?"

"He's not happy about missing swimming till Wednesday, but Nurse said the stitches would heal quickly and he's doing fine. In fact, I went ahead and let him go on the hike this afternoon."

"I forgot to ask how your call with his parents went," Chuck said. It wasn't like him to forget to follow up on a detail like that, but he'd been dealing with a personal issue that had distracted him since Thursday.

"Jonathan's dad was cool. Said he got it that kids get hurt at camp. In fact, he apparently broke his arm at summer camp when he was a kid, so no problem. He said Jonathan's mom would probably have some cookies delivered to camp so their cabin could have a get-well party."

Mike smiled at the idea of Jonathan and his father telling their camp stories over Thanksgiving turkey for the next umpteen years. He went back over Thursday morning's events in his head and his smile disappeared. "I still don't like it," he said. "If we'd made the mistake of having kids handling the belay rope like past years—well, who knows what might have happened. Thank goodness our counselors reacted the way they were supposed to." Mr. Chuck glanced out one of the two open windows that framed the corner of Mike's office and sighed. Last week had been long and full of distractions, but it was Sunday, the start of week two of the final session. Surely the worst was behind them.

"Well, Chuck," Mike said, leaning back in his chair and getting into a comfortable slouching posture. "Aside from how things were handled this past week, I think we should talk about the bigger picture of the climbing wall incident."

Mr. Chuck turned back from looking out the window. He'd been momentarily distracted, thinking he saw something, but knowing all the campers were on their afternoon hikes he ignored it. "Bigger picture?" he asked, after one more quick glance out the window.

"Yeah. I've got a concern I want us to talk about."

"Go on."

"I was visiting with Charlie at breakfast. He raised a thought that runs along the same line as something I'd been toying with."

"What's that?"

"I'm thinking we might want to take a closer look at some of these recent incidents at camp."

"How so?"

"Well, Charlie suggested that we might try to connect the dots between the two incidents this week and the three pranks in session two and even go back and think about the Parent's Day thing that happened at the end of session one. He's thinking that maybe we've got one person—a 'grumbler,' perhaps? You know, someone who's either trying to get our attention or is maybe intentionally trying to sabotage the camp's reputation."

Chuck thought about it for a moment and shook his head. "I don't see it. First of all, the Parent's Day stunt was just mischief, pure and simple. Kid stuff. The things that happened in the last session, well, yes, they were out of the ordinary for camp shenanigans but they were in a different class from sinking a kayak and greasing the top of a climbing wall." He paused to consider his words then shook his head again. "No, I don't think there's a connection. At least not yet. But I do believe whoever sabotaged the kayak also messed with the climbing wall. And I'd say both of those were pretty serious stunts—something we need to get to the bottom of before they really do become an issue for our camp's reputation."

"Okay," Mike said, considering his boss's opinion. "I'll set my conspiracy theory idea aside—not sure I totally agree yet that there's no connection, but okay. Then we need to talk about this week." Mike sat up straight in his chair and rested his large arms on his desk as he leaned in towards Mr. C's chair. "You do feel pretty comfortable about ruling out some camper as the culprit behind the kayak and climbing wall incident, right?" Mike asked.

"You tell me, Mike. You've been around these kids the past nine years. I'm thinking they both look too sophisticated for a camper. The grease stunt, maybe. But the kayak cover-up? That's beyond even a fourteen-year-old. As a pair of stunts—no, they don't seem like something a kid could pull off."

"I agree. So that means we've either got an intruder or someone on our own staff who's messing with us."

Mr. Chuck thought for a moment before replying. "Yeah," he finally said, "but that just doesn't make sense, either. What responsible adult working for this camp would be crazy enough to put our campers, and our camp, at risk like that?"

"More importantly, why?" Mike added.

"Well, I noticed a few minutes ago you called our culprit—what was it—'the grumbler?'"

Mike grinned. "Yeah, maybe a discontented grumbler."

"So, maybe someone really does have a grudge of some sort." Chuck paused and shook his head because the idea really was perplexing. "Guess we ought to look back the past two years and see if you can find some staff grievance that maybe didn't get resolved. Maybe something we thought got handled but wasn't. Or, I don't know, do we have someone on our staff who was a former camper and they've got an old grudge to settle?"

"That sounds a little too complicated . . ."

"Yeah, you're right. But it works on TV. I've seen that before. Okay, maybe not an ex-camper but if we don't get to the bottom of this, we're going to be sittin' in a really bad way if something over-the-top that doesn't qualify as a 'camp prank' happens next."

"Totally agree, boss," Mike said, standing up to get started. "I'll pull the old files and see if I can find anything worth chasing."

Chuck stood and glanced out the window once more. Now he was starting to feel paranoid. "Let's talk more about this after supper tonight, Mike. And tell Charlie thanks from me—for bringing it up. He might have turned a light on for us."

Mike nodded and Mr. C headed out the door. He was anxious to make a quick return to his own, very cold, air-conditioned office!

Outside Big Mike's window an individual was sitting on the walkway that ran along the south side of the administration building. He was leaning casually against the wall a short distance from Big Mike's window, safe and out of sight, chewing a big wad of bubble gum. After taking another sip from a Dr. Pepper he'd brought from the snack bar, he began to think through the discussion in Big Mike's office he'd overheard.

"The Grumbler . . ." the gum-chewing individual repeated the title softly to hear it aloud, then turned it over silently in his mind a few more times. *"Everyone needs a good nickname,"* he thought, *"and maybe I've just found mine: the Grumbler!"*

Satisfied to finally have a legitimate nickname, "the Grumbler" stood carefully and picked up his backpack—which was particularly heavy this afternoon. A satisfied smile led to the loud pop and snap that made bubblegum so rewarding. The Grumbler walked to the back of the building and got on his BMX mountain bike. There was yet another prank to set in motion this afternoon and it was getting late!

13

GHOST RIDGE

Hiking in the Texas Hill Country in the summer is hot, so Tyler and Alex were taking a quick water break while they waited for the rest of the boys from Cabin 9 to catch up.

"This is brutal, my friend!" Alex said, looking up at the sun in a cloudless sky. He glanced back down the trail then wiped his forehead with the wet towel draped around his neck.

Tyler finished chugging his water bottle then stuffed the empty in his day pack. "Reminds me of hiking out at Mac's uncle Eric's place out in the desert," he said. "Except that when you're out there, you can expect the AC in his trailer to be cranked down to a cool 65 degrees when you get back."

"Yeah, well, at least there's the pool here when we get back today." Alex paused and took another drink. "Think we've got enough man-points to let the rest of the guys catch up with us?" he asked with a grin on his face.

"No doubt about the man-points." Tyler laughed, then glanced up ahead. The next leg of the trail was about to take a steep, final climb up to the highest point of Ghost Ridge. "I think that's a great idea," he said and nodded his head toward the uphill path ahead. "In fact, we could probably hike with Charlie for a while if you don't mind letting everybody just go past us here in a minute."

Alex studied the trail ahead for a moment and quickly caught Tyler's point. He grinned then looked back down to the bend in the trail below them and spotted Jonathan and his best friend Sean just coming into sight. The rest of the boys weren't too far behind. "Sure. Let's do that," he said and quickly put the towel back around his neck. "Let's let Mr. J and Sean take the lead for a while."

Once all the boys of Cabin 9 had passed them, Alex and Tyler fell in with Charlie for the challenging scramble to the top of the ridge. When they got there the view was amazing. Below them and to the southwest they could see the snaking path of the Colorado River and in the other direction they could see about a half dozen canyons falling away from the ridge ahead.

"Feels like the top of the world," Tyler said, overwhelmed by the view.

"This is my favorite part of the trail," Charlie replied, grabbing a quick drink from his water pack. "That water way off there in the distance is Lake LBJ. Named for the first US president from Texas—Lyndon Johnson. He had a famous ranch not too far from here."

"Guess you're pretty used to this hike by now, right Charlie?" Alex was impressed with the view but was mainly glad they'd finally made it to the top. He'd studied the topo map and knew the trail would be level up here as it followed the ridge line until they got to the canyon that would lead back down into camp.

"The first week or two of camp is the worst," Charlie said, "but once you get your lung capacity built up, it does get some easier." He looked at Alex and winked; "But not *a lot* easier."

As they started walking again Alex decided to ask more about how the investigation was going.

"Just between us three?" Charlie asked, cautiously.

"Absolutely. Neither of us are motormouths."

Tyler nodded, too. "What's said on Ghost Ridge stays on Ghost Ridge," he added with a sincerity that made Charlie comfortable enough—for now, at least.

"I talked to Big Mike and he said he'd been thinking the same thing, that maybe some of this is related. Sounds like there was some paperwork to be filled out and he'd had to call J's parents, but for now it's still just a Camp Tonkawa internal thing. Not calling in the sheriff or anything big like that."

"Does he think it's a camper doing this stuff?" Tyler asked.

"Not sure. But Alex and I were talking yesterday and I think there's a string of smaller incidents since the first camp session this summer that might be related. Hadn't looked at it that way until the two biggies this past week. So, if that's the case, and they are related, then it can't be a camper."

"Why?" Tyler realized he'd missed something.

"Well, because we've only had a couple of double-session campers and they're little guys in Cabin 1."

"Oh, sure. So you think there's a crazy counselor out there?" Tyler asked. He realized that was a stupid idea as soon as he'd said it.

Charlie laughed. "No, I doubt it's a counselor. No one would do anything crazy like that. But maybe it's an outsider somehow getting in, trying to get the camp in trouble or something." Charlie was nervous that he may have said too much of what he'd been thinking. "That's really not very likely, though. The camp's pretty secure, so I can't imagine how anyone could get in."

"So, that would leave someone on the staff—right?" Alex asked, prying.

"Dunno," Charlie said. "Probably need to change subjects since I don't know any more than you do at this point and it would all just be speculation."

Tyler and Alex took the hint and dropped their questions for now. After a few minutes of hiking in silence they rounded a bend and could see the next quarter mile of trail, including the suspension bridge.

"What's that?" Tyler asked, pointing to the odd-looking bridge.

"Oh, that's the trail's hanging bridge. Fun and scary at the same time. Gives us a shortcut straight across the canyon from side to side." He pointed down into the deep draw below them. "The trail used to wind around down to the left just ahead, and then you had to hike down that steep hillside and then you had to climb your way back up the other side again to get back to the west ridge line. The cable bridge cuts out a really tough part of the old trail."

"So we're going to end up on the trail right over there?" Tyler asked, pointing to a spot way across on the other side of the canyon from them.

"Yup. Over there where that big rock overhang looks kind of like a parrot beak—see that shape? Just beyond Parrot Rock the trail starts back down into the next canyon and that takes us back to camp."

Tyler stood for a minute studying the suspension bridge they'd be crossing in a few minutes. He'd never seen one before. "So, is that bridge like . . . safe?"

"Dude, these kinds of bridges are like everywhere in the world!" Alex said. He was surprised Tyler didn't know about them. "Super simple. You stand up the pylon posts on either side, toss or carry ropes across to the other side and then you drape the two upper cables over the posts and then anchor them on both ends. Those cables support the weight of the walkway planks strung across on the two lower cables. Totally safe."

"Alex is right," Charlie said. "We built it over spring break just before my first year here at the camp, so the bridge is practically brand-new."

Tyler looked at the bridge again and tried to imagine going across it. It looked a bit spooky but then again, *he'd managed to land an airplane earlier this summer* so a wiggly bridge high above a canyon shouldn't be too scary—*right?*

As the hikers walked single file along this narrow part of the trail, they could see the first group of girls from Cabins 4 and 6 and the boys from Cabin 3 approaching the bridge. Behind them were Mac and Monica's friends from Cabin 8 and Cassie and the Eagles from Cabin 10. Charlie's campers were already sitting on rocks waiting for the long line to get moving.

The Cabin 5 and 7 boys were still coming up the trail behind Alex, Tyler, and Charlie. Alex could see there was going to be a real traffic jam as the hundred or so campers would have to wait their turn to cross the swinging bridge single file.

Charlie noticed Alex was puzzling through the details. "You're wondering why's everybody waiting?" he asked, anticipating Alex's question.

"Yeah. It's gonna take like, forever to get all of us across. What are they waiting for?"

"When we hike this trail we always wait to move everybody across the bridge, single file—as a group. Kind of like a safety check to make sure we haven't left anyone on this side of the ridge before we head back down to camp." Charlie started to leave then turned and gave the two boys a wink to let them know he really wasn't worried about leaving anyone behind. He jogged up to the front of the line to meet up with the other counselors.

Once the boys from 6 and 7 had caught up, they'd been told to go on ahead of Cabin 9 while the Grumpy Bears chilled out seeing who could throw a rock the furthest across the canyon. When they got tired of that, they decided to drink some water and eat their granola bars while they waited their turn to be last across the bridge.

Tyler still couldn't get over the view. He took it all in and then told Alex how much better it was being here at Camp Tonkawa this summer instead of being stuck in his mom's old apartment in Kansas City like he'd been this time last year. *Sooo much better!*

14

A DIFFICULT CALL

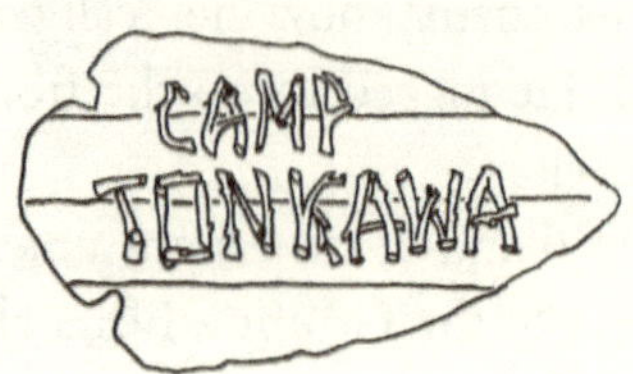

Mr. Chuck was glad to be out of Big Mike's hot office, but now the blast of *very* cold AC on his damp, sweaty skin sent a shiver down his back. He glanced out his office window then sat down at his desk. He'd always found it helpful to make a few notes before a tough phone call, and he knew this was going to be one. He needed to share the concerns Big Mike had raised with his boss: Ms. Sandra Morrison-Parker—chairperson of Camp Tonkawa's board of directors. He rehearsed his points in his head one last time as he waited for Sandra to answer her phone.

"Hi, Chuck," came a cheerful voice on the other end of the phone. "Haven't heard much from you this summer—other than last Monday . . . is everything all right?"

"Howdy, Sandra," he replied, "Funny you should ask. We had a little incident here Thursday. Any gossip gotten back to you about it yet?"

"No, I thought I was just making small talk. What happened?"

"Well, on Thursday morning—when the boys were starting their obstacle course, we had another extreme prank. I didn't bother you with it at the time because, well—if I called you with every prank that kids came up with it'd drive you crazy."

"Right. So what kind of a prank?" she asked, now wanting the specifics.

"All of the grab-holds at the top of the climbing wall had been coated in lithium grease. Three of the first four campers scaling the wall lost their grips."

"Did anyone get hurt?" Sandra asked, interrupting him.

"They all had safety ropes and spotters, but one of our older boys banged his shoulder pretty good. Another camper split his chin open and had to be driven over to Burnett Regional to have it patched up—they superglued it in lieu of stitches, but he's going to be fine."

"Guess that's a relief."

"Yeah, busted chins are part of any given summer, but not from greased handholds!"

"Nobody else hurt?"

"The other two boys got some bumps and a scare but they're fine."

"And that's on top of the kayak thing that happened on Monday?" she asked carefully.

"Yes. That's in addition to the sabotaged kayak." Chuck paused before continuing. "So that brings me to why I'm calling. Mike and I have been talking and we think we may have something bigger going on here."

"Bigger than a psycho camper on our hands?" she asked, teasing. "C'mon, Chuck—out with it. You and Mike love running that camp and don't need me looking over your shoulder. What are you thinking?"

"You might remember when you were here for session one Parents' Day?"

"The M-80s?"

"Right. Massive, over-the-top . . . set a new best for serious attention-getting stunt."

"How a camper could have got ahold of that many M-80s and created that much noise and confusion is still hard for me to imagine." She was silent for a moment then added, "That little stunt had a couple of seasoned Marine vets diving for cover *and* it cost us two legacy campers whose grandparents made it perfectly clear their grandkids would not be returning next year or ever."

"Yes, well . . . I thought all along that it was probably the work of an overachieving camper. Now I'm not so sure. A couple of weeks later in session two we had two pranks we'd never had before."

"Like the three big nasty rat snakes in the boys' shower room?"

"Yes," Chuck acknowledged. *Sandra had a good memory for details.*

". . . and the superglue in the soap dispensers in the girls' bathroom?" Sandra paused again. "You do know my attorney—Travis, still hasn't been able to settle out the liability claim with two of the parents on that one, right?"

"Yes, I do know that, Sandra."

"Just checking. But, yes, those did go beyond the more traditional firecrackers in toilets, shaving cream between the bedsheets, laxative-laced chocolate candy, and mouthwash bottles spiked with . . . well, the mystery ingredient seems to vary by year, doesn't it?"

"It does," Chuck said, trying to bring the conversation back on track. "So here's where I'm at," he continued, "up until about an hour ago I'd convinced myself that this rash of bad behavior was simply extreme. Exotic? Certainly. Getting dangerous? Well, yes, potentially. But until now neither Mike nor I had really considered it as a series that was ongoing. Perhaps even the work of a single individual."

"Even though you never found a culprit."

"Yes. Even though we never found out who was behind each incident."

"Which is actually very unusual for you and your team," Sandra added, "to not have figured out who was responsible."

"Which maybe should have told me something sooner, if I hadn't wanted to just believe they were nothing more than a few more camp pranks."

"And a week into session three we've now added two more extreme pranks, and these two were actually pretty dangerous."

"Yes."

"So, you and Mike are starting to see if connecting the dots, instead of looking for a wayward camper or two, gets us closer to figuring out what's going on?"

"Stuff as deliberate as sinking a kayak and messing with thirty-foot-high climbing walls . . . well, that gets us out of the kid space and suggests there might be something else going on here."

"And that's why you've called."

"Yes, that's why I wanted to call you. Mike and I think that maybe someone or some group is trying to make us look bad. Maybe looking to create a news event, even?"

Sandra said "hmm" and thought for a moment. "You have any ideas? You've been running that camp for us for almost twenty years now and you've seen the best . . . and the worst of kids' stunts. I can tell this has you rattled."

"That's why I called, Sandra. I don't know who would be driving this or why, but I think it's time we think this through from a different angle. If we're dealing with someone who's this careless . . . well, we might have something really serious going on here. Who knows what else might happen these last two weeks of camp."

"Agree. Sounds more serious than we thought." She paused. "If you'd like some outside help, I can certainly make a few calls, bring in a private investigator?" she offered.

"That might not be a bad idea. I'm going to do a full staff meeting during movie night tonight. Maybe there's someone on staff with a beef I don't know about. Maybe someone will step up who's heard or seen something. But if I can't shake loose a lead, we should probably get someone in here to help us."

"It's a fine line, Chuck. With social media and news reporters anxious for a wild story . . . well, something like this could *really* spiral out of control fast if we can't get to the bottom of it. But you know that."

"I do, Sandra. Last thing we can afford is to scare off our alumni parents and legacy campers, or have worried moms yanking their kids out of the current session."

"Well, business aside, we need to err on the side of keeping our kids safe, of course. I do appreciate the heads up—you did the right thing to let me know your concern. Call me in the morning and we can circle back after you've shaken the tree with your staff."

"Will do."

"In the meantime, Chuck, I'll make a couple of calls to our board and maybe to a friend or two to make sure we've got this covered just in case something bigger does happen later this week."

"Thanks, Sandra."

Chuck ended the call and leaned back in his chair. The oversized map of the camp hung on his wall. It was a huge ranch, he reminded himself. Four square miles big. The cabins and mess hall and main part of the camp were very secure from all the nearby public roads. That was reassuring. But the longer he studied the map and traced all the amazing trails the camp had developed over the years, the more aware he was that there were isolated parts of the old ranch that might offer a way in and out . . . lots of ways that a determined intruder could get in . . . if this *was* the work of an outsider. He stared at the map then silently shook his head. *No,* he decided. *There's got to be a more obvious answer.*

15

THE BRIDGE AT GHOST RIDGE

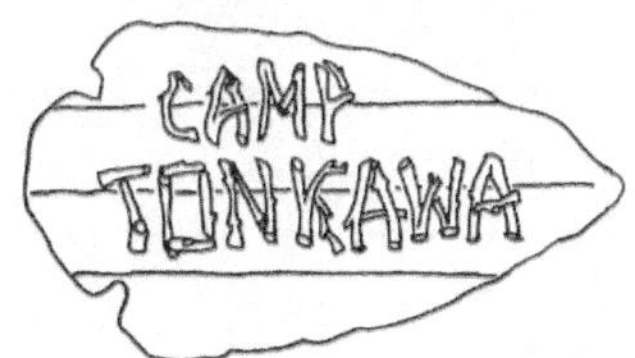

Kelley and Leslie were comparing head counts with Charlie and Carson while Donnie, Jesse, Bubba, and Zoe kept an eye on the campers. The kids were getting restless and were long past ready to cross the suspension bridge and start down the trail to get back to camp.

"Looks like everyone's accounted for," Kelley finally announced. "Let's get 'em on their way. Jesse, you and Donnie go ahead and get the junior campers on across and the rest of us will follow." Then she added, "And as always, single file and no jumping!"

The other counselors groaned and grinned. There was absolutely no way you were going to keep a bunch of campers from trying to make a suspension bridge as scary as possible. It was part of the fun. Still, they would each remind their cabins to use some restraint as they went across.

Down at the end of the line, Alex put his empty water bottle in his pack and then poked Tyler. "Look, they're finally getting ready to go across up there."

"About time. It's hot enough out here—without having to stand around and wait." Their friends, J and Sean, agreed.

61

Suddenly, they all heard a loud cry of panic followed by a chorus of cries and screams.

"Oh, NO!" Alex said, pointing, as they all watched in horror . . . the suspension bridge was coming apart! One of the two lower cables that held all of the foot boards together was suddenly slipping through batches of boards, releasing half the decking and leaving the side that remained dangling precariously. All along the bridge, kids were clinging to the upper suspension cable while trying to keep a foot on whatever they could. Everyone was screaming.

"Did you see anyone fall?" Tyler asked, scanning the canyon below the bridge to see if he could see anyone.

Before Alex could answer they all heard the voices of Charlie and Carson calling out, telling all the campers to go back down the trail 100 yards and huddle-in-place by the clearing.

"Feather keepers are in charge," Carson called out with authority. "Listen and obey."

The boys from Cabin 9 immediately followed Alex back down the trail to a large clearing on the ridge and all the other campers quickly followed to wait for further instructions. With the curve of the ridge line, they could all still see what was going on. At the east end of the bridge, Kelley and Charlie were doing their best to keep calm and quickly rescue the nearest campers who were stranded on the bridge.

"Donnie, I want you and Bubba to take the rest of the campers back down to camp the way we came," Kelley announced firmly. "The sooner we get the rest of the kids off this ridge the better. Take the Dry Branch cutoff to get back to camp as quick as you can. Got it?"

Bubba nodded as Donnie called out "got it" and the two of them jogged back down the trail, leading the remaining campers to join up with the older campers so they could head back to camp.

Charlie suddenly had a thought and called out after Bubba: "Send Alex from my cabin up here and tell Jonathan he's in charge!" Bubba shot him a thumbs-up and continued his way down to where the kids were waiting.

Carson was already on his walkie talkie, calling the camp office to report the incident and ask them to see if the county sheriff's department could get their helicopter up to the ridge to help with rescues.

In the meantime, Charlie and Leslie were with Kelley at the bridge head. Together they were trying to coax the campers who were stranded on the bridge to carefully make their way back to the ledge using what footing remained on the cable that hadn't failed.

It was tricky and slow, but since the second cable was still secure, it was working. By the time ten minutes had passed the counselors had talked seven of the campers back and off the bridge. Each was rewarded with a big bear hug followed by a bottle of water and more hugs.

"This is going to become a big problem here in a minute," Charlie said quietly to Leslie.

"You mean this isn't problem enough?" she asked, confused.

"No, this camper that's almost made it off? She's the last of the taller campers. There's still about six out in the middle who haven't moved at all. They're frozen, holding on but probably aren't going to be able to make it back here by themselves."

The final girl they'd been talking about made it to the end and jumped off the bridge into Kelley's arms for a hug. On beyond, the next camper was almost halfway across and couldn't move for fear of falling.

Leslie looked out to the middle of the bridge where Jesse, the counselor for Cabin 4, was sandwiched between the remaining two groups of kids: "Jesse, hang tight, okay?" she called out hopefully to her friend. "Just keep the kids calm. We've got this!"

Out on the broken bridge, stranded on the single lower cable that was still left, Jesse wasn't at all sure *anyone* had this! *It was a long way down to the floor of the dry creek gulch below them!* She couldn't even imagine the horror of what was going to happen if one of the kids left lost their grip. But then she reminded herself *she had to be brave for her campers!* She nodded her head to Leslie and then began talking to the campers around her, encouraging the scared kids who were clinging to the cable just like she was. She tried very hard not to look down and sternly warned each of the kids with her to *not* look down—to just hold on because help was on the way!

Leslie smiled, gave Jesse a thumbs-up, then lowered her voice as she looked at Charlie. "Any brilliant ideas?"

"I'm thinking . . ." he said, surveying the situation.

Suddenly they both saw Alex running up their way. "Hey!" Leslie shouted, trying to head off the wayward camper. "He's supposed to be with the rest of the kids heading back down the trail!" she said, staring quickly at Charlie with a frown. The last thing they needed in the middle of a crisis was a nosy camper!

"He's not being nosy," Charlie said quickly, stopping her before she could scold Alex. "I asked Bubba to send him up here. I know it sounds crazy, but he's kind of a brainiac and he might have a bright idea for us."

Leslie continued looking at Charlie with a big question on her face and then over at Kelley who was joining them to consult on what to do next. She nodded it was okay with her and told Leslie and Zoe that having Alex in the mix couldn't hurt.

"By the way, Kelley," Charlie said to her, quickly changing subjects, "probably a good time for you to radio Big Mike and give him an update, right?" His dad had taught him, *Rule number one in life: Always keep your boss in the loop!* "Tell him to get the maintenance crew to locate the wall climbing gear—harnesses, ropes, and carabiners and see how fast they can get up here in the four-wheel-drive Gator. Remind them they've got that old construction trail we cut when we were building this bridge which is probably the fastest way up."

"On it," she said.

Jesse called out from the middle of the bridge. "Guys, this is getting tough out here. We need a plan . . . NOW!"

Charlie looked out at the six stranded campers and their counselor. "Hold on! We're getting some gear up here as quick as we can!"

16

RESCUE

About that time Alex arrived at the bridge head out of breath. He still managed to ask the obvious question anyway: "What can I do?"

"We've got the team down in the camp on their way in the Gator with climbing gear and stuff," Charlie answered, "but the kids out there aren't going to last a whole lot longer. Got any crazy, work-around ideas for an amateur rescue in the meantime?" he asked.

Actually, Alex had already been thinking through how he'd handle this emergency, even as he watched things unfold. He'd noticed the last six campers were terrified and unable to move. He'd tried to imagine what they could do with what they had on hand and already had an idea.

"Belts." Alex said quickly and simply.

"Belts?" Charlie asked, confused.

"Yeah. If we can get a few strong belts and a carabiner we can make a simple, underarm safety sling. Snap a carabiner on it then latch it to a cross-body sling you'll have on. That way, you can walk each kid off the bridge step-by-step alongside you. If they slip, you won't lose them as long as you can hold on yourself."

Kelley nodded and looked at Charlie's belt. She hadn't noticed till now that both Charlie and Carson had switched from web belts to "old-school" leather belts this summer. "Okay, you two, let's have those belts!" she said, and tried to keep from laughing in the middle of a crisis.

Both of them quickly unbuckled and pulled their belts through their pant loops and then strung one through the other to make a kind of pair of loops. They clipped the biggest carabiner they could find onto one of them.

"So you'll cinch the first belt around the kid's chest, under their arms and then that sling will be attached to the second belt to make it easier to move."

"So, I get it! The second belt gets looped to the cross-shoulder strap," Zoe was saying as she saw how it was going to work. "It's not rock climbing grade, but it should let you safely start getting kids off."

"Guess if we need a shoulder harness for Charlie then one of you needs to fork over a web belt," Kelley said, then pointed to Zoe.

The bright green web belt quickly became a cross-shoulder harness. Charlie tightened it then latched the rescue sling's carabiner to it. "Better than waiting around!" he said, convinced this was going to work. "Good thinking, Alex."

He looked out at the skinny cable he was about to go inching across and took a deep breath. "Okay, here we go," he said.

Charlie began walking slowly out to the middle of the damaged bridge, carefully keeping at least one hand on the upper suspension cable the whole way. After what seemed like forever, he made it to the stranded campers. He glanced down and almost lost his nerve but quickly caught himself, looked back up, and immediately caught Jesse's eyes.

"Don't look down, Charlie," she said firmly but softly. "But man! Am I glad to see you!"

Charlie nodded and scooted closer to the first of the three campers between him and Jesse. She was crying and clinging tightly to the upper cable, which was almost above her shoulder.

"Who's this?" he smiled and calmly asked.

"This is Angie," Jesse said. "And, she has been a *very* brave camper

—haven't you, Angie." Jesse smiled at the eight-year-old girl who nodded her head.

"Okay, Angie," Charlie said gently. "We're going to put this loop around your chest and under your arms, just like in the movies, and then we'll get you back over to the end of the bridge and with the rest of your friends, okay?"

She nodded her head that she understood but didn't move. She watched carefully as Charlie put the belt over her head and then slowly encouraged Angie to thread one arm at a time through the loop and then squeeze it tight under her arms so it couldn't slip off.

"Lookin' good, Angie," he said with a smile. "Now, we're going to walk back just like you saw me come out, okay? We'll both just take it slow, sliding our hands along the cable. Got it?"

Angie nodded and took a quick breath then looked over to where Kelley, Carson, and Leslie were waiting at the end. It looked like a mile away but she knew she had the sling on so she followed Charlie as he started making his way back, staying close beside him as she went.

It seemed like it took an hour, but it was really only about six minutes when Angie stepped onto the ridge and into a huge hug from Kelley and Leslie.

"Angie, you were a pro!" Charlie said as he undid the belt and prepared to go back for the next camper. "Give me five, girl!"

Angie gave him a small smile followed by a quick hand slap then turned back to Kelley and suddenly burst into tears. "I wanna go home," she said crying uncontrollably. Kelley held her as Charlie started out on the same, careful walk again, this time to rescue camper number two.

Alex nodded as he caught Charlie's eye and got a quick thumbs-up.

17

HELP ON THE WAY

Mr. C was in the front seat of the Gator sitting beside his maintenance crew chief, Sam, who was driving over the rough trail. The construction trail they'd cut through the canyon two years ago when they built the new suspension bridge wasn't too overgrown, but it was pretty rugged and rocky. In the back were two bags of climbing gear they'd grabbed from the rope shed before heading out. Sam was pushing the Gator as fast as he felt he could over the bumps, rocks, and ruts. *There was no time to waste!* Big Mike and the camp nurse were in the second Gator not too far behind.

"I think we're about to clear the pines just ahead," Sam said as he glanced at his wristwatch. "Should only take about four or five more minutes once we get to the dry creek bed."

The oversized, soft tires bounced over a big rock and Mr. C gripped the handhold tighter. It felt like they were going way too fast for this kind of terrain but he didn't say anything, confident Sam knew what he was doing. He pulled the radio out of his pocket to give Kelley, his lead counselor, an update.

"Kelley, this is Chuck. You copy?"

"Hearing you loud and clear, Mr. C. Any update on help?" She tried to sound confident but was anxious to get access to some *real* rescue equipment.

"We're almost to Dry Bone Creek. Sam thinks we're about four minutes out." Mr. C almost lost his radio but managed to hang on as the Gator hit a big dip and nearly bounced him out. The bags in the back had launched into the air too and now landed with a thud as the wheels landed.

"You okay?" Kelley asked. "You cut out all of a sudden."

"Yeah. We're just taking a few more bounces than normal right now. How many campers are still out on the bridge?"

"Five. Plus Jesse. Charlie just got Angie off and is on his way back out with his makeshift sling to see if he can rescue a second kid."

"Okay, call me as soon as the next camper is safe."

"Roger that, boss."

Mr. C looked over his shoulder but Big Mike hadn't caught up with them yet. He tried to imagine how frightened his stranded campers must feel right now. Then he thought of their parents and the challenges the camp would be dealing with after an accident like this. It would make yesterday's climbing wall incident seem almost trivial. But deep inside, his real worry was the kids, the sudden change in their safety—and none of this was acceptable for a summer camp. Especially not for Camp Tonkawa. His thoughts were interrupted by his cell phone buzzing.

"Yeah, this is Chuck Walker," he answered, not recognizing the number.

"Mr. Walker, Captain Vasquez with the Burnet County Sheriff's Air Rescue Unit. You filed an incident report for Camp Tonkawa? A bridge failure in Cougar Canyon?"

"Yes, sir," Mr. C replied. "It's on the far northern boundary of our camp. We've had a partial collapse of a suspension bridge up on Ghost Ridge Trail."

"Roger that, Mr. Walker. We are in route with our rescue crew. We know where the camp is, of course, but can you provide more specific coordinates for the accident site for us?"

"I'm on my way up there on a four-wheeler with our camp staff.

Can I send you a screen shot of my phone's coordinates? We're less than two minutes away so that should be close enough."

"Absolutely, sir. Can you do that right now while we have this line open?"

Mr. C opened his map, zoomed in, and took a screen shot that included his GPS coordinates then texted it to Captain Vasquez. "Got it?" he asked.

"Yes, sir. Hold please."

There was some discussion in the background that was hard to make out with the noise of the helicopter itself but he assumed he was sharing the details with the pilot. Soon Vasquez was back on the phone.

"Okay, thanks for that, Mr. Walker. I'm advised we're two minutes out and our pilot, Lt. King, is very familiar with that sector. He says he'll land us up on the high ridge line above the trail. Can you brief us on the ground situation?"

"We've got four, possibly five campers still stranded on the broken bridge along with a counselor. Our camp counselors on site have cleared eight, possibly nine campers already and are continuing to attempt a rescue of the remaining kids."

"Copy that. Standby, please."

Sam rounded a bend in the riverbed and the Gator started to climb a steeper grade. He pointed ahead, "I can see them."

Chuck picked up his walkie talkie. "Mike, we've got the bridge in sight, what's your location?"

"Probably three minutes behind you, over."

"Perfect. Just spoke with Air Rescue and it sounds like they'll be landing about the time we make it up to the ridge."

"Copy that," Mike replied. "See you there in a few more minutes. Out."

"Kelley, did you copy that update?"

"Yes sir, Mr. C. I can see you and Sam down below just now. Did they say where they're landing?"

"On the top of the ridge, probably just north of you. I imagine they'll go out of their way to avoid any prop-wash shaking the bridge."

"Perfect," she replied. A moment later she added, "Okay, I can see them now!"

The sound of the chopper was a welcome encouragement as the Gator slowly made its way to the ridge line, up from the dry creek bed. Above him, Mr. C spotted Charlie crossing the cable cautiously with a younger camper—with what looked like a belt strapped under her arms—moving slowly beside him toward the safety of the ridge. He counted and there were still four campers left on the bridge, plus Jesse.

Chuck checked his watch and did the math: twenty-two minutes since Kelley had called the report in. The kids and Jesse had been holding onto the cable for close to twenty-five minutes now, but with the arrival of the rescue team, it shouldn't be too much longer before they were all off.

18

NOT AN ACCIDENT

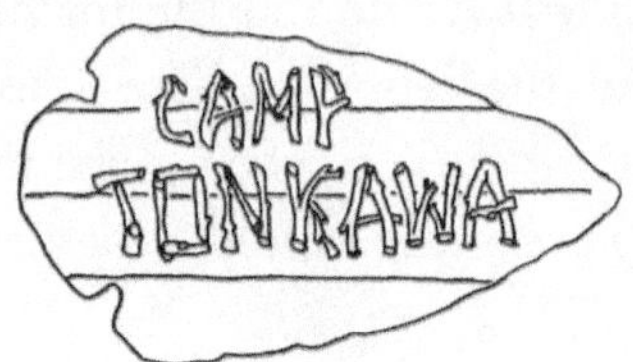

M r. C had just ended his second call of the day with Sandra Morrison-Parker who was stunned at the news of yet another incident at the camp. She promised to contact a friend at the Texas Rangers and brief them since they would likely need to get involved in this. He still had her on the phone when the last of the stranded campers—along with Jesse—made it safely off the bridge.

Captain Vasquez caught his attention. "Mr. Walker, I just wanted to extend a compliment to your camp counselors. My team said their can-do approach to getting started on the rescue work was first class and they were impressed with whoever came up with the idea of using a carabiner and a couple of belts to make an improvised safety sling. Good work and well done."

He nodded his appreciation but was interrupted by Sam. While the rescue was going on, his maintenance chief had made his way down to the bottom of the ravine and back up the far side to where the bridge had failed. He was back now and had a very worried look on his face.

"You're not going to believe this Mr. C," he said softly. He handed his phone to his boss so Chuck could see the pic he'd taken from the other side of the damaged bridge. Captain Vasquez looked over Mr. C's shoulder at the four close-up pictures that Sam had taken of the place where the steel cable had failed.

"That cable didn't just break or come loose," Sam said quietly so only the two of them could hear. "Nothing about the bridge itself failed—that fourth cable that came free was cut. Looks like maybe with a grinder wheel. A perfect, clean cut."

"Whoever did this only left two or three strands of the cable braid to actually fail," Vasquez said, taking the phone from Mr. C and enlarging the picture for a closer look. "There'd have been no way for the bridge to NOT fail once your campers started crossing it."

There was a steely look in his eyes as he studied the photo once again. "I'm sorry, Mr. Walker," he announced firmly, "but this is now a case of aggravated criminal mischief and possibly attempted murder." He looked for his assistant, Deputy Holt, and motioned for him to join them.

"Holt, we'll need to consider this a crime scene." He passed the phone to his deputy to see the sabotage to the bridge cable. "We'll need formal statements from anyone who was here at the moment the bridge failed," he said quickly. "I'll want to talk to that counselor who was out on the bridge as soon as the paramedics are finished checking her out." Mr. C nodded as Vasquez instructed his sergeant to get started cordoning off the scene and set the criminal investigation and evidence collection process in motion.

"If I send you those pics, can I get my phone back?" Sam asked, hopefully.

Vasquez grinned and apologized, handing the phone to Mr. C. "Sure, sorry. It's just that this is a really big deal now. In fact, given the technical nature of this and the resources this is going to take, I'm going to recommend to the county sheriff that we call in the Texas Rangers to handle the actual investigation."

Mr. C nodded. *That was exactly what Sandra had imagined was going to happen.* He quickly sent the pics to himself and then to Vasquez's cell number before giving the phone back to Sam. "How about if Sam takes you and me and one of your team members over to the other side for a firsthand look? I know it's your crime scene, but I need to see it for myself, too."

Vasquez thanked him for the offer and asked Deputy Holt to join them as well. In the meantime he told one of the other officers to organize a conversation with the counselors who'd been present and get statements ASAP. "And check with the nurse to figure out how soon we can do some preliminary interviews with the campers who were out on the bridge. We can do that back down at the camp, but try to keep them separate from the rest of the campers until we get their eyewitness statements. Got it?"

The deputy nodded and headed over to where Kelley and the counselors were standing around, waiting for instructions. Ten minutes later, as they waited with the nine kids who had been rescued off the bridge, Kelley and Charlie both began to understand the full scope of what had just happened. Charlie started to say something but thought better of it when he noticed the kids looking at him. They were just anxious to hang onto anything and everything he might say. He changed his mind and Kelley gave him an approving nod . . . which wasn't lost on either Carson or Laurie.

"Okay, campers," Kelley said, looking at the small group. "We're going to get you back to camp with the nurse.

"Do we get to ride in the golf cart?" One of the girls asked, hopefully.

"Yeah, we'll get a ride in the Gator, but when we get to camp, we're going to the dining hall instead of back to your cabins. The sheriff's deputies will need to have each of you tell them what you saw and maybe ask some other questions. So for now, let's not talk with each other about what happened on the bridge until after they've talked with you, okay?"

There were nods but almost immediately the scene was interrupted. "I want to call my mom!" said Angie, tears forming in her eyes and now frightened again.

"Absolutely, Angie. We are going to get you back down to the camp and then all of you are going to get to call your parents and I suspect they will be here very soon to take you home."

"And you have *all* been totally amazing!" Laurie added, giving the two campers standing beside her another big hug. "Let's see if Nurse Connie is ready to give us a ride back to camp, okay?"

Meanwhile on the other side of the ravine, Captain Vasquez and Sgt. Holt had looked carefully at where the cable had been cut and taken quite a few pictures. They'd also photographed the ground around the bridge's moorings in case there were any telltale tracks or other evidence. When they finished their initial look, they invited Mr. C to take his own pictures.

"Just don't touch anything," Vasquez said politely. "I'm sure the investigators are going to want to see if they can lift any fingerprints."

Sergeant Holt walked along the ridge that led away from the far side of the bridge to see if there was anything unusual. They needed some clues. "Captain, have a look at this," he called out suddenly. He'd stopped to avoid stepping on a track on the trail.

The two men looked closely at what Holt had spotted.

"Bike track?" Holt offered.

"Good guess by me. Take a pic from back here so we don't disturb it! I'm sure the Rangers will want to get a cast or 3D laser photo of it when they get here."

Vasquez walked back over to the bridgehead. "Mr. Walker, I just want to make certain that everyone in camp is *very clear* that this area is officially off-limits. No one, including your staff, is to come up here unless accompanied by one of us or the Rangers. Can you please get that word out by radio to your team right now?"

Mr. C nodded and got on his walkie talkie and asked Big Mike to make an announcement over the camp's speakers so every camper and all the staff knew the hiking trails were off limits until further notice.

When they got back to the other side, they agreed that Kelley and Laurie should use Sam's cart to follow the nurse back with the rest of the nine kids then come back for the rest of them.

After everyone was on their way, Mr. C pulled out his cell phone but then paused. "Mind if I call my board president?" he asked Vasquez. He didn't want to make any mistakes in protocol. "We've got the kids secured, now comes the next challenge—talking to a lot of parents, and I need to get that started."

"Absolutely," Vasquez smiled. "You've got a camp to run and

probably a PR nightmare about to erupt. When you get finished, I'll put you in touch with Shaquille in our communications office. She can help you coordinate a joint statement with our department to the press and public on what happened. But we best be shooting to make a joint statement in the next half hour. News of something like this doesn't hold very long. In fact, I'm surprised one of the news choppers out of Austin hasn't already got wind of this."

Mr. C nodded. *And when once word gets out that the Texas Rangers are involved, they were going to have their hands full!*

19

HEADLINE NEWS

Sandra's number one order was for Chuck and Mike to quickly call the parents of the kids that had been on the bridge and make certain each of those campers got to speak with their parents as well. "When you call, be receptive to whatever arrangements you need to make to connect the parents with their kids—get them home if mom or dad wants them to come home immediately—and I presume most will—or arrange a night with the family this evening at a hotel over in Marble Falls to debrief . . . whatever seems right."

And, number two—but really just as important, she wanted the counselors to use their cell phones to call each of their camper's parents to let them know what had happened firsthand and let them know their child was safe. "Be sure to tell them their son or daughter will be calling them, shortly." By an hour from now, I want every parent to know from *US* what is going on!" In the meantime, she agreed that she'd give the sheriff's communications director a call and arrange for a joint press statement to be released at five p.m.

By the time dinner rolled around, the camp was buzzing with rumors. In the dining hall, Mac, Monica, Kaitlyn, and all the Road Runners from Cabin 8 were excited to share everything they'd heard or

77

seen that day. Any news or gossip was fair game when they got to the table with their food.

"I heard one of the girls from Cabin 4 slipped and was hanging on by only one hand and the helicopter crew had to rescue her in one of those basket things!" Dory announced. She spoke as though she had gotten the word from the helicopter crew themselves.

"I'm not so sure about that," Monica said, dismissing Dory's scoop. "But I did hear that the cable—the one that broke—had been burned through with one of those torches. Sabotaged by some crazy former camp counselor."

"Cassie told her best friend Ellen that her mom had watched the local news and there were five of those black SUVs full of FBI agents surrounding a house in Austin where the guy who did it was having a standoff with the FBI," Elle said, contributing yet another crazy rumor to the day.

"Alex was actually there at the bridge helping," Mac said with confidence. "He said he heard Mr. Sam tell Mr. C that the cable had been cut. Somebody intended to have it break and drop all the kids from Cabin 4 into the ravine." Mac paused to put more ranch dressing on her Tater Tots. "He said the helicopter captain was calling in the Texas Rangers."

"That's stupid!" Dory sneered, assuming Mac was referring to the baseball team. "Why would they call in a baseball team?"

Everyone stared for a minute at Dory then Monica laughed out loud. "No, Dory. The *real* Texas Rangers. Not the baseball team." Monica laughed again then regained her composure. "They're kind of like the FBI, Dory, only they work for the State of Texas on certain kinds of crimes."

"How do you know that?" Dory asked. Her voice was both mad and embarrassed.

"My dad's a cop. Police do cities and towns, sheriffs take care of counties, and if there's been a major crime that needs special help, they call in the Texas Rangers to help investigate what happened. They've got their own crime labs, lots of money, and don't have to do what local cops or sheriffs tell them to do."

Everyone at the table was impressed when Monica finished. "So, when you talked to your mom and dad this afternoon, did they tell you that?" Kaitlyn asked. She was very curious since she was learning something new about Texas.

"No. They just asked me if I wanted to come home or stay—and I said *stay*."

"I heard every one of the campers in Cabin 4 is going home." Mac said, opening a new angle on the story.

"So did they rescue all of them or not? I thought they said one of them fell off and broke her back and had to be airlifted to a hospital over in Austin." Emme didn't sound like she totally believed the story, but wanted to contribute something.

"I think if anyone had actually fallen off the bridge and gotten hurt that bad, we'd all know by now, don't you think?" Mac finished her Tater Tots and took a long drink of iced tea. "Besides, I imagine they'd have closed camp and we'd all be going home if something that bad had happened."

"Yeah, and since Alex was helping, he'd have told us, right?" Monica looked around to see if everyone agreed.

"Yup," Emme said and nodded.

There was a tapping of Mr. C's finger on the tip of the microphone as he checked to make certain the PA system was working. "Well, campers," he began once everyone was paying attention. "We've had a pretty crazy day out on the trail this afternoon. He paused and looked around at all the campers in the room. Most had finished dinner and, for a change, were anxiously paying attention to what he was going to tell them.

"Just to kibosh any rumors to the contrary, no one was physically hurt on the bridge this afternoon." He stopped and made eye contact with the campers at the Cabin 5 table. They were talking instead of listening but got quiet when they realized he was looking at them.

"Let me repeat that. Thankfully, no one was hurt in the incident on the bridge this afternoon." The room erupted in the sudden noise of cheering and applause as the pent-up emotions of the day spontaneously burst out.

Mr. C smiled and waited for the moment to run its course then continued to recount the details of the afternoon. "We had eleven kids and two counselors on the bridge when the accident began Counselor Donnie and his Coyotes had just stepped on to the bridge when it started to fail. Donnie pulled the only one of his campers who was on the bridge in front of him, immediately off the bridge." He looked over at Donnie's table and announced, "Well done!" and the cafeteria began to clap again.

When he held up his hand for silence, the applause died down and then Mr. C continued his recap. "Over the next few minutes another three campers were able to carefully make their way off. Then over the next five to ten minutes, five of our counselors—Carson and Charlie, along with Laurie, Kelley, and Zoe, were able to put together a rescue for another three of the six stranded campers. So by the time the Air Rescue team from Burnet County arrived and took over, there were only three campers left to be rescued, plus Counselor Jesse."

Everyone began to cheer again and then started talking noisily to each other. They were interrupted by Mr. C, thumping his finger on the microphone again to get their attention. "Thanks again, everyone, for doing your part to listen and to respond as asked. Now by this time, most of you have had a chance to call home. I do know there are about twenty-five of you who are still waiting to hear back from a parent or guardian, but we hope to have all those calls wrapped up early this evening."

Mr. C checked his notecard then spoke again: "Last thing, kind of an important thing, in fact. As a reminder, the upper trails are completely closed until further notice. The Burnet County Sheriff's Department and Texas Rangers are investigating the circumstances of the bridge's failure and are treating the area as a crime scene. So just think about the C.S.I. TV shows and respect their authority and control of the crime scene. Anyone caught snooping around up there will be sent home immediately. Everyone got that?"

There were nods and murmurs of "Yes, Mr. C."

"Alright then. Tonight is movie night, so we will still have our movie-under-the-stars as planned. We'll have popcorn and popsicles starting at 8:30 in the amphitheater. Remember, if you have any questions I haven't answered already, be sure and talk to your counselors."

The chatter started back up again all around the dining hall and no one really was paying attention when he said, "That's all, you're dismissed," before leaving the platform.

"What movie are they showing tonight?" Monica asked Mac as they got up to take their trays to the clean-up window.

"No idea," she said and shrugged her shoulders. Anything was going to suit her; she was just glad the camp wasn't getting shut down because she was having too much fun with Monica and her new friends.

20

SUCCESS!

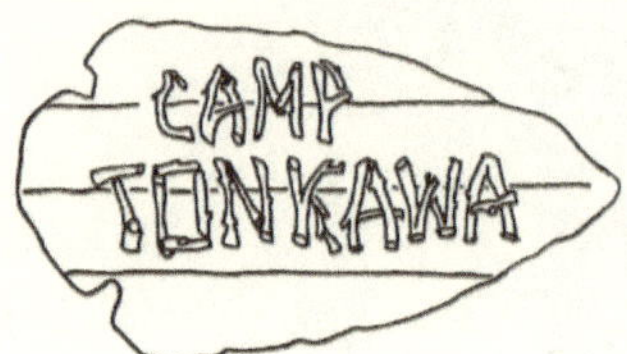

In his pocket, he felt his cell phone buzz, even though he kept it on silent when he was at work. He was dying to pull it out and have a look but his hands were wet and soapy and he was in the middle of scrubbing a five-gallon stainless steel cooking pot. He looked to his left and counted another nine pots before he'd be even close to a chance to sneak a peek at his phone.

But *the Grumbler* knew that it was going to be an alert from his local news feed. He'd been hearing the chatter as the kids came through the serving line this evening and his boss had been upset about "the accident up on Ghost Ridge" earlier in the afternoon.

He wasn't sure which irritated the cook more—the fact that something terrible had happened at the camp . . . or the inconvenience of her and her team being locked out of the kitchen and mess hall for over an hour while sheriff's department officers came and went.

Didn't matter. They hadn't been allowed in until 5:30 to start making supper. That meant only enough time to offer the camp equivalent of fast food, which in this case was canned bean soup with ham chunks, cornbread, and salads. And, pudding cups for dessert, of course.

Fifteen minutes later, he wiped his hands on his apron and looked around. The cook was nowhere in sight so he stepped outside into the hot air. He pulled out his phone and followed the link in his alert to a Breaking News Story. The video clip began with a local reporter who was breathlessly telling what had happened at the camp while video footage—obviously shot by a drone, circled and zoomed in on a broken suspension bridge high above the canyon below.

The voice of the reporter was very matter-of-fact yet held a sense of drama as she spoke.

"A 75-foot cable bridge suspended over a canyon at the Camp Tonkawa summer camp near Marble Falls, Texas, failed this afternoon, stranding nine campers and a counselor as they were crossing. The Burnet County Sheriff's Department was called to the scene and responded by helicopter to rescue the nine children and one adult who had to cling to the remaining cable for over thirty minutes while camp staff and first responders assisted them off the precarious remaining suspension cables. Camp Director Chuck Walker had this to say: 'We are so thankful that none of our campers were injured in this incident and appreciate the head-up response of our camp staff and the swift assistance of the sheriff's department to ensure all of our campers were rescued without harm.'"

The video switched back to the reporter who was posed live at the Burnet Airport where the county helicopter was parked. After a nod to the camera to acknowledge she was live, she concluded her story. "We understand tonight that the circumstance of the structural failure is currently under investigation and that the Texas Rangers have been called in to lead in that investigation. The president of the board of directors that runs this camp offered a written statement saying simply, 'We want to thank the Burnet County Sheriff's Department for their swift response and are thankful that no one was injured in an accident that certainly could have caused significant injury. We look forward to a full and thorough investigation by the Texas Rangers into the cause of the accident and will have no further statement at this time.'"

The reporter looked up at the camera with the helicopter still strategically positioned behind her and gave her sign-off: "This is Lilly Esparza for Channel 2 News. We will keep you posted on additional details of this breaking story as they become available."

The video clip stopped, and he looked around before deciding against watching the clip a second time. *Later,* he told himself and slipped the phone back into his pocket. He allowed himself a satisfied smile. His latest incident could not have gone better! No one hurt—but a big black eye for the camp. And, more important, now there would be super high visibility for the next prank.

A total success in so many ways!

21

GOTTA LOVE A "GATOR!"

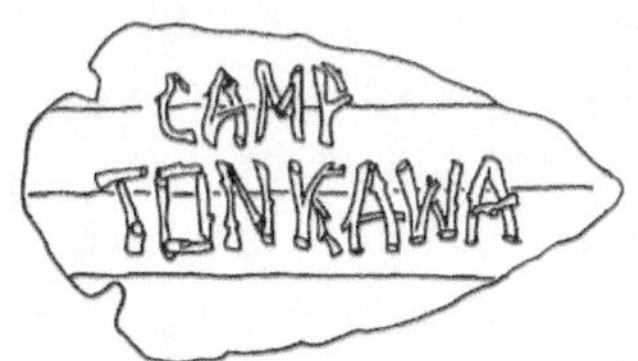

When it comes to navigating the wild brush, rocks and steep landscape of a Texas Hill Country ranch, few vehicles can get around like a four-wheel drive "Gator." Maybe a Toyota FJ40 Land Cruiser or a good 4WD Jeep, of course, but ATV's like a Gator are fun and amazing. Big Mike had called Charlie to his office after breakfast and asked him to take the Gator and three guests up to the ridge line. Charlie was only too happy to help!

Big Mike introduced Sergeant Max Conner and Captain Rene Stone, the two Texas Rangers who had just arrived to Charlie. "The Rangers, here—and Capt. Vasquez," he said and nodded toward the captain who was standing by the window, "they're pretty anxious to spend some time looking around the crime scene. I thought since it's so remote and you know our trails, it would be faster if you could just run them up to the ridge in the Gator."

"Sure, boss. I'd be happy to help!" Charlie replied enthusiastically. He instinctively snatched the Gator keys that Big Mike tossed over to him with a confidence that would have impressed a Major League Baseball talent scout. He dropped them into his pocket. "If you're ready, we can head out right now," he said.

Mike smiled as the three investigators followed Charlie out. He was certain they'd be chatty around one of his counselors than with Sam. And besides, *who knew?* The three might even discuss some useful info that Charlie would be happy to share with him later. It wouldn't hurt for him and Sandra, and Mr. C, to have some early insight on the direction of the investigation.

The bouncy, rough drive up to the ridge was mainly small talk as everyone kept at least one hand tightly gripped on something, *anything*, to keep from being accidentally ejected from the Gator. Captain Stone took the front bench seat beside Charlie and seemed pretty much at ease with the ride in spite of the roughness of the trail. She asked Charlie how he liked the camp, what the campers were like this year, what he was majoring in at college, and then circled back to ask what he thought of Mr. Walker and Mr. Murkowski.

Vasquez was leaning forward, listening and nodding. When Stone was finished, Captain Vasquez followed up with a couple of questions of his own about whether there were any mountain bike trails that had access to the west side of the bridge. Charlie described the network of bike and hiking trails to them and pointed out several parts of the upper trail along the ridge line above them as they got closer to the bridge.

After fifteen minutes, crossing rough terrain and a couple of creek beds, Charlie stopped at the bottom of the ravine under the damaged suspension bridge that hung about sixty feet above their heads. It looked very odd and kind of sad from directly below.

"Wow," Sgt. Conner said as he stared at the bridge and scanned it from left to right, his eyes focused on the 20 feet or so of floor planks that now hung from its west side. He traced the useless boards to the point where a limp length of loose cable hung down, dangling lazily in the afternoon breeze. "Thanks for your help getting us up here, Charlie," he finally said after taking it all in. "You obviously know your way around this part of the camp's property."

"I'll second that!" Captain Stone said with a grin on her face. "Glad we weren't having to pick out that trail ourselves. Reminds me a little bit of the old deer lease my dad used to have."

"Oh yeah?" Charlie asked, brightening at the words "deer lease."

He loved deer hunting and always enjoyed good stories with other hunters. "Whereabouts? Somewhere here in the Hill Country or somewhere else?"

"Up near Sulphur Springs, actually—northeast Texas. It was about twenty-five miles north of I-30 if you're familiar with that part of the state."

"Sure." Charlie replied and nodded. "One of my buddies at A&M has a family cabin up on Cooper Lake near there. That's a pretty part of Texas!"

The captain smiled at Charlie and nodded in acknowledgment but then switched to business as she turned to the two men with her. "Okay, Vasquez, show us what you found."

Charlie knew he should probably hang back and let them get on with their work, so he sat on the front hood of the Gator and sipped water from his camp bottle as he watched them hike up the ravine. He could see now that after the initial thrill of getting to drive the Gator, this was going to be one of those "hurry up and wait" kind of afternoons. So he climbed back in to get comfy in the front seat of the Gator for *the wait*.

22

CLUES

At some point Charlie caught himself staring up again at the underside of the bridge. His mind wandered back to spring break two years ago when he and Carson and a work crew had built it. He smiled to himself. It hadn't been as much fun as partying over spring break at South Padre Island with his friends might have been, but it had paid well and he liked the challenge of learning something new. He remembered being impressed by the simple engineering principles that Richie, the engineering student who'd designed the bridge, had explained to them: "These sorts of bridges have been used for thousands of years all over the world," he'd told them. "Two towers, one pair on each bank are all it takes to successfully hang the top cables which hold the weight of the walkway."

The towers for their bridge were just simple, ten-foot tall telephone poles. They'd dug holes and planted two in the ground on either side of the ravine. They'd drilled big holes in the tops of each rough post and then strung thick braided steel cables across the ravine between them. The cables hung in an arc across the valley between the towers and were anchored at both ends to shorter posts. It looked like a miniature of the famous Golden Gate Bridge in San Francisco.

The underside of the bridge was just two steel cables that were strung through each floor plank to create the actual walkway. Smaller cables ran in a zig-zag pattern between the upper and lower cables on either side. "That smaller steel line between the top and bottom cables lets the the upper cable hold up the weight of the floor boards," Richie had explained. *So simple.*

Charlie had seen pictures of similar bridges made out of heavy ropes and other simple materials. They were used in the Andes Mountains of South America and in the Himalayas of Asia. They could be found in the mountains of Afghanistan and Pakistan and anywhere people needed a fast way to get across a deep ravine: anywhere that people were willing to cross a tiny, narrow walkway in the sky—*without looking down and freaking out!*

Charlie's thoughts were interrupted by Captain Vasquez calling out to him and asking if he could join them up on the western ridge. "I'll be right there!" he answered, taking one last big drink of water before scrambling up the steep, rocky wall of the ravine.

Captain Vasquez gave him a hand at the top as he pulled himself onto the western ridge of the trail. "So, tell me, Charlie—where, exactly does this trail lead to from here?" Vasquez asked after Charlie had caught his breath.

He pointed into the forest of trees in the distance and then traced an imaginary path across the next two ravines and then down the side of the canyon to where the land was less steep and the trail became a winding path through the lower trees. He noted it crossed the dry creek, and eventually entered the main campgrounds near the dining hall and Sam's maintenance shops.

"If you look way down there, closer to the river, you can see the blue roof of the maintenance sheds and the mess hall just beyond the camper cabins," he said. "The trail kind of starts and ends down there."

"Have you ever ridden this trail on a mountain bike?" asked Capt. Stone, looking at him intently as he answered.

"It's a *bite* of a trail." Charlie said, scrunching his nose at the thought of its difficulty. "We did a counselor challenge last year before camp started—you know, a run, hike, bike, and swim kind of thing? I'm a decent swimmer and runner and I can get around these hills on a hike but you've got to *really* be in shape and trained in mountain biking to make that trail all the way up to here. It's a killer and that's no lie."

The two Rangers grinned and nodded, then glanced at Vasquez. "If your theory is right, Captain, then we're looking for a pretty seasoned trail biker, right?"

Vasquez nodded his head in agreement. "At least gives us one possible piece of the puzzle."

The sergeant spoke up: "So, Charlie, you said you were a part of the crew that helped build this bridge? Was that last spring? The year before? It really doesn't look very old."

"Two years ago," he said. "Part of the reason the Gator trail coming up here is still pretty good is 'cause it hasn't been that long since we cut it. In fact, we had to build the trail first, just so we could build the bridge, you know? Took a lot of trips to get all the lumber and cables and stuff up here."

"I can just imagine," Stone said, nodding. "Any idea how many of the counselors who were here to help build it are still here?" She was looking at him with that intense look of hers again. That intensity when she asked a question didn't make him very comfortable. *You really wouldn't want to be in an interrogation room across the table from her if you were a bad guy, that's for sure!* he thought.

"Well," he began, trying to recall the crew that had built the bridge with him, "besides me, my friend Carson was here that spring. Zoe and Bubba, too. And there was Sam—I know he's not a counselor, but he and a guy who used to be a counselor, the two of them, they designed it. He was majoring in engineering at A&M and the bridge was part of his senior project or something. I think his name was Richie. Anyway, I know there were a couple of other former counselors that helped that spring, but they've moved on and I didn't really know them." His eyes met Captain Stone's again. "Does that help?"

"Yeah. It does." She smiled now and the intensity faded. She turned to look across the bridge to the far side that was still intact.

"Charlie, I've got one other question, and that's about tools," Sgt. Conner said as he walked over to where the cable had been cut. "Obviously, we can have a chat with Sam when we get back, but it's pretty clear that this lower cable failed because it was cut pretty clean, probably with a power grinder and a cutting wheel," he said, glancing down to see it once again. "Well, cut clean except for maybe one or two strands of the cable," he said looking back up from the cut. "Whoever did this absolutely understood a thing or two about steel suspension cables." He shook his head and then looked back at Charlie again. "Anyway, let's talk tools. How easy is it to get ahold of serious tools around here?"

"If you're talking about a wrench or a pair of pliers or screwdrivers, pretty easy. But power tools, that's something you'd have to borrow from Sam and he keeps most of his tools under lock and key. He says good tools that aren't locked up, they always learn to walk when you're not looking."

Sgt. Conner nodded his head in earnest agreement. "So true."

"So, you know . . . everyone around here knows to stay out of Sam's shop unless you're working with him. Great guy—but don't mess with his tools!" Charlie concluded.

"Got it," Conner said, grinning at the description. "My father-in-law's the same way." He glanced at Vasquez then back at Charlie. "Thanks for your help."

"Okay, everyone." Captain Stone finally said, checking with each of her two partners. "Are we done here or do we need anything else before we head back?"

Vasquez paused and looked down the trail that led back to camp. "So Charlie, if I wanted to hike this trail back to camp, how long would it take me?"

Charlie considered the question for a moment. "I guess about 25 minutes at a good pace. That is, if you don't accidentally take the Snake-Pit Detour. The trail's pretty well marked if you're familiar with trails, but if you happen to come to a massive burr oak along a super-steep drop, you'll know you missed your turn and you're headed for the snake pit. Just be sure to turn around unless you really, *really* like rattlers." Charlie winked at Vasquez who smiled back knowingly.

"Okay. I'll meet you all back down at the camp in a half hour or so. I just want to get the lay of this trail and see if our suspect might have dropped anything on their way back from sabotaging the bridge."

"No problem," Stone said, nodding her approval. "Conner and I will head back in Charlie's *deer-lease limo.*"

Charlie grinned proudly and the three of them made their way back down the ravine to the Gator while Captain Vasquez disappeared into the woods following the upper trail.

"So what's your preference, Charlie?" Stone asked as they climbed into the Gator. "Rifle or bow?"

"Bow, of course!" he replied without hesitation. It's the only way to enjoy deer hunting as a true sport."

"Agreed," she said with a big smile. She reached up and grabbed ahold of the edge of the roof above her for the rough ride back to camp. "Let's roll."

23

WHERE'S THE MOTIVE?

"Are you asleep yet?"

Alex recognized Tyler's whisper from the next bunk over from his. "Nope," he replied. "Guess you're not either, huh?"

"Are you kidding? I'm wide awake trying to figure this out—I mean, this is some kind of crazy going on! You think there's some killer clown or some nut-head on the loose somewhere out there?"

"I don't think you need to freak out . . . and no, I don't think we're in the middle of a slasher movie, Tyler." Alex smiled. Tyler was usually calm and collected but Alex could see the events at camp this week had finally rattled him.

"Well, all I know is that Monica told Mac that her dad had told her there were about twenty cops combing the woods looking for an escaped convict who'd bought a hacksaw at a hardware store in town earlier this week. That sounds pretty serious, so I don't know what to think!"

"Calm down, Tyler. That's just all gossip and reminds me of that old pass-along story game we used to play. Every time the story gets retold, someone gets part of it wrong or adds to it until it doesn't even come close to reality."

"Then I can ignore Monica's 'killer clown' theory?"

"Yeah, I think you can cross that one off your list." Alex grinned to himself in the darkness of the cabin.

Tyler was silent for a few moments, then whispered another question: "So, you've been pretty tight with Charlie the past two days. What does he think is going on?"

"Hmm," Alex muttered. "Charlie drove a couple of the Texas Rangers up to the bridge in one of the camp's Gators just after breakfast." Alex paused and glanced at the other bunk near them. Jonathan was already sound asleep, so he continued. "I guess they let him see where the cable was cut—and no, it wasn't cut with a hacksaw." He paused and looked at Tyler in the dark. "Dude, that cable is like an inch thick or so. It's heavy-duty, braided steel cable—you couldn't cut that with a hacksaw unless you went after it for an hour or more!"

"Whoa."

"Yeah. Charlie said the cut was as clean as a hot knife on a stick of cold butter . . . except for the three strands of wire that had been left to fail once there was weight on the bridge. The Rangers told him it looked like someone had used a grinder cutoff disk."

"You mean like the grinders they use in Eric's shop when they've been welding?"

"Yeah. But probably the cordless kind—like you'd use at a construction site. I'll bet there's a couple of 'em here at the camp's maintenance shop and I'll bet Sam's probably missing one."

"Sounds like an inside job, then?"

"Not sure," Alex said. He wanted to be careful about speculating about who might be responsible—especially since no one had really pointed to any specific suspects yet.

"It's probably kinda dangerous—and also pointless to try and guess who the culprit might be. We ought to hear more in the next couple of days though."

"Sure hope so," Tyler said with a touch of resignation. He realized there really wasn't much else anyone knew, yet. But it was helpful to hear a few real facts instead of all the crazy gossip Monica was spreading.

Tyler had run out of questions. After a minute of silence, Alex offered one more comment to Tyler in a loud whisper: "There's one thing missing here."

"What's that?"

"Motive."

"Meaning . . . ?"

"Meaning, who stands to gain from whatever is going on?" Alex asked. "This isn't a one-off, you know, like when someone puts together a plan and then goes out and does something crazy and then they're either caught or something goes wrong, or worse."

"I don't get what you mean." Tyler said, looking over toward his friend in the dark.

"Well, this looks like a very deliberate *series* of events. Someone has put some real thought into all this. And even though they've been dangerous stunts, there's been some caution and reserve in what's actually happened."

"Cutting a bridge doesn't sound very thoughtful or careful to me!" Tyler said, confused.

"Okay, sure. But think about it. Whoever cut the bridge only cut one cable—or most of that one cable. They didn't intend for the whole bridge to fail and in fact, I think they were counting on a slow enough failure that everyone would hold on to what was left and get rescued."

"Sounds pretty sick to me."

"Agreed. But there's always motive in a deliberate plan, and right now I'm missing why someone would go after the camp this way. I wish I had my laptop . . . or at least my phone so I could research a couple of questions I've got."

"Maybe Charlie would let you use his, tomorrow. Couldn't hurt to ask, right?"

Alex thought about Tyler's idea for a minute. "You might be right. I'll think about that."

Tyler noticed a dim LED light suddenly turn on in the small staff room in the corner of their cabin where Charlie slept and kept his stuff. "We better shut up," he whispered as softly as he could. "I think we woke 'the giant' up." There was a slight snicker in his muffled voice; *the Giant* was the nickname the boys had given their counselor, Charlie. The thought brought a grin on his face in the dark.

"See ya in the morning," Tyler said quickly.

"Yeah, see you in the morning," Alex replied. He said nothing else but he still couldn't fall asleep. He just kept staring at the dark ceiling of the cabin.

What's the motive? he kept asking himself. *There's got to be a motive that makes this all make sense!*

The last time Alex checked his watch it was two a.m. and he was still wide awake—but Alex must have fallen asleep shortly after that.

NEWS MOVES FAST ... TOO FAST

"**Y**ou checked your news feed this morning?" Sandra asked with a worried tone in her voice. Big Mike and Mr. C were on a conference call with her to discuss the investigation going on at the camp. Mike slid his phone across the desk so Mr. C could see the story from the San Marcos TV station on his mobile app.

"Uh, give me a sec, Sandra. We only just got the campers underway for the morning so I haven't had a chance to look just yet." He quickly scanned the first couple of paragraphs of the story while Sandra told gave him the highlights from her perspective.

"*Classic Texas summer camp the target of a near deadly sabotage!*" She said dramatically, repeating the lead story she'd seen on her morning news. "They even flew a drone over our property—*without permission!* to get an aerial shot of that broken bridge. Great cinematography if you're filming a suspense movie, but pretty terrible publicity if you're running a legacy summer camp whose campers include the sons and daughters of a who's-who list of attorneys, doctors, and corporate executives!"

The exasperation in her voice betrayed the frustration she was feeling at how suddenly and unexpected this turn of events had unfolded. Mr. C quietly slid Mike's phone back across the desk to him.

"Well, whoever is behind this certainly got the attention they were looking for," he agreed.

"And it's quickly spinning out of our control and that is unacceptable."

"What can we do to help at this point?"

"I spoke with Elsa this morning," Sandra continued. "Told her to get on this and fast. She's to see what she can do to get some sort of a reasonable narrative around it all. Worst thing you can do in a situation like this is to be passive. Time to take control of the narrative!"

"Elsa, your PR guru?" Mr. C asked, for Big Mike's benefit.

"Yes, Chuck, THAT Elsa. She'll be calling you when I get off. I want you to give her a full briefing and don't worry about confidentiality, tell her everything you know and help her with anything she asks for. Anything. If she can spin a beached oil tanker and a stolen Van Gogh she can surely help us get this under control."

Mr. C made a mental note to explain Elsa's professional resume to Big Mike so he'd know what Sandra was talking about. But Sandra had access to the right person. Elsa was a professional fixer when it came to helping media sources "better understand a useful point of view" as a news story was developing.

"So, Sandra . . ." Mr. C began, hesitant to ask the question he was about to ask.

"What, Chuck? Don't be coy at a time like this. What's on your mind?"

"I've been trying to wrap my head around a motive for this. I honestly don't think we've got any discontented campers or past counselors with a grudge or a whacko-parent out there that we somehow offended. I talked with the lead Ranger last night and she's telling me that whoever cut that cable probably has a reasonable engineering background to have calculated the degree of failure involved in that cut."

"I know. I got the same update from the deputy head of the Rangers myself last night," Sandra said.

"So . . . have you got an angle on why someone would want to make us look so bad? I mean, we're just a kids' summer camp for goodness' sake. Someone out there is taking a lot of risks to make it look like we're a bunch of inept fools running a dangerous camp. Why?"

Sandra was silent for a moment then asked simply, "Is your door closed?"

Big Mike glanced over his shoulder then reached out to close Mr. C's door. "It is, now. Why?"

"Because all of this might have something to do with the Major Hoffmeier Compact. You know, the legal document that created Camp Tonkawa and the camp's board." She paused. "I hate to sound paranoid, Chuck, but I believe someone wants to get access to the camp's land . . . but their only way to do that is to destroy the camp's reputation first."

"Woah," Mr. C muttered softly.

"I don't think this is over yet, Chuck," Sandra said. Mr. C sensed a rare hint of uncertainty in the voice of his normally very self-confident boss.

THE HOFFMEIER COMPACT

Carson, Zoe, and Charlie were sitting at one of the camp picnic tables with Alex and Tyler. It was craft time and today's project was to build an eco-friendly bat house.

Over the course of this week, each camper was supposed to build three of them so they could take them home and offer them to a local city park. Bats love mosquitos and with enough bat houses in a park . . . well, controlling mosquitos with bats rather than with insecticides was a great opportunity to try a new approach!

But it was no coincidence that there were three counselors sitting with these two campers this morning. Charlie was anxious for his friends Carson and Zoe to hear what Alex had found out. Tyler was included since he was Alex's best friend.

"Okay," Charlie began in a low voice, offering some background, "I know it's a little bending of the rules, but Alex is something of a detective nerd with good credentials. I let him borrow my laptop for a half hour this morning. He wanted to research some ideas he had about what's been going on here at the camp this summer. He and I thought you might want to hear what he came up with; it's kind of interesting."

Zoe glanced over to the two tables where her campers were busy working on their bat houses. She nodded. "Sure. What's up?"

"Alex?" Charlie said, cueing his camper to start.

Alex wasn't easily intimidated but he was kind of surprised to be briefing three counselors instead of just having a casual conversation with Charlie. Nonetheless, he began with a name they all knew: Major Hoffmeier. "This camp is the former ranch of Major Simeon Hoffmeier. Y'all know that—it's part of heritage night the first week of camp and it ties this all back to the Tonkawa Indian tribe."

"First peoples," Charlie corrected him.

"Sorry, first peoples," Alex acknowledged. "Okay, so Hoffmeier was an amateur anthropologist. He was pretty intense and was also a collector of early oral histories of a bunch of the first people tribes in this part of Texas. After realizing what a heritage the Tonkawa people had in this area, he wanted his ranch to be a legacy to that heritage—so, he put together a kind of complicated will that left this part of his ranch to a land trust and a board of directors that would operate a kids' camp on the land to honor the people of the Tonkawa Tribe."

"So far, none of that is news, Charlie," Zoe said, looking at Charlie with curiosity. *"Where is this going?"* she mouthed silently to Charlie when no one was looking at her.

"Hang in there," Charlie said and then nodded for Alex to continue.

"It took some digging, but in the Burnet County digital archives I found a copy of the compact that was filed with Major Hoffmeier's will back in the 1930s."

"That's the legal document that created the land trust for the camp," Tyler added, hoping to be helpful.

"Very enterprising," Zoe said, impressed.

"Let me guess," Carson said with a smile. "It said he wanted to set up a land trust with a board and turn the ranch into a camp."

Charlie gave him a sour look for teasing Alex, and he backed off. "Okay, Alex. What did you find in that document that maybe we don't already know?"

"Well, if you read the whole thing, what do you think the reversion clause looks like?"

Zoe looked at Carson and then at Charlie. "What's a reversion clause?"

"It's what happens if something changes the original plan." Tyler said, stepping in with the factoid he had just learned himself only a half hour ago.

Alex grinned at Tyler then continued. "If, for whatever unforeseen circumstance, the camp can no longer operate as a self-supporting, non-profit business and ceases to be a camp under the terms of the grant, then the land doesn't stay with the camp's board."

"Okay, but why?" Carson asked.

"That ensured the land could never be sold to benefit the board." Alex looked at Zoe and Carson to get their reaction. "In other words, it can never be redeveloped or sold, it can only be a camp."

"So . . .?"

"Well, if the camp can't be a camp anymore, then the land reverts back to the blood heirs of Major Hoffmeier."

"Kind of a stretch, but I suppose you know who the heirs are, right?" Zoe asked, growing increasingly impressed with Alex.

"The heir. Like only one." Alex smiled. "There's only one living blood heir at this point."

No one asked a question, they just waited for Alex to continue. "That's because Major Hoffmeier's two oldest daughters died without kids and his only son was killed in the Pacific during World War II."

"But the son who died in World War II, he had a kid?" Zoe asked.

"Right. Edwin was married before he left for the Pacific. Ironically, Hazel, his daughter—who would be Major Hoffmeier's granddaughter, she was born the very same day Hoffmeier's son Edwin was killed during the invasion of Iwo Jima. Weird, huh?" Alex shook his head.

"I'd call it tragic, Alex," Zoe corrected him.

"Agreed," he conceded. "So, anyway, Hazel grew up, married, and then she had a daughter named JoEllen, who was born in 1969. There's no record of who the dad was, but later, JoEllen, Hoffmeier's great-granddaughter disappeared in Canada. But before she left the U.S., she had a son. He was born in Austin, Texas in 1992, just before JoEllen moved up north to Canada."

Carson did the connections. "Okay, so that kid would qualify as a blood heir if anything went belly up for this camp, right?"

Zoe jumped in. "And so, you think there's a thirty-something guy out there who's decided to ruin this camp so he can inherit his great-grandpa's ranch?"

"Great-*great*-grandpa," Alex corrected her. "Yeah. Why not? It's one of the oldest motives there is for mischief and mayhem . . . inheritance greed."

"Sounds too easy," Zoe said, shaking her head. "The Rangers probably already know this and even know the guy's name. Seems like it would be pretty easy to run that angle down and do something about it."

"Well, I already know his name. He's Dillon P. Clarke," Alex said. "But here's the black-hole thing: the kid disappeared with his mom when she left for Canada back in 1998. No record of him online. Can't find where he is or what he even looks like."

"Or if he's alive?" Zoe observed.

"Whoa," Carson said, holding up his finger to ask Zoe to hang on. "I like where you're going, Alex." He suddenly had a new respect for Charlie's young camper. "Don't you see how that would all make sense, Zoe?" He shook his head and looked back at Charlie. "Even if you don't know where he is or what he looks likes it makes a great story, doesn't it? When are you going to let Mr. C know?" he asked.

"Well," Charlie hesitated, "I guess we hadn't gotten that far, yet."

"Think again, my friend. Your camper here might've just hit a home run. I'd say run, do not walk, right over and see him now."

Alex turned to look at Tyler. He nodded. This was too important to keep to themselves.

DIRTY DISHES

It was Thursday, the day that Mac and Monica had been dreading since the camper duty calendar had been posted on Monday. That's when they'd discovered they'd been assigned "KP." Alex said it was called "kitchen patrol" in the army, but any way you named it, it was just kitchen duty and their turn had finally arrived. To be sure, there were worse assignments on the schedule. Dory got stuck on trash detail which included ALL the girl's restrooms AND all the green trash bins scattered all around the campgrounds. Kaitlyn and Riley had been assigned to set tables and clean up the dining hall after breakfast, lunch, and supper today.

The shared misery of assignments was of only limited consolation to Mac and Monica, though, since their job meant they were missing snack bar time this evening. "No pink passion fruit frozen yogurt tonight." Monica said glumly as she sprayed the food off another rack of yucky plates.

"No coconut gummy worms and strawberry frozen slushee." Mac said, shaking her head.

"No Swedish gummy fish on top of that pink passion fruit frozen yogurt."

"Nope."

While everyone else in camp was buying their favorite snack or drink, Mac and Monica were rinsing plates and plastic cups and racking them to feed through the camp kitchen's industrial dishwasher.

"Drink cups, 135; plates, 135; 39 serving bowls plus all the dirty forks and spoons and at least two racks of miscellaneous other stuff." That had been Alex's estimate of things after he and Tyler had done KP the week before. One supper's mess would end up filling about two dozen big, stackable plastic dishwasher racks according to Miss Nancy —the camp cook. And most of it was covered in every imaginable combination of left over food stuff.

"This is just so totally gross!" was Monica's simple and on-point assessment after loading their twentieth rack.

"Better than emptying trash," Mac countered, trying to find the bright side.

"Maybe, but after seeing this I might not want to eat for a week."

"Tell me that tomorrow morning when they have chocolate chip waffles on the menu."

"What? Really? We're having chocolate chip waffles tomorrow?" Monica asked with excitement.

"YES, REALLY!" Mac said in mock astonishment. "With whipped cream, even!" Mac decided she must be the only camper that bothered to look at the next day's menu. It got pinned to the bulletin board every afternoon but when she would mention what they were having, her fellow campers imagined that she was clairvoyant or something.

Mac glanced at the giant stack of cooking pots and utensils along with all the big stainless steel pans that were used on the serving line. At least all the kitchen food prep stuff was washed by the paid kitchen staff. Presley, one of the cook's two hired assistants was responsible for cleaning up all that stuff tonight.

"Who knew it took this much work to feed us every day!" Monica said as she finally finished rinsing the last tray of dinner dishes.

"I guess that's why they make us do this." Mac said. She figured there was always a reason for just about anything that was hard to do, even if it was boring. "At least we're getting close to being finished. I'll be back in a minute, I'm gonna take these two trays of glasses to the pantry and put them away."

"Well, don't take too long," Monica said suspiciously. "We've still got three more trays to go through the dishwasher."

"Chill, girl. I'll be back in a min," Mac replied. She picked up the two large trays and headed to the hall on the other side of the kitchen. A short hallway led to both the walk-in fridge and the walk-in freezer as well as to three small storage rooms. The cook called the first two rooms her "pantries," but they looked more like oversized closets to Mac.

The larger of the two was lined with wire shelving racks where all the canned, boxed, and bagged food stuffs were kept along one wall. On the other side, all the paper goods were neatly stored on another rack of wire shelves. Next door to the food pantry was a second, smaller room with more wire shelves for storing the cooking pots and the steam-table pans, along with shelves for other gadgets and equipment, stuff that belonged to the cook. The third room really wasn't much bigger than a walk-in closet. It had two racks of shelves along one short wall where all of the cups and plates and smaller utensils were stored between meals. The cook just referred to that space as her "crockery closet" when she gave them a quick kitchen tour and job assignments.

Mac was taking the tray of cups to the crockery closet but when she turned the corner she got confused and stepped into the open doorway of the food pantry by mistake. Presley, the cook's assistant, was on his cell phone and when he looked up and saw her, it startled him and he gave Mac a pretty ugly scowl. He was not happy to have a lost kid-camper interrupting him.

"Wrong room!" he snapped impatiently and glared at her.

"Sorry!" Mac said, backing up to turn around. "Got the wrong door." She was embarrassed for her mistake and quickly figured out which was the correct door instead. She set the two trays of glasses on one of the wire shelves, beside four other trays just like them.

When she did, she stopped for a moment to replay the accidental interruption in her head. As she thought about it, the situation suddenly struck her as odd. First, she couldn't imagine why the cook's assistant would be on his phone right now. *Why would he be taking a break before all his pans are done?* And then, her embarrassment quickly turned to indignation. *And what was with the dirty look? That was just mean and totally uncalled for! After all, it was just a simple mistake.*

She was getting ready to leave and go back to the kitchen to give Monica a self-pity rant, when she overheard Presley speaking in a loud whisper. He seemed very agitated. Mac paused to listen, just nosy enough to want to know what was being said and if it might have anything to do with why the cook's assistant had been so crabby to her.

"It's none of your business HOW I get this done," she heard Presley say. "I'm going to do it my way and I don't need any input or help from you, got it? And, when it's done, we've still got a deal and you better hold up your end of the bargain!"

Now Mac didn't know what to do. If she walked past the open pantry room door, Presley would realize she'd overheard his conversation. *What to do?* Suddenly she remembered a conversation she and Tyler had been having with Alex during one of their afternoons at the pool earlier this summer. Tyler liked to call them "Alex Rambles." Alex could go on and on about something he'd read whether they wanted to hear it or not.

"Spy-craft" was the topic one afternoon. He'd been educating them on what he called "trade craft" that might come in handy some time. *Right.*

"Distractions make for diversions and they confuse people more easily than we realize," he'd said. "A good distraction can mask the reality of a situation, like a magician's sleight of hand." Suddenly, that gave Mac a brilliant idea!

Looking up, she pulled the top tray of plastic cups over to the edge of the shelf just far enough for the whole thing to fall tumbling to the ground with a terrific amount of clattering and noise. She added her own shout of embarrassment and frustration: "Oh, no! Arrg!" to add to the drama.

"What happened?" Monica called as she came running to the closet, following the sound of the commotion. When she spotted Mac, she immediately saw the mess: the tray lying on the floor and plastic cups scattered everywhere.

"I tried reaching too high and they slipped!" Mac said, making up a story to cover for all the noise.

"Aw, Mac! Now we're going to have to wash all those again!" Monica said, frustrated with Mac's clumsiness.

"Help me pick them up, okay?" Mac asked and got down on her knees and began reloading the tray. "At least they're clean, right? All we'll have to do is run them through the sanitizer again."

"Yeah, right . . . I guess. But this isn't rocket-science, Mac, all you needed to do was put the tray on the shelf."

Presley appeared in the doorway watching the two of them and now laughed at the mess Mac had made.

"Figures," he said. "Amateur Hour with The Junior Kitchen Help! I'll leave you two to clean up your own dumb mess, I've got pots to wash!" It was clear he wasn't the least bit concerned about their plight. And, he had no idea the drama had been a ploy of avoid suspicion. *Wow . . . Alex was right about distractions!*

Mac watched him head back to the kitchen, then gave Monica a very obvious and overacted wink.

"What's that for, Mac?" she asked, a puzzled look on her face.

"I'll tell you later, girl." she replied, grinning. But then she added, cryptically, "I'm not as clumsy as you think I am."

She carried the rack of cups back to the wash counter and glanced over at Presley. He seemed totally unaware of anything around him as he looked intently at the pot he was scrubbing. But Mac was certain she'd stumbled onto something significant.

Presley was up to something. She just wasn't sure what.

27

BAT HOUSES—ROUND TWO

"I'm thinking bat houses probably are *not* a priority at the El Paso Parks and Rec Department," Monica casually observed, just in case anyone was listening.

"Never know," Tyler replied. He was using the staple gun to attach the roof to his second bat house for the week.

Mac was using the electric burner pen to draw her best impression of a bat on the outside of her bat house. The acrid smell of singed cedar wood hung over the table. "Mac, that stinks. Aren't you about finished?" Tyler asked. "I mean, seriously . . . how many bats do you really need to draw on your house, anyway?"

She looked at the scene she'd created on the front of her bat house and counted four winged critters and decided it would be a more balanced composition if there were five. "One more should just about do it."

Alex shook his head and started gluing the inside hidden pieces into the frame of his next bat house.

"Oh sure, Alex," Monica said, "show us all up by already starting on your third one."

"Fourth," he countered. "My uncle has a ranch in San Agustin and I figure he'd like to give these a try." He finished gluing his last stick

109

down and when he was satisfied, he put the lid back on the glue bottle and then pushed his project over to the middle of the table to cure.

"So," he said, satisfied with his work and turning to Mac, "you told us you had a story from last night in the kitchen. When are you gonna to put us out of our misery and tell us what happened?"

Mac looked at Alex and then at Monica, who just shrugged. She decided now was as good a time as any. "Something weird happened when we were washing up the dinner stuff," Mac began.

"More like creepy if you ask me," Monica added.

"I was taking two racks of the glasses to, you know, that 'crockery pantry' Miss Nancy calls it."

"Yeah. I know what you mean," Tyler said, remembering his KP duty with Alex from earlier in the week.

"I made a mistake when I was going to put the trays away. I went into the food pantry first by mistake . . ."

"That's not much of a story," Alex said, interrupting and pretending to be disappointed.

"I'm not finished!" Mac said, a little upset at being made fun of.

"That's good," Alex replied with mock relief, "needs more to make it a decent story!"

Mac glared at him. "So I accidentally stepped into the food pantry and I surprised the cook's assistant. He was on his phone instead of washing pots and pans like he was supposed to be doing, and I think he wasn't expecting to get interrupted."

"I believe that is the definition of an interruption, right?" Alex said, laughing.

"Do you want to hear the story or not?"

"Too late to say '*not.*'"

"Cut it out, Alex, and let Mac tell her story," Monica said firmly.

Mac relaxed and continued. "Anyway, I go to the right room to put the racks away and I can still overhear the guy's phone conversation. Not intending to eavesdrop or anything, but he was telling whoever was on the phone that *it was none of their business HOW* he got whatever he was talking about done. *I'm gonna do it my way and I don't need any help from you.* And then he said, *And when I'm done you better hold up your end of the bargain. Understand?!*"

Alex was quiet for a moment while he thought about that. "Which guy said that?" he finally asked.

"That creepy guy who's the cook's assistant," Monica replied. "Perry, Preston, something like that."

"You mean Presley?" Tyler asked.

"Yeah, that's it!" Monica nodded her head.

"You remember the dude that had to wash all the cook's pots?" Tyler asked Alex, trying to help him place the person Mac was talking about. "He was maybe thirty or so with the blonde hair and round glasses? He's one of the two assistant cooks. The other guy is younger and from somewhere in Europe. He has a funny accent."

"Yeah, no," Alex paused, "sure, I remember him." he started playing with the bottle of glue on the table, spinning it around in circles while he was thinking. "Say it again—what you heard him say."

"It's none of your business HOW I get this done, I'm doing it my way and don't need any input from you, got it?" She paused for effect, "And, when it's done, you better hold up your end of the bargain!"

"How old do you guess Presley is?" Alex asked Tyler again.

"I dunno, has to be at least thirty, maybe older. He's for sure older than Mac's other cousin, Cory, and he's like twenty-nine, I think. Presley likes his bubble gum, though. That's for sure." If you noticed nothing else about the otherwise non-descript guy that worked in the kitchen you couldn't miss him blowing bubbles and popping them loudly when he sucked them back in.

"I remember when we first got here, he was hanging out over by the kitchen on a trick bike wasn't he?" Alex asked. "One of those BMX trail kinda bikes, wasn't it?"

Tyler didn't remember but wasn't surprised that Alex had, he always seemed to notice and remember the weirdest little things. He shook his head. "Dude, I have no idea. But come to think of it, I did see him on a green BMX one afternoon this weekend."

"Okay, so lemme play this idea out a sec." Alex set the bottle upright and looked directly at Tyler. "Charlie said that Captain Vasquez guy from the sheriff's department was looking for a suspect who did mountain biking, right?"

Tyler nodded in agreement, watching Alex's face.

"And when I was telling Charlie and Carson and Zoe about the idea of a family heir maybe out to ruin the camp's reputation so they could get the land back, that missing heir was born in 1992 . . . so he'd be about thirty something, right?"

"You did, but you said his name was Dillon Clarke." Mac interrupted. "I remembered that detail because I had a teacher in fifth grade named Dillon."

"Hmm, yeah, but actually it was Dillon P. Clarke, so it still works 'cause he might be going by his middle name. What if he got a job here at the camp just so he could sabotage things without getting caught?"

"I think that's a pretty big stretch, Alex." Tyler shook his head. "How could we know that, anyway? This guy could be totally innocent and just having an argument with a friend about selling something that has nothing to do with what's going on here." Tyler wasn't convinced they could have simply stumbled onto such a significant coincidence.

"Well, I think he's creepy. I say we turn him in to Big Mike." Monica was excited at the prospect of being able to do something that might be heroic.

"No, we can't do that. We don't have any proof," Mac said, shaking her head. "We'd need more to go on. Besides, I don't want to look stupid if we're wrong."

"What if there's some simple proof?" Alex said slowly.

"Like what?" Mac could see Alex had another big idea about to be served up.

"What if the cut-off grinder is in his locker?"

Tyler remembered the room off the dining hall where all the staff had lockers. Most of the counselors kept their stuff in their space in the cabins, but the other camp employees each had a staff locker where they could keep their personal stuff.

"How would we check that?" Monica wondered out loud, not used to working with Alex on his big ideas.

"I've got an idea," Alex offered, a smile now on his face as he glanced at each of his friends. "But if we do it, we have to keep it a secret, even from Charlie."

"I'm not sure I like that, Alex." Trying to find out what was in Presley's locker didn't sound like such a good idea to Tyler. "Isn't that burglary or something? Besides, shouldn't the Rangers figure that out?"

"It's burglary if you take something," Alex countered. "We'll be spies, doing reconnaissance work for the Texas Rangers to help them solve a crime. If it's there, we'll let them know."

"How are you going to get into a locker?" Mac asked.

"Leave that to me, but I'm going to need everyone's help to pull this off."

Mac looked at Monica who was smiling and clearly excited to do something bold. Tyler was concerned that this could be trouble but he trusted Alex's instincts, as long as they were looking but not taking anything.

Mac finally nodded her head. "Okay, but I don't want to get kicked out of camp—we've been having too much fun."

"Don't worry. I'll pull together the details and we can make this little operation happen during snack time tonight when everyone else —including Presley, is distracted."

They all agreed and sealed their silence with a round of fist bumps.

Suddenly, bat houses didn't seem to hold the same interest. They were going to be part of a spy job!

28

—————

NEWS IS NEWS - ONLY WHEN
IT'S NEWS

A s promised, Sandra's PR expert, Elsa, had worked her magic with the news outlets. Despite all the attention which the fallen bridge had created on Sunday evening and most of the day Monday, no one was actually injured. So, like so many evening news stories, once the shock was gone, interest faded quickly. Two local news stations had a brief, two-paragraph update about the investigation on Tuesday, but no video. By Wednesday—*nothing*.

Elsa let Sandra Morrison-Parker know that if there were reporters out there hoping to make a name for themselves with a big, investigative journalism angle, they hadn't appeared yet. That was a relief to Sandra and the board. And, it was precisely why she kept Elsa on a *very* expensive retainer. She knew how to manage a crisis! On the other hand, Sandra knew this probably wasn't over yet. At least not until someone figured out who was responsible. Her update from the Texas Rangers was focused on someone with a mountain bike but that was about it.

Unknown to all of them was the interest of another person, someone who had also noticed how quickly the news had faded. He was *not* pleased. He was the "person of interest" the Burnet County Sheriff's

Office and the Texas Rangers were looking for. That person had expected the bridge event to create a hive of investigative reporters quickly pouncing to destroy the camp's reputation. But that hadn't happened! That left him both surprised and disappointed. He knew the game wasn't over yet, but in the meantime, he'd overheard a conversation from Big Mike's office that the cops were trying to identify a BMX bike track found up near the bridge. He hadn't been careful enough, it seemed.

Oops.

He'd decided it was best to hide his bike under some tarps and old life jackets in the back of the old storage shed near the new boat house. *No one would be looking for a bike in that old unused shed!* Unfortunately, that meant he was now on foot since he didn't own a car. *Maybe he should go into town and buy a cheap, used bike at a pawnshop or off a local on-line resale site. Something that didn't look anything like his old BMX! Or would that be too suspicious?*

Dang!

But there was more. On his way to the kitchen yesterday—before his lunch shift, he'd seen two Texas Rangers talking to Sam in his shop. He hid and listened to their conversation. They wanted to know if he was missing a grinder. He'd grinned to himself as he could see Sam shaking his head. He was glad he'd decided to just buy a cheap cordless grinder instead of "borrow" one of Sam's.

A dead-end lead for the Rangers!

The Grumbler chugged the second half of his energy drink and dropped the empty can into the trash bin. Time to get back to the kitchen. As he stood, his phone buzzed in his pocket.

"Hullo?"

"Listen here, you little goofball. A little birdie just told me the Rangers are looking for a 'person of interest' who might have been seen riding a BMX trail bike on Farm-to-Market Road 2134 near where it goes over the low-water crossing of South Fork Creek around 2:30 p.m. on August fourth." The voice paused. "They said the person was riding a green BMX trail bike and had on a gray hoodie and a black backpack on his back. He was wearing a pair of aviator-style sunglasses."

The Grumbler swallowed hard and said nothing as he quickly pulled off his sunglasses and stuffed them in his backpack.

"Well look you, little dimwit, I'm just wondering if you got yourself tagged when you were pulling off your stupid stunt with the bridge."

"Bogus."

"Not you? That's a relief."

"No way anyone's got an ID. They're fishing."

"You better hope so. Not only is the deal off, but you are high, dry, and a total *unknown* to me if this falls apart on you."

"No, dude. You want this way too bad to walk it," he replied, a silent smile on his face. He was suddenly suspicious that maybe his buyer wasn't being totally on the level with him. Was he messing with his head? Was there really a description of him out there? Had someone really seen him on his bike over where the Ghost Trail briefly ran alongside FM 2134? He hadn't seen anything about that on any of *his* newsfeeds. *The Buyer's just baiting me,* he decided.

"You just make sure you don't go and kill someone with your whacko scheme," the voice continued. "I'm not buying blood land. Don't convince yourself I'll buy it at any cost. I won't buy a PR nightmare."

"What, you think I'm stupid?"

"Well, I'm not so sure." There was a brief pause. "Just don't go crossing a line on me . . . 'cause I'm not kidding. I'll walk so fast it'll leave your head spinning."

The line went dead as the Buyer hung up.

Yeah, like anyone this close to getting their hands on this prime ranch land was really ever going to walk! No way, the Grumbler muttered to himself.

He checked the time on his screen before he slid the phone back into his pocket. *Ten-forty-seven. Dang! Now he was two minutes late for his lunch shift.* He blew another huge bubble then snapped it as he jogged to the back door of the kitchen.

What the heck, so what else was new?

29

JUST A QUICK PEEK

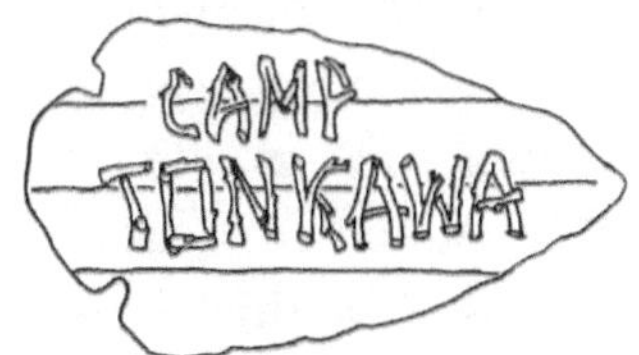

Alex's plan was simple. They'd each get their snack and then casually wander over to the breezeway hall between the administration building and the mess hall. The backside of the breezeway wasn't as well-lit as the rest of camp so it would be easier for one of them to slip into the locker room and the others serve as lookouts.

"Where did you come up with a key?" Tyler asked as they met up with their slushee drinks, candy bars, and Monica's yogurt.

"I had a quick look this afternoon at the brand and the numbers. Presley's locker is number 14 and the lock is a number 2856. The camp only uses one brand of locks and Sam keeps replacement keys by number . . . so I kind of helped myself to a #2856 while he was getting me a replacement LED light bulb for our cabin."

"Dude, one of these days you're going to get so caught pulling one of your stunts!"

"Meh. Maybe," Alex said, shrugging and handing the key to Mac. "Presley should be tied up washing pots and pans for at least another half hour but we'll keep an eye out just in case."

Mac took the key and examined it. Sure enough, it had the

number 2856 stamped on it. "Locker 14?" she asked, just to make sure she'd heard right.

"Yup. Now Monica, we need a relay, so you need to be sitting on the floor in the breezeway, leaning against the wall near the locker room door eating your frozen yogurt."

"Which is really starting to melt!" she said, annoyed.

"Yeah, whatever. If you hear either me, or Tyler say something like *'The Astros are really going to put the hurt on Phoenix this weekend, Parsons is really on a hitting streak'* then you'll know someone is coming and you should say something out loud to yourself like, maybe, *'Dang, I'm out of Swedish Fish, I knew I should have gotten more on my yogurt!'*"

Mac spoke up. "And I'm supposed to know that means to hurry up and leave?" It was obvious, but Mac thought she should better ask.

"Duh, yeah!" Alex said with a pained look on his face.

"Okay. Let's do this before I lose my nerve," Mac said. "Here, Monica, hang on to my slushee till I'm out." She handed her friend her cup that was still over half full. "Wish me luck."

"You can do it, Mac. As they say in show biz: *Break a leg.*" Tyler winked at her and offered a fist bump.

"Thanks, I think."

Mac and Monica stepped into the breezeway. They both looked around suspiciously, wanting to make sure no one was watching. Monica sat down against the wall to be Mac's lookout. "Go get her done," she said, and then set Mac's drink cup on the sidewalk beside her.

Mac stepped into the locker room, key #2856 gripped between her fingers.

There were six aisles of lockers with a bench that ran the length of each short aisle. Convenient if you needed to sit down and change shoes or set something down. Locker 14 was in the first row to the right as you came into the room. The rest of the rows went on back from the door all the way to the end wall of the room. *Who knew the camp needed this many staff lockers!* Mac thought.

She stuck the key into the lock and turned it. She heard it click and quickly lifted the sliding latch to open it. On the shelf at the top of the locker she saw at least six boxes of bubble gum—a lifetime supply, and a tube of something that looked like grease. Hanging on the hooks were a couple of lightweight hoodies—a grey one and a black one. There was a black backpack stuffed on the floor of the locker and under the backpack was a skinny, red and blue, battery-powered tool with a round disk. "Bingo," Mac said softly to herself. "The grinder."

"Oh, ah . . . oh man!" Monica stammered, suddenly unsure of herself. "Too many Swedish Fish on my yogurt. Dang, should have gotten more!"

Mac realized Monica was in a panic and having a hard time remembering her lines but she knew exactly what she meant. She quickly closed the locker door as quietly as she could, dashed to the back row of lockers at the end of the room. She stepped up onto the bench and squatted down, trying very hard to not breathe too loudly. She heard the voice of the assistant cook tell Monica, "You campers aren't supposed to be here. This is off limits, so scram, go eat your yogurt somewhere else!"

Mac waited to hear Presley put his key into the lock and open his locker but a sudden, terrible thought rushed over her. She looked down at her empty hands. *She'd left Alex's key in the lock!* She heard the locker door open slowly and then close again.

"Someone in here?" Presley called out in a sinister-sounding voice. It wasn't so much a real question as it was an accusation.

Mac tried to work out how this was going to end. She realized it wouldn't take him long to check each row of lockers . . . till he found her in the last row.

What was she going to do? She'd just worked out a plan in her head, that that once she heard him get to the next-to-the-last row, she'd make a mad dash down along the opposite wall and then break right and head for the door. Hopefully it would catch him off guard and he wouldn't catch her before she got away!

But then, suddenly, everything changed—Nancy, the cook, came marching into the locker room and yelling at Presley: "Presley Clarke, get your butt back to work, NOW!" The steps stopped. "I'm sick and tired of you slinking off to do whatever you're doing every time I turn around. Now, get back to the kitchen and don't even think about leaving until every pot is done and all the work tables are so clean, I could use them for brain surgery! YOU HEAR ME?"

Presley obediently left with the cook and Mac quickly went back and retrieved the extra key, which was still in the door of Locker 14. *"Way to go, Mac . . . that was dumb!"* she said to herself as she poked her head out into the breezeway to see if the coast was clear.

"Hurry up and get out of there!" she heard Tyler hiss in a super-loud whisper from the dark end.

Mac didn't waste a second and dashed towards her friends. When she was safely with them, she looked back and noticed her slushee cup, sitting where Monica had left it.

"Guess I won't be finishing my slushee tonight," she said, shaking her head. She caught her breath and then proceeded to tell the others what she had seen in Presley's locker. Then she admitted what had happened with the key when she'd panicked. "So, I guess he knows someone is on to him. Sorry, Alex. Looks like I'm not the best spy in the world." She paused, then added brightly, "But . . . at least we know he's the one behind all this."

"Right," Tyler said, giving Mac a shoulder hug as consolation. "And you heard the cook yelling at him, right? She called him Presley Clarke. Alex had it right."

"We may be right, but now we've got to figure out what that means," Alex said as he looked at his three friends then stared at Monica. "And if Presley Clarke is half as clever as I think he is, then he knows that whoever left that key in his locker door is likely a friend of Monica's."

"Sorry, Monica," Mac said, starting to get frightened again. "Let's get back to the rest of the campers, okay?"

30

A TIMELY PHONE CALL

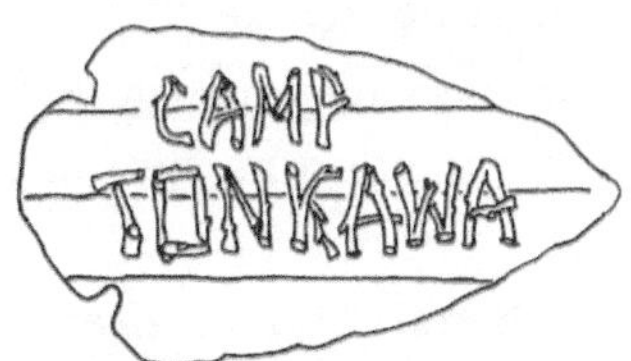

Sandra Morrison-Parker hung up from the call she'd just finished. She smiled to herself and shook her head. *What a remarkable conversation,* she told herself before glancing at the clock. It was 9:45 and she knew she now had an important call to make—*no question about that!* But before she did, she took a moment longer to reflect on the call. It gave her a sudden sense of satisfaction and confidence to have a big piece of the mystery solved—and to realize it had been solved by a quartet of kids! Each generation had intelligent, resourceful people—she'd long known that. But sometimes it helped to have that belief affirmed. *Alex Ortiz was going to be one of those people!* She smiled confidently.

The world will still be in good hands long after I'm gone!

Sandra had always taken pride in surrounding herself with intelligent people. People who were good at assessing a situation, coming up with a recommendation, and then keeping her in the loop while they executed a plan. But she knew that it all started with having common sense. To be a top-of-game player meant—among other things, that sometimes you had to quickly recognize when you were in over your head and needed help. More important, you had to also know who to call at that point. Alex ticked all those boxes. He knew he was in over his head so he'd had the good sense to call her for advice instead of clumsily ad-libbing and creating a disaster.

Her next call would be to her friend Ben with the Texas Rangers. They had a delicate situation on their hands which would need a soft touch to end well. She knew Ben could handle that. Quickly, safely, and without creating a new, bigger problem at the same time. Sandra scrolled through her phone, found Ben's contact and number and touched it. She knew it was late, but this couldn't wait. As it rang, she reminded herself this would be her fourth conversation with Ben in the last three days. At least this call would be different. She wouldn't be asking for help, she had information for him instead. And not just any information, this was case-breaking!

"Hey, Sandra," came Ben's cheerful, deep voice as he answered. "What's got you on the phone this late in the evening?"

"Well, Ben, I just finished a remarkable conversation with a thirteen-year-old junior detective over at the camp. He's managed to crack your case for you."

"Really?" Ben replied, skeptical but anxious to hear more.

"Let me give you the full download, but first you need to know, this information comes from four kids who probably have crossed a few boundaries that I need to tell you about up front."

"Hmm . . ." Ben's caution light went on in his head.

"But you're a smart guy," she reminded him. "I'm sure you can figure out how to use the information to create a clean solution that will keep you, your team, a county prosecutor, and a judge happy . . . if you know what I mean."

Ben smiled, knowing Sandra had always understood when to step lightly and allow the professionals to do their job. "Okay, understood. So what exactly have your junior detectives discovered for me?"

31

7:00 A.M. BRIEFING

The five Texas Rangers who'd been sitting in the briefing room stood at attention when Captain Stone walked in.

"Thank you, Rangers—and good morning! You may take a seat." Rene Stone was still caught off guard by the formality of respect from her friends and colleagues when she led a briefing, but it was a great tradition all the same. She smiled at the team then opened her laptop. The large screen on the wall to the left behind her immediately lit up with the Texas Ranger logo and this morning's date.

She turned her attention to the five Rangers present. "Smith, Tran, Waters, and Alvarez, you've been asked to join Sgt. Conner and me to see if we can quickly resolve the case of the criminal sabotage of the bridge at Camp Tonkawa this past Sunday." She looked up to make personal eye contact with the two women and three men assigned to assist her.

"We received a breakthrough tip late yesterday evening. Sgt. Conner has done a tremendous job working that tip overnight. He's put together new information to share with us. Sergeant?" she said, cueing him to take over.

"Thank you, Captain, and good morning, Rangers," Max said as he stepped to the front.

"Good morning," they replied in unison—following their tradition.

He advanced to the next slide in the presentation. A Canadian passport photo of a young man wearing a navy blue sweatshirt appeared on the screen.

"Rangers, let me introduce Mr. Dillon Presley Clarke; age 31." He clicked again and some vital details appeared on screen alongside the photo. "Mr. Clarke is a naturalized Canadian citizen but he was born here in Texas in 1992. Clarke immigrated to Canada in 1999 with his mother and took a Canadian passport in 2013 at the age of 21." He glanced up then continued: "Clarke returned to the U.S. three years ago to attend the University of Minnesota as an engineering student and dropped out after a semester. We're still working on details of his past two years but we know that he took a job with Camp Tonkawa this summer as a kitchen helper, joining staff in late May."

Max paused, then announced: "We believe Clarke to be the person of interest being sought by the Burnet County Sheriff's Department in connection with Sunday's bridge incident at Camp Tonkawa." There were some whispers as several of the Rangers commented to each other about this development since the case that had been widely reported in the news.

"Overnight, we were able to secure a warrant from a judge in Burnet which allowed us to review Mr. Clarke's phone records. What we've uncovered so far is multiple calls and texts exchanged with one particular cell number in Austin over the past four months belonging to a Mr. Derrick Ball. Mr. Ball is a real estate developer and controlling owner of Hill Country Estates LLC. Our first priority this morning will be to make contact with Mr. Ball and see where that discussion takes us."

He looked around and asked if there were any questions. There were not, so he noted that banking records should be available before ten this morning and then handed the presentation controller back to Captain Stone.

"Let me be frank," Stone said when she returned to the front. "We now believe we have a very tight connection between Mr. Clarke and the bridge sabotage and possibly to a pattern of other incidents at the camp. We believe we'll be able to better understand a motive after we talk with Mr. Ball. Since we've not yet uncovered any smoking gun evidence linking our suspect to the bridge incident, we're going to place Clarke under surveillance instead of arresting him just yet. We want a tighter case, though we suspect the most critical evidence has possibly been already destroyed."

"What's the story on that?" asked RuthAnn, one of the newly assigned rangers.

"We contacted the lead staffer at the camp around five this morning and asked him to do an owner's search of the suspect's locker. Two items that had been seen in the locker by a camper yesterday evening were no longer there. However, we've been informed that the suspect was likely aware a camper had seen the contents of his locker, so he no doubt cleared it out overnight."

"So we're not planning to arrest Mr. Clarke and bring him in for questioning at this time?" Corporal Tran, one of the newly assigned Rangers, asked the question.

"No, Corporal. We actually want him to assume that he has gotten away with something. He needs to believe that only a single camper knows what was in his locker. If we get something useful from Ball— and the young man doesn't suspect we're on to him, yet—then we may be able to catch him planning his next move."

Captain Stone smiled and the rangers nodded their agreement.

"Tran and Smith, the two of you are going to head over to the camp this morning in an undercover capacity. Your cover story is that you're safety inspectors that have been sent by the camp's insurance company." RuthAnn and Corporal Tran acknowledged their assignment with a nod.

"Our biggest priority is to speak with Mr. Ball. I'm convinced he's got some idea about what's going on. When he realizes the Rangers are involved . . . well, I suspect he'll prefer to cut a deal rather than risk being pulled into criminal liability for our suspect's dangerous actions. Right," Captain Stone finally announced, signaling she was wrapping up. "Sgt. Conner and I will focus on Mr. Ball after we wrap up here. Tran—you and Smith, you're to make a plan for your on-site investigation and be there by lunch today. Corporal Alvarez, you and

Waters will begin building case notes and going through bank records when they arrive. I'll also want you to liase with the Burnet County Sheriff's Department. We need them up to speed very soon on what we've found and our *hands-off* plan of action so there are no mix-ups!" Everyone nodded that they understood. Nevertheless, Stone asked the obvious: "Any questions?"

There were none, so she smiled and announced that they were dismissed. She once again noted their discipline and tradition as they stood at attention while she picked up her laptop and left the briefing room. *It wasn't an ego thing,* she thought to herself as she closed the door behind her; *it was the pride that came from being part of a team with such a rich heritage* that made her smile.

32

TOOTHPASTE AND TALK

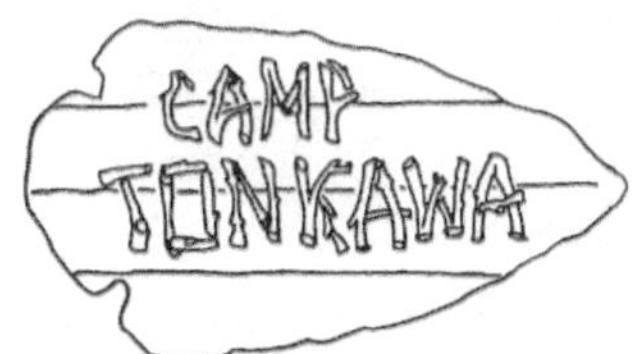

Alex was brushing his teeth when Tyler walked into the boys' shower house. There had been too many other campers around for the past fifteen minutes for Tyler to ask Alex about last night and he was getting impatient. When Sean grabbed Kyle's toothbrush and camp bag and took off running back to the cabin waving it, Kyle took off after him to get it back. With the shower house empty now except for him and Alex, Tyler quickly asked how last night had gone. "What did Charlie say when he found out?"

"He was cool. He listened, didn't give me any grief, or anything, he just took me to see Big Mike. After he heard Mac had seen the grinder, Big Mike called and talked to Mr. C. He asked a couple of questions then had me get on a call with him and Miss Sandra."

"What did she say?"

"She listened and after asking a couple of the same questions that Mr. C did, she thanked me but told me and Mr. Chuck that she wanted to tell the Texas Rangers about everything before they did anything at all and that my initiative was recognized but I needed to back away and let the investigators take it from here."

"So, are they going to arrest him or what?"

"No, man. She told them to absolutely, under no circumstances, let Presley know they are aware of ANYTHING! She was like—don't even act like you know the dude 'cause she doesn't want him suspecting that they know anything at all about what went on with his locker."

"Woah!"

"Yeah. She wants them to play dumb this morning and only react to what the Rangers tell them to do."

"That's gonna be weird, isn't it? I mean, they know he's got the grinder in his locker and they aren't going to go get it?" Tyler thought that didn't sound like the way to solve anything.

"Sure, but think about it. If Presley doesn't think they know about it then he might go ahead and work on whatever he has planned next—then they could catch him in the act. Besides, I guarantee you he got rid of that grinder last night after he got off work! It's probably out in the bottom of the river by now. They've only got a circumstantial case at best. But if he keeps with his plan and they catch him, well, they they've got him, good."

Tyler realized this made sense and wasn't sure why he hadn't thought of it himself. "So they're going to set a trap?"

"Well, that's what I was going to suggest that we do if this hadn't gotten so dangerous. You can be sure he's got something else planned."

Tyler had been thinking the same thing but hadn't said it. "Probably at tomorrow night's powwow."

Alex rinsed his toothbrush, dried his hands, collected his stuff to put into his toiletry bag, then tossed his towel over his shoulder. "I think that's exactly what he's got planned. And, assuming the Rangers don't show up today with a search warrant and tip him off, I imagine Presley will think he's dodged a close one and keep on plan."

"He's odd," Tyler said, picking up his own stuff to head back to their cabin. "And a little bit scary."

"Maybe more than a little bit scary," Alex corrected him. "I think he's pretty dangerous and maybe more unpredictable than anyone thinks."

33

A SURPRISE VISIT

Sergeant Conner was driving himself and Captain Stone to Round Rock, Texas, just north of Austin. He and Stone had planned a surprise visit to the office of Derrick Ball, a regional real estate developer.

While Conner was driving, Stone decided it was time to get Sandra Morrison-Parker and the camp staff on the phone to brief them on the plan. She liked having a junior officer drive; it gave her time to make calls. She dialed Morrison-Parker, first, to be certain she was available, then placed her on hold while she tied in Chuck Walker, the camp director. Mr. Walker needed a few minutes to locate Mike Murkowski so he could join them.

"Okay, Captain Stone—Mike and I are both here now," Mr. C finally said. "What can we do for you?"

"First, thanks for your time and cooperation in our investigation," Stone began, "and in particular, Mr. Murkowski, thanks for the early morning check of Mr. Clarke's locker for us. We weren't at all surprised that the evidence was no longer there, but that's fine for now."

"I should have thought of that last night," Sandra offered. "I told Mike and Chuck to hold off doing anything till they heard from you. My apologies."

"No apology necessary. You did the right thing, Ms. Morrison-Parker."

"Please—it's Sandra. Everyone calls me Sandra because I find hyphenated last names so cumbersome!"

"Okay, I'll make an exception from my decorum . . . Sandra."

"Thank you. Now, dear—what is our plan of action?"

Stone was caught off guard by Sandra's take charge approach but smiled to herself. *Better to work with a professional who understood how to get something done. It was so much harder to work with someone who stumbled over their own shadow trying to help but always kept getting in your way!*

"Big picture and key point for the morning is that I need the three of you to know we intend to give Mr. Clarke every reason to believe that he has not been discovered." She paused to make sure that had registered with her three stakeholders. "We want nothing to change from yesterday or earlier this week. We know he's out there—but we DO NOT want him to figure out that anyone knows." Stone paused again, "You all okay with that?"

"As long as you're confident no one else is going to get hurt in the meantime," Sandra replied tentatively.

"I think we have a few days before he strikes again and we're working an angle to give ourselves some insight into Mr. Clarke's next move."

"Okay, then." Sandra conceded.

"This is a difficult approach for a lot of people, but I want to limit our exposure. At this point, no one really needs to know who we believe is responsible. So we're going to limit this involvement to only the three of you and my team. That means no briefing of the counselors, staff, or anyone else at all. We're all good with that?"

"Got it," Big Mike replied. He knew it would be impossible to set a trap if any of the counselors or staff knew what was going on. Nancy, their cook, would for sure be a weak link if she heard that one of her kitchen staff was the prime suspect but was to be left alone. No chance that was going to happen!

"We have two undercover Rangers who'll be showing up at the camp around lunch today. Their cover story is that they're insurance inspectors checking out safety at the camp on behalf of your insurance carrier, okay?"

"So they'll be here today?" Mr. Walker asked.

"Yes. They're doing their background work this morning and clearing it with your insurer, but you should expect them just after lunch. You can go ahead and let your staff know that you've been advised that your insurance company is concerned and are sending out some inspectors. That will mix things up a bit and serve as a good distraction for what we'll be working on in the meantime."

"Makes sense," Big Mike said approvingly.

The four of them talked through a few more details and answered a couple of questions that Mr. C had. When there were no more questions, Stone wrapped up the call.

"I'll be back in touch later this afternoon, but for now, remember: insurance inspectors and nothing else. Thanks again for your help on this."

"Not at all," Sandra replied. "We'll let you drop off the call while the three of us discuss internal next steps, okay?"

"Perfect!" Stone said then hung up. She set her phone down on the center console and looked out the window for a moment as she thought through a dozen details that were playing out in her head.

"That sounded like it went well," Max commented as he turned his pickup truck into the parking garage of a large commercial office building.

"Part one is set," Stone said, smiling to her sergeant before looking out the window again. "Now to see if we can get some cooperation from Mr. Ball."

34

BAD KARMA

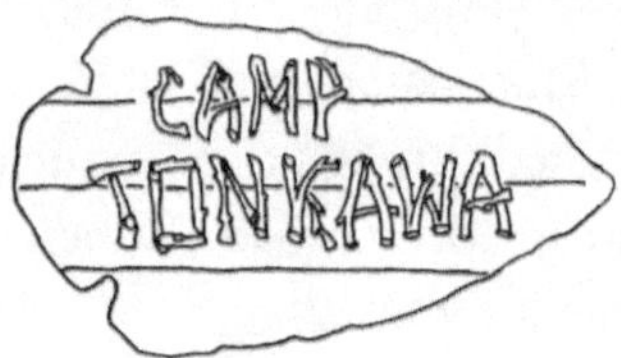

Charlie and Leslie were both standing in Big Mike's office while Mac and Alex were seated in the steel folding chairs facing his desk. Big Mike had been rehearsing the performance that he and Captain Stone had agreed on during their call with Sandra and now it was showtime.

"Mackenzie, Alex, we need to have a talk," he began, giving them his best, stern, *you're in trouble* face and voice.

Alex and Mac looked at each other and Alex squirmed in the uncomfortable chair.

"Last night, Mac, it's my understanding that you broke into the personal locker of one of our staff members and later made accusations about what you believe you saw in that locker. We did not find what you said you saw in the locker. In spite of your intentions to somehow be amateur detectives, breaking into a staff locker is unacceptable behavior for a camper here at Camp Tonkawa. Period."

"But we were trying to help . . ." Alex protested before he was cut off mid-sentence.

"You were meddling in an active law enforcement investigation and possibly obstructing the course of that investigation, Alex. Furthermore, the story that you told our camp director last night turned out to be false. And, despite your honest intentions to help—the fact remains that you stole a locker key from our maintenance operation and gave it to Mackenzie and that is totally out of bounds for camper behavior."

Big Mike was struggling to keep a straight face, knowing what he knew, but this was the plan they had agreed to. It was critical that Alex and Mackenzie and their friend Tyler stay out of the way of the Rangers' investigation for the next several days. They were sharp, but their amateur sleuthing could actually endanger them at this point, as Captain Stone had clearly pointed out this morning.

"But it's true, I saw . . ." Mac began—

"Stop right there!" Big Mike interrupted. "No more accusations. We are not going to say one more word about what you think you did —or didn't see!"

He looked up at Leslie who, unlike Charlie, was totally in the dark. "Leslie, I'm sorry, but a comment was made last night that you are not aware of and we are not going to repeat it here. Again, I know it's confusing but at this time, what Mackenzie told Alex—which he in turn told to Mr. Chuck and to me is confidential. After discussing it, Mr. Chuck has determined the content of that conversation is not to be talked about at all."

Leslie was confused but nodded her head reluctantly then glanced at Charlie who was looking very concerned.

"Charlie, same goes for you. No chatter about what Alex shared with us last night. Not with Leslie, here . . . not with anyone. Am I clear on that?"

Charlie wasn't used to being reprimanded. He thought he'd done the right thing last night. But now . . . well, he didn't know what to think. *Was something going on?* As he quickly thought through that idea, his eyes brightened and a slight smile crossed his face. He found himself nodding that he understood. *Oh, yeah,* he thought, *I think I know exactly what little psychological op is playing out here!*

"Good." Big Mike relaxed a bit and leaned back in his chair. He turned his attention back to Alex and Mac. "The good news for you two is that Sandra Morrison-Parker really, *really* likes you both. She insists that you two be given a second chance in spite of my opinion that you should both be sent home immediately." He glanced out his window quickly to collect his resolve. *This was going very well!*

He turned his attention back to Mac first, and then to Alex. "You both get to stay in camp at her request, and Alex—over my protest, she insists that you get to keep your feather."

Alex was stunned. *What had just happened? If Big Mike was so mad at them, why were they really getting to stay in camp and why didn't he have to give up his feather?* The best he could manage was a mumbled "Thanks." Then upon further reflection he added, "Sorry. I hope I didn't screw up the investigation."

Mac looked at Alex. She was bewildered at a response that totally didn't seem like her friend and caught a subtle wink from him that no one else would have seen. She decided to follow suit and ask later why he'd done that.

"Yeah, okay," she began, "I'm sorry, too. I shouldn't have been so nosy." Then she turned to Alex and added a bit of drama to her acting: "Way to go, Alex, thanks a lot for getting us both in trouble!" Then she looked at Leslie—and decided to act like she was upset, like she was so embarrassed she was about to cry.

"Can we go now?" she demanded, loud and defiantly.

Big Mike decided the whole encounter had gone pretty much perfect but was about to unravel. "Yes, you all can go," he replied quickly. Then he added, "Just remember, if I hear that there's been any further discussion about any of this or what you claim you think you saw, you're both outta here and heading home without appeal. Got it?"

"Yes, sir" the two said in unison before standing to leave. Alex gave Mac a sly thumbs-up before turning to walk out the door with his counselor.

Mac grinned to herself and decided she should be nominated for an Oscar for her over-the-top performance!

35

NOT FINISHED . . . AT LEAST NOT JUST YET

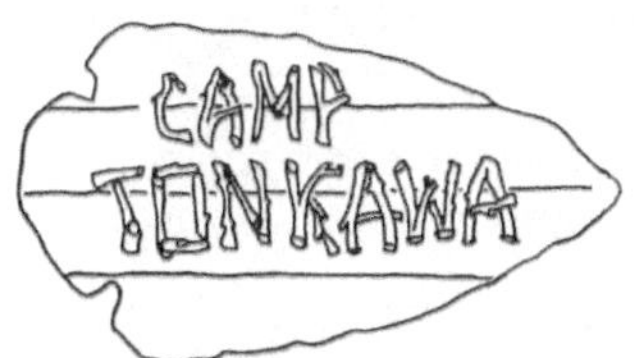

Alex and Charlie walked back to Cabin 9 quietly, neither of them saying a word. Alex's brain was working through a dozen ideas, trying to decide his next move. Charlie was feeling bad for Alex but wasn't sure if he needed to just give him space or see if he wanted to talk about what had just happened.

Charlie finally broke the silence. "Look, Alex—I'm sorry about what happened back there. You know I totally believe you, right? I mean, if you and Mac went to all that trouble to check out if the grinder was in that guy's locker and you say it was, then I believe you. I'm really not totally sure why Big Mike was acting so weird back there."

"Not a deal," Alex said softly.

"Well, but it kinda is a deal. You've put so much of this together yourself and it seems like you've given the investigators exactly what they needed to get to the bottom of this. I just didn't appreciate Big Mike not giving you any credit."

Alex stopped walking. "Look Charlie, it's okay. Really, it is."

Charlie was looking at the kid who seemed to be taking this all better than he was. "Are you sure?"

"Look, man. You and I both know what was going on back there,"

135

Alex continued. A big grin emerged on his face. "We gave the cops everything they need and then some. Probably broke the case wide open for them. But I'm sure they told Big Mike and Mr. C to keep us kids out of the way. They had to make sure we got the message." He watched Charlie's face carefully, then added, "Right?"

"Yeah," Charlie said slowly, realizing that Alex had read more into what was going on than he had. "Yeah, sure, that's no doubt what was going on."

"Of course it was. I'm supposed be all scared and sorry and worried that I'm gonna get kicked out of camp and get out of the way while they put together their own trap. I get it, okay? Fine with me."

"You think they know it's Presley but just want to spring a trap?"

"Absolutely. It's what I'd have done if this didn't get so far off into criminal kind of legal stuff."

"So, Alex, I'm guessing you're not out of the game on this by a long shot, right? Is that a good assumption on my part?"

"You said it, not me, boss. I've been told I might get kicked out of camp if I get caught doing anything else helpful."

"Got it. So, your big objective is to simply avoid getting caught now, right?"

"Pretty much. Is there anything about all this that I don't know that I should?"

"Only thing that might be helpful is Presley's bike." Charlie looked over his shoulder toward the office then suggested they keep walking.

"The investigator from the sheriff's office seemed pretty focused on bike tracks they'd found up near the bridge."

"I wondered about that," Alex nodded. "When we first got to camp, the cook's assistant was everywhere on his tech bike . . . a really sweet ride if I say so myself, even though a board is more my thing—if you know what I mean."

"Yeah, give me a long board any day!" Charlie agreed. "And just to let you know, he's been that way all summer. Always hanging out on his bike between shifts in the kitchen. Then, all of a sudden yesterday, it's like the bike suddenly didn't exist."

"Exactly." Alex said. "I'm betting that somehow or another he realized the bike might have left some tracks and decided to hide it."

"And you think you're going to find it."

Alex grinned and looked over toward Cabin 9 for a moment. "Well, boss, let me just say that what you don't know can't incriminate you, so I cannot confirm or deny the answer to that question."

Charlie laughed and shook his head. "Alex, I hope you don't get caught," he said. "Not that I think you will, but I'm going to miss having you around here if you do get caught and sent home."

He paused then got a more serious look on his face. "Just don't do anything stupid, Alex. And for goodness' sake don't disturb any evidence or do anything to make Presley think you're on to him."

Alex smiled but nodded that he understood.

"And I can assure you that Big Mike was totally serious. If anything goes south and he finds out you're involved, you'll be heading home and I'll probably be looking for a new summer gig."

"Got it, boss. No screw ups."

Charlie shook his head and laughed. Then briefly held a finger to his silent lips before they continued their walk to Cabin 9.

36

IS IT A WIRETAP . . . OR A WIRE-TRAP?

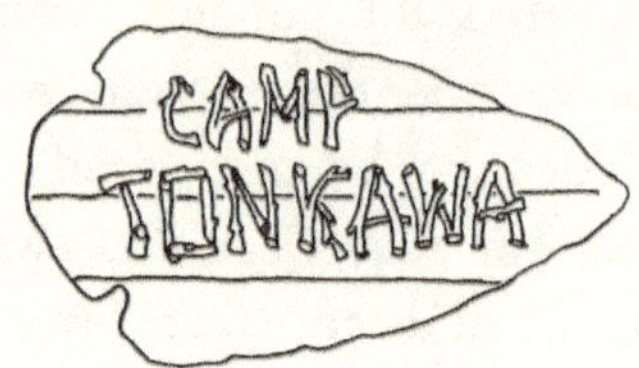

Presley was in his bunk room in the staff cabin with his door shut, working on some wiring for his next "prank" when he heard his phone play the Canadian "Maple Leaf" anthem. He looked at the screen and wondered what Derrick wanted this time. It seemed like the guy was becoming an unreliable partner in his plan. And yet, he *was* the guy with the money. The guy who was going to make this all worth it. *Better take the call.*

"Yeah?" he asked dismissively, not bothering to say hello.

"Yo, Dillon," came the reply. "How's your week going?"

This seemed a little odd to Presley, but he reminded himself that he had introduced himself from the outset as "Dillon" to the developer to avoid mixing up his two personas. Still, it seemed odd for him to phone him since nothing had changed since their last call.

"So, things have been pretty quiet this week after all the fireworks last weekend. You doing okay or just decided to lay low for now?"

Hmm, Derrick didn't usually want to know much about what he was up to—just the opposite. He didn't want to know much and even seemed pretty upset with him last time they'd talked. Presley's inner radar was feeling a little prickly.

"I'm fine," he replied. "Cook's keeping me busy. Nothing much going on here. How's your investment syndicate holding up? Everyone still on board with that new development you told me you were working on?"

Truth was, Derrick had told him very little about his work other than to let him know that the funding for the deal between the two of them was going to involve a pool of three or four investors due to its size. Sixty-five million dollars was a lot of money to put together.

"Um, sure. All's going great. The team is just very anxious to be able to close the deal. For now they're okay staying in the dark but I'm just starting to get a bit nervous about timing, you know?"

Presley laughed to himself. *Same old Derrick.* "Well, there might be some developments in the works . . . you know, along the lines of what we've discussed in the past. I'm hoping that we can be having a deeper discussion of our interests soon. Depends on how things go in the next couple of days."

"Next couple of days?" Derrick asked with a kind of hopeful, expectancy in his voice.

"Yeah. Next couple of days. Things always seem to get exciting here at camp on weekends so I assume we'll have a better idea after this weekend." Presley paused to see if Derrick was finished or what.

"Okay then, Dillon. We'll continue to hold on tight and wait to hear from you. Assuming there won't be any bad news this weekend, will there?"

"Not sure what you're talking about, Derrick. What kind of bad news?" Presley was starting to wonder if something was up with his buyer. He was ready to wrap this up anyway, so he did. "Look, gotta go. Talk to you later."

He hung up the call and stared at his phone for a moment. It seemed to him like it took a moment or so longer to disconnect than it normally did.

He shook his head. *Whatever.* He had more work to do to get ready for Friday night, but he certainly wasn't going to let on about anything related to his plan for an excellent, super-prank. At least not to Mr. Derrick Ball! *No way.*

~

At her desk, Corporal Waters took off her headphones and looked over at Captain Stone. "You get anything out of that, Captain?"

Stone shook her head. "Just that the guy's a little on the paranoid side, maybe suspicious. Tells me it didn't go the way he was used to conversations going between him and Mr. Ball. In any case, if we had one of those high-dollar profilers listening in, I think the main thing they'd tell us is that we're dealing with a guy with a super big ego and outsized sense of self-importance who's got something big planned for this weekend."

"I'll get on the phone to our contact at the camp and get a better picture of what 'big things' are coming up in the next couple of days," Waters volunteered. She was excited to be on her first big investigation and anxious to contribute to getting a solid case on this Presley guy.

"Perfect. In the meantime I'll brief Smith and Tran on what we heard before they head over to the camp." Stone paused then added: "And be sure to get this transcribed as quickly as possible so we can get a copy over to Captain Vasquez over at the Burnet County Sheriff's Office. Got it?"

"On it, Captain!"

Stone smiled as she left the room. *Corporal Waters is going to be a great Texas Ranger.*

37

BREAKING THE RULES

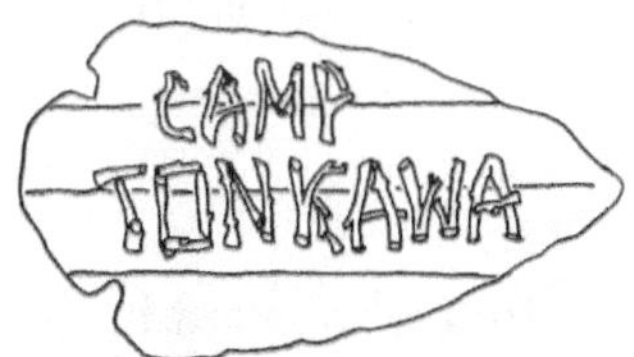

Alex and Tyler were in line, waiting for their turn to run the obstacle course. All of the handholds on the climbing wall had been degreased and rechecked before the timed qualification runs were to begin today. While they were waiting, Jonathan felt obliged to ask the obvious question to both Charlie and Carson: "Did you check out the entire course? I mean . . . we're sure there aren't any real gators in the pond if we fall off the handholds?"

And before either counselor could answer, Eldon wanted to know about the stink tunnels: "You've checked them for snakes, right?"

That was quickly followed by a raucous shouting of other questions concerning nearly every inch of the course. Carson finally blew his whistle, and everyone immediately got quiet. "Yes," he said. "We've checked the entire course for any challenges that shouldn't be there."

Charlie added, "look, we know you're all concerned about more surprises, but Big Mike still thinks the greasing of the climbing wall may have been a bad prank and that the bridge incident is possibly unrelated. The authorities are looking into all that, okay? In the meantime, we're gonna have some fun and see who our top eight campers are going to be for tomorrow morning's rematch."

"So, is everybody ready?" Carson asked.

A loud shout mixed with "ready" and "yes" and a lot of just yelling and hoots and noise was heard from all the boys. Charlie got out his stopwatch and clipboard along with his walkie talkie while Carson watched with his whistle at the ready as well. He checked in with Bubba and Donnie who were at the finish line. "Think we're ready to start at this end," he radioed.

"Copy that," Bubba replied. "All set at this end, too."

"Okay, confirming that Heat One is Louie, Eldon, Liam, and Kyle, you copy?"

"Uh huh. That's what I've got. I'll start my stopwatch as soon as I hear your whistle."

Charlie nodded to Carson who raised his hand and caught the eye of each of the first four starters, then dropped his hand as he blew the whistle. The four boys were off for the wall. This time the boys from the second heat were handling the belay ropes for the boys in the first heat.

"Move it, Kyle!" Tyler shouted, encouraging his friend from their cabin to climb faster.

"Go Beavers!" yelled all the boys from Cabin 7, urging on Liam. It was getting noisy and everyone was excited.

As soon as all four boys were up the wall, standing on the upper ledge, they quickly changed their safety carabiner over to the long rope they'd each been assigned. It was time for the big, thrilling swing across to the zip line nest which would be their next stop on the course. When they each got to their zip line, they transferred their carabiner yet again, this time to the pulley on their steel cable. When they were ready, they launched off their towers to ride the zip line for almost 300 feet. This was the best part of the course!

At the end of the zip line they landed on the big air bags and quickly took off their safety harnesses to get ready for the mud run. The four boys who would be in the third heat were waiting to take their harnesses back to the start where they'd wear them when it was their turn to climb.

Alex and Tyler were the last two in the line for Cabin 9. It would be a while before it would be their turn and no one was paying attention, so Tyler asked Alex what he'd decided.

"About the recon down to the river front?" Alex asked.

"No, about your upcoming trip to Mars, dufus!" he said, shaking his head. "Of course your recon."

"Yeah. I'm in. It makes sense that the bike has got to be in that old boat house. Nobody uses it anymore; it's right there by the kayak shed —so if he screwed with Mac's kayak, he'd likely have hidden his drill in there, too. And third," he said, looking away from the wall to Tyler for a quick glance, "it's the only place big enough to store something as big as a bike where no one else, like Sam for instance, could find it."

"From the looks of it I'll bet even Sam hasn't been in there for a couple of years," Tyler said. He recalled how totally abandoned the old boat house had looked when they'd walked down to the river to check out the kayaks this morning. Alex was always good at coming up with a logical reason to be in a place he shouldn't be when he wanted to be there anyway. Having a look at the kayaks was this morning's excuse.

"When are you going to do it?" Tyler asked. He paused because the next heat of climbers was getting set to go. After Carson blew his whistle, he turned and asked Alex the question again.

"Well, I figure Presley is tied up in the kitchen until after lunch."

"Go on—"

"So, I'm going to walk in with everyone for lunch but duck out after I get my food. I'll put my tray on the table and make like I'm heading for the restroom. If I'm not back in time, you can pocket my PB & J for me. You know, so I can eat it later. And be sure and get rid of my tray, too. Okay?"

"Got it," Tyler said and nodded his head. "And if Charlie asks about you?"

"That's easy. You know nothing. We didn't have this conversation. That's why he's a counselor and gets paid the big bucks!"

Tyler laughed, knowing the counselors did this for the fun of it and not a lot of pay, but he understood Alex's plan. "Okay. Just be careful and like Charlie warned you, don't screw anything up for the investigation. Just a look-see and no-touching—right?"

"Yup. Just want to see what's in there."

The two of them continued to cheer each of the boys in their cabin as they took their turn. Soon it was time for Tyler to go retrieve a climbing harness. "See you at the other end!" he said, then jogged off toward the end of the zip line.

"Indeed," Alex said confidently. "And don't forget to try and break J's record this time around."

Tyler gave him a thumbs-up as he headed out.

It was lunchtime and everyone in camp was in the massive dining hall making lots of noise and enjoying their peanut butter and jelly sandwiches—or honey and butter for those with a food allergy. Alex hoped that Tyler would remember to bring the bag of nacho chips, too —if his brief look around the boat shed took longer than he'd planned.

The shed was in a grove of juniper trees that had grown up around the old building. It had once been the main home for the kayaks and all the boating gear for the camp. The side that faced the water had two, long sliding doors that could be opened to expose almost the length of the building to make it easy to store canoes or kayaks on racks along the wall. Alex figured those doors hadn't been opened in a long time and probably wouldn't budge without digging out some of the dirt and silt that had accumulated around them.

But on the backside, off the path that led past the old boat house to the newer kayak shed, Alex had found a back door. Oddly, the latching hasp on the door didn't have a padlock. Instead, it just had an old kitchen knife dropped into the hasp's padlock loop to keep the door from swinging open. Alex put on the latex gloves that he'd "borrowed" from the nurse's first aid box. *Don't want any fingerprints of mine messing with Presley's prints if I'm right!* he thought.

He unlatched the door and carefully set the kitchen knife on the ledge just inside the door and then pulled it mostly closed behind him. Flipping on his handy camper flashlight, he started looking around the dark room. One thing was for sure: it was a mess! Lots of unused things: paint cans and broken equipment no one had wanted to either fix or throw away. Junk was everywhere . . . along with cobwebs. *LOTS of cobwebs!*

Alex knew Mac wasn't afraid of spiders, but if she was the one doing the looking around in here right now—well, he was pretty certain she'd be creeped out and maybe leave right about now. Then again, he reminded himself that from what he'd heard, she'd done a pretty amazing job in the old silver mine earlier this summer. He thought better of it. *Probably wrong. I imagine she'd be doing exactly what I'm doing,* he decided. *But Monica . . .* he laughed to himself at the thought of Monica in here with the cobwebs and spiders and who knows what else. *Monica wouldn't be caught dead in here!*

As he moved the beam of his light around the dark room, casting shadows, he caught sight of an old paint tarp draped over something along a side wall. It was tucked behind a broken swim ladder. Alex carefully worked his way over to see what was under the tarp.

He lifted the edge: *Bingo! A bike!* And on the ground under the tarp he also spotted a cardboard box. He shined his light into the box and wasn't surprised to find a battery-powered drill, along with a few drill bits. There was also the grinder and the tube of grease that Mac must have seen in Presley's locker. He wished he had his cell phone so he could take a picture for proof, but he didn't. *Instead, I've got one of those dumb, SIM-less camp photo phones!*

He held it up and snapped about five or six pics. He wasn't going to touch anything, but this time he was going to have proof!

When he'd finished, Alex carefully rearranged the tarp the way he'd found it and took one last look around. Satisfied, he worked his way back to the door. He found the kitchen knife and after he got back outside, he closed the door shut, latched the hasp and stuck the knife back in like it had been when he got here.

He checked his digital watch. He'd been gone eighteen minutes. *Perfect!* There was plenty of time to reappear at lunch . . . and maybe even time to have a few of today's Oreo cookies. Alex texted Tyler's watch with a single word: *done.* Then he took a quick look up and down the trail before stepping out from behind the shed. *The last thing he wanted to see was Presley . . . so, better to check than be surprised!*

But there was no Presley . . . no one anywhere in sight, in fact.

Convinced he was in the clear, Alex headed back to the dining hall. He touched the pocket of his camp shorts as he walked quickly, his heart racing. *Yup, his camp camera phone was safely in his back pocket!*

38

SOMETHING'S UP

It was the hottest day at camp for the year, so all the campers were excited for swim time in the huge pool this afternoon. The previous record was yesterday which was 101 degrees at 1:00 p.m. Today it was 102, so the water was a welcome relief to everyone.

Charlie and Carson were keeping a close eye on their campers as the horseplay and competition began to pick up. They were interrupted as both of their phones buzzed at the same time. A quick look gave the same message from Big Mike:

"2:15 Sr Staff mtg, my office."

Carson glanced at Charlie and then across to the other side of the pool and spotted Zoe and Kelley. The two of them had just looked up from their phones as well and were glancing over their way. The four of them, also known to the campers as "the Elders," made up the four-person senior staff. Carson nodded his head when he'd caught Zoe's silent attention and got a nod back.

Charlie checked the time. "Man, it's already five after two—that's pretty short notice, isn't it?"

"Something must be up."

"Guess so," Charlie mumbled. "But twice in one day?"

"I better go tell Mason he's in charge while we're gone." Carson dropped his phone into the pocket of his unbuttoned shirt and stood up.

"Ditto," Charlie nodded. "I'll flag Alex."

After both of them had alerted their feather keepers, Carson and Charlie caught up with Zoe and Kelley.

"What now?" Zoe asked as they walked quickly toward the camp office next door to the dining hall.

"It must be pretty important to pull all four of us away during pool time!" Kelley was not amused.

"Anyone do anything stupid this morning—that you know of?" Carson asked.

The other three laughed because that was exactly what each of them was really expecting.

"Well, I know there was a lot of yelling going on between two of the girls in Cabin 4 after lunch, but nothing Jesse couldn't handle," Zoe volunteered.

Kelley just shook her head.

"Nothing I know of either," Carson said. He opened the door to the front hall of the camp office and after walking to the end of the narrow hallway he knocked on Big Mike's door. It was usually open but was closed when they arrived.

"C'mon in," Mike shouted through the door and they all filed in.

Big Mike was perched behind his big, steel desk like usual, but Mr. C was there too, standing beside the window. At Mike's small, round conference table were two people that none of them recognized. The table was usually covered with Big Mike's file folders and binders and work stuff—all of it haphazardly stacked. Kelley noted that it had suddenly been cleared off and looked surprisingly professional. She also noticed that Big Mike's window was closed and the AC was cranked on high. *What's with that?*

"Go ahead and grab a seat—and Zoe, pull the door, will you?" Big Mike instructed.

Mr. C seemed particularly nervous as he glanced out the window then back towards the two people at the table. The woman and the man smiled at the four counselors but simply nodded and didn't say anything.

"Okay, team," Mike began when the door was closed, "We've got a situation and we need to get the four of you up to speed on it—okay?" He glanced over at the two strangers, then back to his senior staff. "First of all, this is highly confidential—for your ears only. Got it? None of the other counselors, no other staffers, no one else at camp hears what we're going to talk about, understood?"

The four of them glanced at each other and nodded, wondering what was up.

Before beginning, he looked at Charlie and apologized for having to put him on the spot with Alex, his camper this morning. "But actually," he continued, "this off-the-record meeting is kinda a continuation of where we left off from that. It'll make sense here in a minute, but we had to get our 'junior detective camper' to back off, okay?"

"Sure, okay." Charlie glanced at Kelley.

"First, lemme introduce Sergeant Smith and Corporal Tran from the Texas Rangers," Big Mike announced and looked over to the two strangers to introduce themselves.

"Sergeant Smith," said the tall woman with her back to the wall. She had red hair and even though she was smiling, Charlie could imagine you really wouldn't want to cross her. She looked tough.

"Corporal Tran," added the man sitting next to her. He lifted his hand from the table to the tip of his forehead to offer a sort of salute.

"So here's the deal," Mike continued. "These two Rangers are here the rest of this week working undercover, right? We'll be getting the word out at supper tonight that they're safety inspectors from our insurance company." Mike glanced over at the "safety inspectors" and at Mr. C before stating what was now obvious. "Other than Mr. C and me, you four are the only people at Camp Tonkawa who are going to know who these two really are."

"So, why are you telling us?" Zoe asked, confused about why they were being drawn into the ruse.

Sgt. Smith answered her question immediately and bluntly. "Because we think our suspect has planned another incident to follow up on their bridge tampering. We believe it will take place as part of your campfire powwow tomorrow night."

Cpl. Tran picked up where Smith left off, saying that "based on intel that we now have on Mr. Presley Clarke—your camp's kitchen assistant—we believe he intends to create another large event very soon and most likely tomorrow night. We believe the bridge incident, the kayak sinking and the tampering with the obstacle course were a prelude to something far more dangerous which will be designed to make parents very unsure about the safety of the camp."

Smith added, "We believe Mr. Clarke's ultimate goal is to sufficiently sabotage the reputation of the camp so that it is forced to close. Without getting into too much detail at this time, he likely believes that forcing the camp to close will in turn, benefit him financially."

Tran looked at each of the four counselors. "You four are going to be our eyes and ears over the next few days as we look for evidence to affirm our suspicion—without tipping off Mr. Clarke that he is a suspect. That's why we're keeping everyone else in the dark."

"And," Big Mike added, "since the four of you are in charge of the big campfire event and the theatrics that make it exciting for the kids, we believe that if you are particularly observant, you might likely spot something 'out-of-sorts' that might help us anticipate what our suspect is actually planning . . . so we can prevent it, of course."

The four counselors nodded that they understood and then looked at each other.

"So, for now we're just keeping our radar up for something related to the powwow pyrotechnics?" Zoe asked. The pyro effects was basically her show.

Sgt. Smith interrupted Big Mike before he could respond. "Look. We think Presley Clarke is a rogue loner. If he were fifteen years younger, we'd profile him very differently but what we're looking for here is an airtight case against him instead of a case built on circumstantial evidence that gets tossed and ultimately lets him get away. The man's thirty-two years old and acting like a frat boy doing dangerous pranks." Her annoyed attitude suddenly changed to cool confidence. "We believe he has a very deep financial incentive to ruin Camp Tonkawa's reputation . . . permanently. But we don't believe he is nearly as clever as he thinks he is and will likely make a mistake. You four are going to help us catch him."

Zoe, Kelley, Carson, and Charlie each nodded. It was becoming very clear now. The investigators wanted to set a trap and they were going to be right in the middle, helping them.

Kelley spoke up. "You think he's planning to create a major problem with the fireworks for the great stag's entry tomorrow night—right?"

"From what your director and Mr. Murkowski have described, that certainly sounds like where Clarke would create the most impact." Sergeant Smith paused to glance over at Corporal Tran. "Tran and I are going to be poking around undercover, asking risk assessment questions as insurance investigators, trying to put together a bit more of the case, but also keeping an eye on Clarke."

"In the meantime," she added, "if you spot something, anything—say something. I want you to put my number and Tran's in your phones and call either of us directly if you think you notice anything. Anything at all! Don't second guess, just call and let us decide if it's important, okay?"

"Got it," Zoe and Carson said at the same time. They turned and looked at each other and laughed at the coincidence.

"Okay, you four need to get back to the pool before everyone starts asking questions," Big Mike said. "Get Sergeant Smith's and Corporal Tran's numbers in your phones then head on back. We'll talk more later."

They each created two new contacts in their phone then shook hands with each of the two Texas Rangers.

"Cool," Zoe said as she turned to leave, "I've not only shaken hands with a real, live Texas Ranger—two, in fact, but I've also got them on speed dial!" She smiled big and winked at Carson who nodded back before holding the door open first for Zoe and then Kelley and Charlie.

39

A REALLY BIG "BANG"

The Grumbler was sitting on the porch of the dining hall when the four Elders left Big Mike's office. *Another meeting,* he thought to himself, then smiled. *Just wait. Life is nothing but meetings unless you take the bull by the horns and get rich instead.*

"Get Rich Instead!"—that was Presley's personal motto these days. He paused to consider it again and then admitted to himself that it really wasn't original. He'd adopted it after listening to a guy named Jack Jackson talking on the web about ways to get rich and take it easy. It turned out that most of Jack's ideas had been pretty stupid. The number one idea was to simply go out and create a website like his and then get people to click from your website to his website to watch his webinar called *"Stop Dreaming and Get Rich Instead."* He promised to pay you a share what he charged "your guest" to view the video.

Karen, his girlfriend, had laughed when he'd told her about it. "A pyramid scheme," she'd called it. "The only person who makes any money in that kind of a scam is the person at the top," she'd said.

Still, Jack Jackson's worthless video had reminded Presley of how much he hated his boring job. He was thirty-two and every day was the same: Go to boring meetings and take notes for his stupid boss and then go back to his desk and find the answers to the boring questions his boss asked him to research. He'd decided it would be much better to *"Get Rich Instead!"*

But how?

The answer came last fall after his mother died. He and his girlfriend had gone back to Canada for his mom's funeral and to clean out her apartment. Karen had wanted to look through the old cedar chest his mom had kept.

Presley never liked the chest, thought it looked ugly. But it had belonged to Grandma Woods and his mom kept a lot of her personal things in there. So he and Karen had gone through the chest and found lots of old family stuff. Stuff about his mom's life when Presley was a little kid, before she'd moved to Canada. Stuff she'd never wanted to talk to him about.

Karen found a picture album of his mom and his dad in there. His mom never really talked about his dad, only that he'd run away to New York City right after Presley was born. That's why his mom had eventually packed up and moved to Ontario. The pictures all looked nice and happy enough, but he knew pictures can hide the truth.

He'd also found out their family was from Texas, and that the family had been rich at one time! In fact, his great-great-grandpa had once been a big Texas cattle rancher. *Imagine that!* Since Presley was really good at online research—*after all, that was the main thing he did in his boring job!*—it hadn't taken long to find out what happened to all the family money. It was crazy, but his mom's great-grandpa had just given it all away. *Seriously?*

The crazy old man had sold half his ranch and given the other half away to be a summer camp! There was more to it than that, of course. Sure, he'd found out about the will and the Hoffmeier Compact that had set up the camp. But the old man had left that reversion clause in there, hadn't he? Why, it was almost as if he knew that someday he'd have a great-great-grandson who'd want the ranch back!

Right?

And while it was true that he'd left a pretty big chunk of money to his son and his son's wife, they'd lost it all in the 1950s. *His family certainly wasn't rich after that!* He'd figured out that was where Grandma Woods fit in. Hoffmeier's son and wife had one kid—

Presley's grandma. He remembered the older woman who'd come to visit him and his mom in Canada, once. She was a widow by then—his mom had told him she'd been a nurse when she was younger. Grandma Woods had wanted him and his mom to move back with her to Arizona. It had been a really weird visit with lots of yelling and arguing before his grandma had finally left to go back home. He and his mom had stayed in Ontario.

But opening that old chest had changed his life. Everything just sort of fell into place in his head. "Get rich instead" didn't have to be a dream, it could be his reality!

When he'd told Karen about it, she thought he was crazy. They'd broken up after that trip. Turns out she wasn't as anxious for him to get rich as he was. But now he knew there really *was* a simple way for him to get rich: he just had to find a way to get his family ranch in Texas back!

Presley glanced around the deserted grounds by the dining hall and reminded himself he was wasting time, again. Today's task was to figure out how to "borrow" one of Sam's Gators. There were five big, bad "firecrackers" he'd built and had hidden in the old boat shed. He needed to get them each placed in the woods before tomorrow night's powwow. He also needed to wire them into the same control board the counselors would use to set off their own fireworks.

Five, twenty-gallon blue drums aren't impossible to handle, but he really needed a Gator to make things easy. *But how am I going to get the keys to one of the Gators without Sam knowing?*

Just then, he noticed Big Mike walking out of the camp headquarters building. Big Mike was chatting with a couple of very official-looking people who were carrying digital tablets. They were pointing here and there and asking lots of questions. Presley shook his head and told himself how lucky he was to not be doing something like that this summer!

Then he suddenly got an idea: *Big Mike never locks his office. He looks like he's going to be walking the camp with those outsiders for a while.* Sam wasn't the only person with keys to the Gators! Big Mike had keys, too—right? *If only one of his key sets disappeared, it wouldn't be missed, would it?* Presley stood up and glanced around once more before walking briskly over to the office.

He'd be in and out in no time!

As he walked, getting keys reminded him of today's second task, another loose end he needed to wrap up: that unexpected key in his locker and the silly girl saying dumb stuff sitting outside the locker room the other night. She was clearly a lookout for someone who'd been messing with his locker. He was going to need to keep an eye on her and figure out what to do about her and whichever friend of hers had been snooping in his locker. He hated loose ends, but that one could wait until after he'd gotten the keys to a Gator!

40

___

EXTRA WIRES

Zoe was a detail person. That's what her father had told her and one of the reasons she had decided to major in accounting. More specifically, forensic accounting—she loved a good mystery. She'd found out from a family friend that the most important person in major criminal investigations was a forensic accountant. Someone who could follow the path of money through receipts and records and figure out who the real bad guys (or girls!) were. With any luck, this time next year she hoped to be working for the CIA or the FBI, training to be one of those experts.

This morning, though, she was checking her wiring for the big fireworks finale at tonight's powwow. It was a job she had taken very seriously for each powwow this summer. Fireworks were fun to watch and fun to launch but like anything this dangerous, you had to respect the details and take nothing for granted!

Part of the prep for each show was her wire check. All of the ignition wires that led to the various launch boxes were neatly and methodically arranged to easily inspect them from end-to-end. No one but her was supposed to mess with any wires. Period. That made it all the more intriguing that there were five wires she didn't recognize on the massive terminal board that was controlled by her firing panel.

156

"Carson, did you add anything new to tonight's show?" she asked. That wasn't likely, but the change in wiring made no sense.

"Nope." Carson replied. He set aside the box of M-80 firecrackers he'd been unpacking to have a closer look with her.

Zoe pointed to one set of wires that came in from launch box C. There were twelve launch boxes and each one could hold up to four dozen rockets, which meant up to forty-eight wires for each box if they were fully loaded.

"Look," she said, tracing five wires that had been screwed onto the board's terminals for the Number 12 firing. "Number 12 is the opening of the finale, right?"

"Yeah, that's the firing for the dozen sky rockets that go off just before all of the M-80 clusters."

"Right. The M-80s, they're Number 13." Zoe paused to look more closely at the wires. "But you haven't added any skyrockets, have you?"

"Nope. We've got to save the rest for the final powwow next Friday." He looked more closely at the wire. "Hang on," he said, "I'm not sure I recognize that wire now that you mention it." Carson walked over to one of the shelves in the fire control shed and picked up a roll of lime green wire.

"See, this is the stuff I've been using—lime green."

"Hmm," Zoe said. "And these new ones are more of an old-fashioned forest green. Different wire."

Carson nodded his head and then agreed: "Yup, not mine."

"Guess we should chase the wires and see where they go, right?"

"Any other time, yes," Carson said cautiously, then suggested, "but this might be the break the Rangers were looking for, you know?"

"Yeah, I was just about to take back that idea of us hunting this down ourselves." She pulled her phone out of her back pocket and called Sergeant Smith's number. "I agree," she said to Carson while she waited for Smith to pick up.

"Whatcha got, Zoe?" the Texas Ranger asked as she answered her phone.

"Carson and I are over at the firing shed getting ready for tonight's fireworks and we've got some unexpected wires. Wanna come have a look?"

"You bet!" she replied, covering the phone's mic to get Tran's attention. "We'll be there in a minute. Don't touch anything! You never know if something like that's been booby-trapped!"

"Got it. We'll wait for you to get here."

~

Corporal Tran had been a Marine and his assignment had been ordinance. He'd briefly trained on bomb disposal so he knew explosives inside and out. "From this end, I'd say we're looking at something pretty basic," he told Sergeant Smith. "No power load at this end, only the ground and detonator leg so I don't think we're looking at anything sophisticated enough to have a fail-over type like an electronic trap might."

"Which means what for the rest of us?" Smith asked with an amused look on her face.

"Likely just intended to take the firing line like any other fireworks but deliver it somewhere out there in the woods." Tran said, a touch embarrassed at his enthusiasm.

Smith nodded her head then looked over to Carson. "And you don't have any of this color wire at all in your stuff, right?"

"Nope. I've got lots of other colors to help keep things straight, but only one roll of green and it's as lime green as a pair of Nikes."

"So do you want me to go ahead and disconnect them?" Zoe asked.

Smith looked at her watch: *Ten-fifteen.* It was going to take an hour or more to get a bomb-disposal squad up to the camp and that was going to draw a lot of attention and totally blow their strategic objective of not alerting Presley Clarke. "Give me ten minutes," she finally said. "Tran, you stay here with Zoe and Carson while I have a quick chat with the captain."

After what seemed like an eternity to Zoe, Sergeant Smith returned. "Tran, Captain Stone believes your onsite assessment is sufficient for us to secure the firing shed and lock down all the ignition circuits so we have a safe search environment. She said she'll brief the disposal team on what we've got and bring them in from the north end of the camp's property. I'll work with Mr. Murkowski to ensure their discrete arrival through the woods to deal with whatever it is these wires are connected to. In the meantime, once you're secure here, I want you to trace those lines with Carson and photograph what you find. Zoe, you'll stay here to ensure no one returns, and I'll be back as soon as I've got details worked out with Murkowski. You good with that?"

Zoe nodded. "By the way, you know, this had to have been done overnight last night, right? No one would be silly enough to show up here at the shed in broad daylight and these wires weren't here when we were testing circuits late yesterday afternoon."

"I totally agree with that assessment. In fact I'm certain of it, or I wouldn't chance leaving you here for a single minute by yourselves," Smith smiled.

41

WHAT HAVE WE HERE?

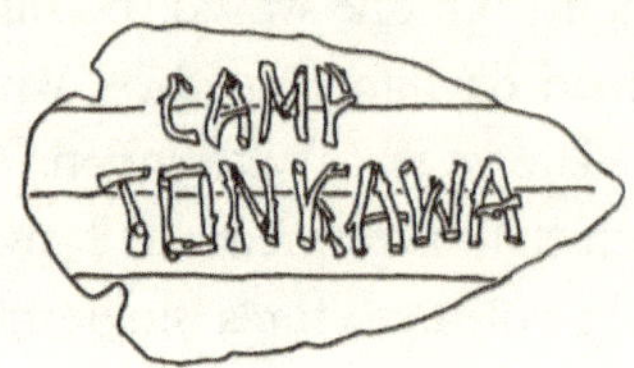

Charlie thought Big Mike was looking particularly flustered. It was only a half hour until all the campers were due to show up for lunch, so he had no idea why he was getting called into Mike's office for another special assignment. "Dang it, where's my key?" Big Mike muttered loudly as he searched his drawer once again.

Not wanting to interrupt, Charlie just waited.

"I don't see the key to Gator One, so here's the key to the old one," Big Mike finally said, tossing a key to Charlie.

"Where to?" Charlie asked.

Big Mike regained his composure. "Here's the deal, Charlie. The Rangers got a call from Zoe a little while ago when she and Carson found some extra wires hooked up to the fireworks panel. A bomb squad from the Rangers is coming in from up on the North Ranch Road so they won't be seen. I need you to go meet them and take them the back way to the powwow grounds to meet up with Sergeant Smith. Got it?"

"Yes, sir."

"And by the way, when you pick up Gator Two can you have a look-see in Gator One to see if I left a key in it? Doesn't seem likely but I can't find my key."

"Will do, boss."

The trail to the North Ranch Road used some of the same, bouncy track that the bridge road took. It turned north, though, when it came to the lower side of the Chief's Peak and became a logging and firefighting road—that ran parallel to the power line easement all the way out to the Texas Farm-to-Ranch road which marked the north side of the property.

When he got to the gate, he found Captains Smith and Alvarez. Beyond them he saw a Burnet County Sheriff's SUV with dark windows. He guessed whoever was sitting inside was enjoying some cold AC.

"Charlie, good to see you again," Stone said as she shook his hand over the top of the gate.

"You, too," he replied. "Let me get this opened up for ya'll." He pulled out the key ring Big Mike had loaned him and found a special firefighter's key for the gate's padlock. Moments later he stood back while the SUV slowly rolled through and past him.

Stone climbed into the Gator, and Alverez sat down in the second-row seat. "Okay. Guess we are going to discretely head to the fireworks shed, right?"

"That was my understanding," Charlie smiled. He passed the SUV which then followed him toward the camp's powwow grounds.

"So, what's up with all this?" he asked after a minute of silence.

"Tran and Smith found five suspicious containers in the woods about forty-five minutes ago. That was after Zoe had spotted some wires she didn't recognize attached to her fireworks control board."

"She's pretty top notch. I think she's imagining herself working for the FBI or something when she finishes her CPA," Charlie said, bragging on his friend.

"One of the most important jobs in law enforcement," Stone said with a soft smile. "All the guns and car chases and clever work of medical examiners make for great TV. But what most people don't know is how many cases are built by a forensic accounting expert!"

She glanced over at Charlie as the trail suddenly degraded into a rough mess of rocks. When the Gator stopped bouncing she added,

"She shouldn't have to look long to find a great job if that's what she's wanting to do."

When they finally arrived at the clearing in the woods behind the powwow circle, the doors of the SUV opened and three men in heavy body armor suits emerged. "Bomb-disposal 'Lite,'" Stone said to Charlie. "We think we're dealing with something we can isolate without a lot of danger, but if we're wrong, we'll go ahead and bring in the Really-Big-Bomb-Van."

Sergeant Smith met her boss and gave her a briefing on the location of the suspicious barrels they'd found. Charlie overheard one puzzling clue from Smith: "The suspect may have been trying to be clever or create their own fail-safe, but the five wires Carson and Zoe spotted because of their different color, they'd actually been connected to their own fireworks and five of their own wires had been wired to the barrels."

"Interesting," Stone murmured as she and the three bomb team experts started to follow her to the first of the five barrels.

"Want me to just leave you the Gator key?" he asked Stone.

"Great idea, Charlie, thanks. Now all of you should get back to your camp assignments. We'll talk about our next step later this afternoon."

THE BEST (AND WORST) THINGS HAPPEN AT LUNCH

"She's not an insurance inspector," Alex said in a hushed voice to Tyler. None of their friends at the table were paying attention anyway. The rest of the guys were trying to decide if Jonathan was going to kiss Cassie before the end of camp next Friday.

"What are you talking about?" Tyler asked, trying to shift his focus from Jonathan to his friend Alex's latest pronouncement.

"The woman over there with Big Mike and all the Elders. Charlie said she and that other guy were insurance inspectors that were checking things out. Here to see if the camp had overlooked safety standards after the reports of the bridge collapse."

"So?"

"So, insurance inspectors don't pack heat."

"What does that mean, Alex?" Tyler asked, exasperated that he was missing the other conversation that was going on about Cassie and Jonathan. *Personally, he thought it was Liam that would get a kiss from Cassie, not Jonathan. What's Alex's deal, anyway!*

"Dude, she's loaded. Look at her ankle when she moves her leg." He paused a moment, then said, "Now! See what I mean?"

Tyler had no clue. The woman sitting at the end of the table across from Big Mike had a pair of loose-fitting black slacks and hiking shoes. *So what of it?* "Still don't get it," he said.

"Concealed weapon. Lower-leg holster."

Tyler looked more closely. He was suddenly intrigued since he finally understood what Alex was trying to get him to see. "Okay, yeah . . ." he said, tentatively, seeing the lower leg of her pants maybe bulge a bit when she moved her foot. "I think I see what you're talking about."

"You know what this means, right?" Alex looked at his friend, not convinced he really did get it and prepared to explain what it meant if he had to.

"I'm guessing you think she's a cop? You think this is all related to the stuff that's been going on?"

"Exactly," Alex said, relieved that Tyler was catching on. "I'm guessing she's a Texas Ranger. Besides, my mom's company hires insurance inspectors for jobs all the time and they don't spend more than a couple of hours at a place. These two people have been here since Charlie and the other Elders got called in to Big Mike's office after lunch yesterday. Remember? All four of them went wandering off while we were swimming."

Tyler hadn't noticed and was always amazed at the little things that Alex did notice. It was kind of crazy how Alex could always figure out things that no one else saw—or most times things no one else even cared about. "You're cooking up another plan, aren't you?" he finally said, realizing where this was going.

"I am," Alex said simply.

"And . . . ?"

"I've got a couple of pictures I think our friend 'the insurance inspector' might like to see."

"You mean you decided not to show 'em to Charlie?"

"Couldn't. It would've gotten him and me both in trouble. Me for poking around when I was warned off and him for not keeping a closer eye on me." He smiled. "Can't make life miserable for Charlie."

While they were talking, Big Mike got up and took his tray to the dirty dishes window but the woman who appeared to have a leg holster stayed at the table with the guy who was also supposed to be an insurance inspector.

"Think they're both Rangers?" Tyler asked, now curious.

"Would make sense," Alex said. He looked around the table and noticed everyone was finished, just waiting on Charlie to come back. When he looked back over to the far table, he saw Charlie and the other Elders had finally stood up to get rid of their trays. That was his cue.

One of Alex's jobs as feather keeper was to dismiss his table. "Okay, campers," Alex announced, "Looks like the boss is finished so let's clear the table and meet back at the cabin in fifteen minutes. Got it?" The rest of his Cabin 9 campers started scooting chairs out and talking louder. That was as close to an acknowledgment as Alex was going to get. He waited to be last in line.

When the rest of his campers headed for the door, Alex delayed and then gave Tyler a silent nod to let him know to go on without him. When they were all outside, Alex walked over to the table where the two Texas Rangers were sitting alone now, talking to each other.

"Hey there," he said politely as he took an uninvited seat at their table. Hardly anyone was left in the dining hall by now, but that didn't stop Sergeant Smith and Corporal Tran from taking a quick look around to see who might notice this unexpected encounter with a camper.

"Pardon me—but, can I help you?" Tran asked, preempting Smith.

"No, not really," Alex said with a big smile on his face and a ton of self-confidence. "But I think what's on my camp camera phone here just might be of help to *you*." He slid the phone across the table with the first of his shed pictures already pulled up on the screen.

Smith did a kind of double take when she realized what she was looking at. After swiping through the half-dozen pics, she slid the phone over to Tran for a look.

"And just who are you?" she asked with a touch of bewilderment on her face.

"Alex. Alex Ortiz. I'm the kid who provided the info to Sandra Morrison-Parker about the locker and the cutter and who was told to stop being so nosy and mind my own business and let the professionals handle this." He grinned then added, "And I'm guessing from the heavy-duty ankle-wear you're both sporting—well, I'm guessing that y'all must be the professionals they were talking about."

This made Smith laugh. *So this was the kid she'd read about in the briefing memo.* She nodded and reached out her hand to shake Alex's. "Pleased to meet you, Alex. I happen to have read quite a bit about you. And, actually, I think you may have saved us some time with your amateur detective work."

"Please tell me you didn't touch anything?" Tran said nervously as he passed the phone back to Smith.

"Nitrile gloves . . . of course!" Alex said quietly with a big grin.

"Of course," Smith replied, nodding her head. She looked around at the near-empty dining hall. "Well, even if *you* were clever enough to spot us, no one else around here—including the camp staff—is aware of our true identity. So, if you want to tell us discretely where we'll find this stuff and then say your goodbyes—QUICKLY, that would be helpful."

"Got it," he replied. "There's an old boat shed down by the river. Used to be the camp's kayak and canoe shed before the new one got built. I took these pics after lunch yesterday. All this stuff should still be there."

"Hmm," Smith said, looking at the pics once again.

Alex paused and glanced around once more. "Okay, I'll take off, now." He glanced at Tran then back at Smith and grinned. "So, when I stand up you can tell me to say hi to Angie for you . . . she's my mom. I'll just tell my friends I spotted one of my mom's pals and thought I better be friendly and say hi!"

"Good cover," Tran said, approvingly. "Considering a career as a CIA Spook someday, Alex?"

"Never know," he said with a hopeful look on his face. Alex stood up and came around the table to give Smith a neck hug like he would an old family friend. As he left, Smith dutifully gave her greetings to Alex's mom and the scene played out the way Alex had suggested. At least, he hoped it had.

～

From the kitchen, Presley had been keeping a closer eye on things today than most days. The fact was, on most days he simply couldn't stand the campers. They were noisy, they were extremely rude when they brought their mess to the dirty tray window, and some of the boys seemed to go out of their way to make butter and food sculptures for him to clean up.

But today, he was on a mission to figure out the name of that girl who'd been in the breezeway Wednesday night—the one with the yogurt. He was certain she'd been a lookout. When he saw her coming through the food line with Cabin 8, he realized that she and her friend were the same two that had worked in the kitchen with him Monday night. *That's why she'd looked so familiar in the breezeway!*

He'd paid careful attention as they filled their trays and then he heard one of their friends call one of them Monica and the other one Mac.

Monica and Mac. He recognized Monica as the one in the breezeway, and he recalled Mac was that *awful* girl who'd walked into the wrong room when he was on his phone and then dropped a tray full of plastic drink cups.

Now that lunch was over and he was rinsing trays and dishes, he had time to think . . . something he was certain he was good at. His original plan didn't include Miss Monica and Miss Mac getting in his way. Doing something about nosy campers hadn't been top-of-mind but it was now. This was going to require something creative. An idea started to take shape as he looked around the kitchen.

He glanced out the dirty tray window to see if there were any campers left and noticed one of the boys from Cabin 9 sitting at the table with the insurance inspectors. *Why is he sitting with the inspectors?* Presley knew that boy's face, *He was the feather keeper for Cabin 9, wasn't he?* He wiped his hands on his apron and walked over to the cook's cork board. He found the posting: "Feather Keepers in Charge by Cabin."

Yup! There was his face and his name: Alex Ortiz—Cabin 9.

What was that kid doing, talking with the insurance inspectors when nobody else was around? He looked more closely at the man and woman the boy was talking with. They both looked a little nervous.

He glanced at Alex again and suddenly a lightbulb went off in his head; for the last two weeks he'd seen those two girls hanging around with this Alex kid. Him and one other boy. *Maybe the boy who'd had kitchen duty with Alex for supper last Thursday?*

Maybe Alex is somehow a part of the snooping in his locker? Presley thought about that some more and it began to feel like a revelation. *Yeah. What if he's a part of it, too? What if he was the one in the locker room Wednesday night? Maybe he's telling the insurance people about what he saw in his locker Wednesday night?*

Now he was starting to feel paranoid. He knew from experience and reflection that paranoia was his worst enemy. He always made his worst decisions when he felt threatened, but he couldn't help it—he couldn't set the idea aside: *What if he knows and he's telling the inspectors about him?* He shook his head. *Clearly, he needed to deal with three campers now. Not just two! And that—well, that was going to complicate things for tonight.*

43

____

THE SHOW MUST GO ON

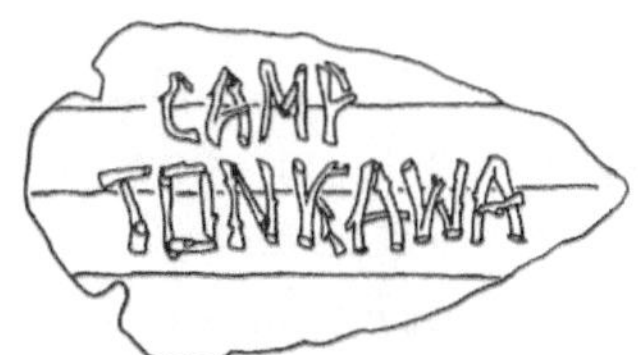

"It's your call, Captain," Vasquez said. He was sitting in the mobile command post trailer, across the table from the four Texas Rangers. They were parked just off the remote Farm-to-Market Road on the north side of the camp to avoid being seen.

"We've got the evidence in hand and the lab techs told us they found plenty of fingerprints when they dusted the hidden bike and tools," Tran said, recapping the work they'd done that afternoon. It had helped that most of the campers were out on an afternoon hike while the team had been working.

"So, we've got pretty serious charges here, in the bag," Stone acknowledged. "What still worries me is the difference between these pieces of circumstantial evidence and the really big motive at work here."

"You're looking for a 'smoking gun,' so to speak," Vasquez said sympathetically, "right?"

"Yeah, I guess I am. I want to be certain we get this guy properly for not only for the risks he created but also for the intent to defraud the terms of the land trust involved here."

"Well, the explosives have been removed. We replaced them with

169

barrels that look the same—filled with plain old water in case Clarke makes a final check of his plan," Sgt. Smith offered.

"So, there's no real threat to the kids if the powwow goes on as planned," Tran added.

"I mean, it might be interesting to see just what Clarke does at the end of the show when nothing big blows up. He might just put a 'bow' on the case, you never know." Vasquez looked at Captain Stone and smiled. "I know exactly what you're leaning toward; it's what I'd do if it was my case, too."

"You do indeed," Stone replied, a smile spreading across her face. "Let's go ahead and maybe he will put a bow on the case for us!"

"I'll have deputies in the woods at each barrel site taking pictures and video. If Clarke comes around for a look-see, we'll have that well documented," Vasquez said.

"Perfect. And let's have a pair of uniformed deputies show up just before 'showtime' to be on-hand. No early warning to staff, have 'em show up about nine, find Mr. Murkowski and just be present. Can't second guess every detail, so they're our backup just in case anything unexpected happens." Satisfied, Stone turned to the rest of the team gathered around the table. "Everyone in agreement?" she asked.

Each person nodded and spoke a word of agreement. When everyone had spoken, Sergeant Conner checked his watch. "It's three-thirty. I think I better give Murkowski a call and confirm we are a 'go' for his powwow."

"Do it." Stone said, nodding her head.

44

PASSING NOTES

Well, isn't this cute," Dory said, laughing as she handed a piece of paper to Monica. It was folded four times and had a single staple in the center of it to hold it closed to prying eyes. The name "Monica" had been written on one side. "Reminds me of fourth grade, right? Looks like someone's passing you a note, Monica! A secret admirer from Cabin 3?" She giggled and so did two other girls who overheard her. They all knew the campers in Cabin 3 were third and fourth grade boys.

"Great, thanks," Monica said, taking the note and looking at both sides of it.

Dory was right, she hadn't gotten a note like this since she was in Ms. Strong's class in fourth grade. "Where did this come from?" she asked, not recognizing anything about it."

"Dunno. The feather keeper from Cabin 7 gave it to me over at supper and asked me to pass it along."

"Oooo," Kaitlyn said with a fake enthusiasm, "Maybe Liam is looking for a rendezvous at the snack bar tonight?" she teased.

"As if!" Monica gave Kaitlyn the *stink-eye* before shaking her head. She took her note and walked outside to find Mac, who was sitting in one of the Adirondack chairs in front of their cabin, trying yet again to read the book she'd brought to camp.

"You know you're never going to get past page twenty-two before we go home," Monica said. She plopped down into the chair beside Mac.

"Especially not if I keep getting interrupted and have to start over." Mac looked up and offered an insincere glare before grinning and putting her book down. "What's up?'

"Just this," Monica said, handing Mac the note.

Mac looked at both sides of it and sized it up as everyone else had: "Looks like some third-grade boy has a crush on you."

"I was going to be generous and make it fourth-grader."

"Whatever." She passed it back to Monica. "You going to open it or just keep it as a camp souvenir?"

"Think I'll open it."

Mac waited for Monica to read it to her. When she didn't, she cleared her throat really loud. "Well??"

"So, have a look. It's from Alex and he wants us to meet him in the camp kitchen at nine, just after snack time, but before we go to the powwow. Says to use the backdoor and don't worry if the lights are out, he'll have his flashlight."

"Lemme see." Mac took the note to read it for herself. "Hmmm," was all she said at first. "Where did you get this?"

"Dory," Monica replied. "She said the feather keeper from Cabin 7 gave it to her after dinner."

"Well, Alex's writing has always been pretty awful looking, but this is worse than usual."

"I wouldn't know," Monica said, taking the note back. "Should we go?"

"Probably ought to. He's likely playing private detective again. Sometimes I wish he'd stop, but we'd better see what he's got going on."

"Guess you're right." Monica paused and read the note one more time before folding it back up and stuffing it in her pocket. "At least he said *after* snack time."

Mac laughed and nodded her head. She knew exactly what Monica was thinking. "Yup, girl. You'll still get to have your frozen yogurt and Swedish gummy fish!"

"You know it!" Monica said before stretching out in the chair to watch the sun as it began to settle below the ridge line in the distance. *This was the prettiest time of day!*

45

A DANGEROUS RENDEZVOUS

Alex hated missing snack bar time. He was racking his brain to try and figure out what on earth Monica and Mac had found in the kitchen that was so important that he needed to miss snack bar to meet them. The note was actually from Monica, but it was short and to-the-point:

Meet me and Mac at the camp kitchen just before snack-time. Need to show you something!

He walked around to the back door of the kitchen. The lights were off but the door inside the screen was open. He opened the screen slowly and peered into the dark. It felt like he was stepping into a scene from one of those horror movies he used to watch. *What were Mac and Monica doing in here so quietly? Shouldn't they have brought a flashlight?*

"Mac?" he hissed in a loud whisper, "where are you?" There was no answer. "Monica, you in here?" he asked in a louder whisper, but still no answer. *What to do?* His instincts said run, *but what if Mac and Monica really are here? I can't just run away all scared of the dark, right?*

He thought he heard the gentle shift of air as if a body had just walked past him, but it was so dark who could tell? Suddenly the door shut in the dark. "What's going on?" he said in a loud whisper. *If this was Mac's idea of a stunt, he was starting to get mad.* Just as he was about to call out and tell Mac to either come on out or he was going to turn on the light, he felt a hand slap a piece of duct tape across his mouth and then push him across something, causing him to trip and fall forward. Almost as soon as he hit the floor there was a knee in his back and someone was on top of him. They grabbed his hand and wrapped a piece of duct tape around his wrist. He tried to swing with his other hand but being face down on the floor, it was like fishing in the air. A moment later that hand had been grabbed and the rest of the duct tape closed around his other wrist as well.

He tried to kick and roll over but it was no use. It was dark, he couldn't see, and couldn't get the person off his back. As he silently realized how helpless he was, he began to panic. There was really only one possibility: *Presley. But how could Presley have known anything about him?*

Presley, or whoever had tricked him into coming into a dark kitchen, was now sitting with their full weight on his back. Alex heard the sound of more duct tape being unrolled. He tried his best to squirm again, but his captor had already started wrapping the tape around his ankles. Once, twice, three times.

Alex lay there helpless and realized he was about to cry. *No!* he told himself. *No tears. Get your head clear and stay alert!* But that didn't answer his two pressing questions: *Why me?* and *who was crazy enough to do this to a summer camper?* Suddenly whoever had attacked him got hold of his legs and started dragging him across the tile floor. He heard a big door open and was awkwardly shoved into a very cold room.

This isn't good! he thought to himself as he heard the door close.

46

SNACK TIME

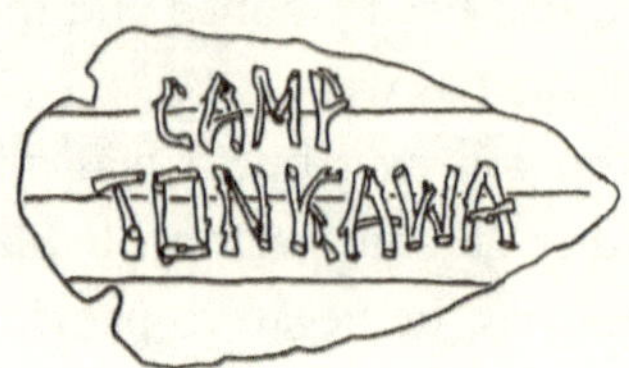

Tyler couldn't find Alex. He and Jonathan had been talking about tomorrow's kayak race rematch between Cabin 9 and Cabin 7. This time the race was going to be cumulative relay style: four boats per team and after the first two kayaks were off, the next kayak could start only after the race master downstream waved the flag that their team's prior boat had crossed the finish line.

"Kind of like track—you know, the 400-meter relay," Jonathan said. "Comes down to the lead-off and the anchor . . . first and last. You've got to lead us off with as much spread as you can earn us . . . then Sean and Micah will do whatever they can to hold the middle, and then I'll make up whatever distance they lose."

"Or, you can build on the lead they add and help us really win big!" Tyler said.

"Okay, yeah," J said, nodding his head. "I like the way you think, Tyler!"

It was only after he and J had gotten to the snack plaza and he'd gotten his iced slushee drink and fruit rollups that Tyler realized Alex wasn't already here. *Where was he?*

He spotted Mac and Monica over with their tribe so he knew the three of them couldn't be off on another of Alex's "secret missions."

Tyler wandered around some more and even had a look down the breezeway to see if he spotted him there, but no Alex. Now he was really starting to worry. It just wasn't like Alex to go missing at snack time. He sat on one of the benches to listen to Liam telling everybody an embarrassing story about someone from Cabin 5. Tyler drank about half his slushee and got himself a mega-brain freeze. When he'd finally recovered, he looked around once more before it dawned on him where Alex must be: *Charlie had probably recruited him to help with tonight's fireworks.* Tonight's show was supposed to be really big and totally awesome! He probably needed a hand at the last minute— *yeah, that was where he was. No doubt.*

He went and found Jonathan and the two headed over to wait in line for their cue to go in with the rest of the campers in their cabin. *Tonight was going to be amazing!*

47

MORE DUCT TAPE, PLEASE.

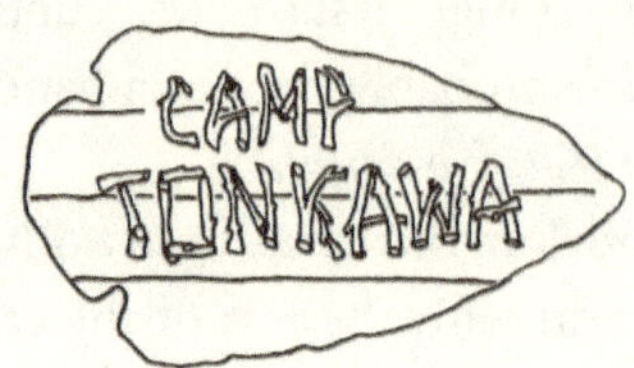

Mac checked her digital watch. It was a couple of minutes till nine.

"They're starting to line up," Monica said. "If we're going to duck, we better make our move now before someone notices us."

"Let's do it," Mac replied and stepped into the shadows closer to the buildings before making her way around to the back of the buildings with Monica following close behind.

"Alex better have brought his flashlight for this little escapade!" Monica said, sounding annoyed that they might miss the big opening to the powwow and be stuck in the dark as well.

"He thinks of everything . . . don't worry," Mac assured.

When they got to the screen door, they could see the inside door was already open so they pulled the screen door and stepped in, being careful not to let it slam behind them.

"Alex, you in here?" Mac asked in her loudest whisper voice.

She paused, expecting a reply but none came.

"C'mon, Alex, enough kidding around. Where are you?!" Monica hissed loudly.

"He's in the walk-in refrigerator," came a man's voice in the dark, just as the back door closed and a single light came on over the cook's stove. In the eerie, dim light they saw Presley standing beside the door with one finger held to his lips. Before they could run or scream his voice gave them pause: "Scream and I'll move him into the freezer instead. Cooperate and you can simply visit with him for the next half hour. I just need to finish my big show, then I'll let the cook know where to find you."

Mac and Monica were stunned and neither of them knew what to do, but neither of them screamed.

"What do you want?" Mac asked, angry and not sure what else she could do or say. It was all too bizarre.

"Like I said," Presley replied with a smile on his face, "I just need about a half hour to finish what I've started."

"He's crazy," Monica said, glancing around quickly to size up their options.

"Yeah, maybe a little," he replied. "I had a good thing going until you and your friend got nosy. But no matter. As long as the three of you can stay out of trouble for the next half hour, all will be fine."

He glanced at his wristwatch, and Monica thought it looked like it was an old Rolex like her dad's. "Nice watch," she said in a steady, cool voice, trying to buy some time for Mac to come up with a brilliant way that they could escape and rescue Alex . . . if he really was here.

"It is a nice watch," Presley said, flattered. "A Rolex Submariner from the 80s. A gift, actually. Something my dad left for me."

"How do we know you've got Alex in the fridge?" Mac asked, realizing they might just have stumbled into a trap that they could still escape from.

Presley's eyes moved to the prep table in the middle of the room. Both girls followed his glance and noticed a roll of gray duct tape on the table.

"I'm on a tight schedule," he said. "So, as much as I'd love to chat, I've got things to do and you have a friend who would just love some company."

Looking at Monica, he addressed her by name. "You're Monica, right? Tell you what, Monica, how about you open the fridge door really quick and confirm that Alex is fine. A bit cold, but he's fine."

Monica hesitated. "Well go on!" he snapped. "I said I'm on a schedule, go see for yourself then decide if we've got a deal or not."

Mac watched as her friend opened the door to the walk-in fridge. Alex was sitting on a five-gallon canister of butter and looked pitiful—and cold. He glanced up and Monica could see a glimmer of hope in his eyes. She nodded to Mac.

"So here's the deal," Presley continued. "I don't want to create delicate issues, so I need both of you to just go ahead and put some duct tape over your own mouths, then one of you . . . Monica, you can duct tape Mac's wrists and then I'll finish up your wrists and then you can all just wait for the next half hour until the "troops" come to rescue you. Got it?"

It was a cold deal but both girls had seen how agitated Presley was getting. They didn't want to, but they nodded to each other in agreement. They each put the duct tape across their mouths, as loosely as they thought they could get away with. Then Monica gently put a single wrap of tape, loosely around Mac's wrists.

"Look, girls, this isn't a TV show. This is serious stuff. Three wraps and tight enough to be a nuisance. NOW!"

Mac was relieved that at least he wasn't tying their hands behind their backs—they ought to be able to get free pretty easily once they were in the fridge. Mac stretched her arm out for two more wraps of tape. After the formality of three quick passes around Monica's wrists, Presley directed the girls to join Alex. There were only two five-gallon buckets in the fridge, so Alex stood up to let Mac and Monica both have a seat. He waddled sideways to sit on a shrink-wrapped pallet of ranch dressing jars.

"Now then, that wasn't so hard, was it?" Presley asked. "Behave yourselves and before you know it, you'll be out of here," he said with a wink and a frightening grin. He closed the door and quickly slipped a padlock through the latch which he clicked closed. He smiled to himself. *That was too easy*, he thought. *And I really could care less if they quickly untaped each other; they won't be getting past that padlock anytime soon!*

But Presley wasn't quite finished. The big event for the night had a grand finale that was going to be spectacular! In fact, he decided just this afternoon to upgrade the show from spectacular to super-spectacular! He took a crescent wrench from his back pocket and worked quickly to disconnect the gas line that ran to the kitchen's stove from its main shut-off valve. The smell of gas began to fill the room . . . a dangerous fireball just waiting to happen.

He moved quickly to leave, but paused at the door, proud of his plan in an odd sort of way, then said aloud: "Well, I really must be going now. Hate to leave a party, but I've got things to do and places to go!" He carefully closed the back door to the kitchen so there wouldn't be a premature spark. *Choreography is everything!* he reminded himself.

48

WHERE IS EVERYBODY?

Micah and Kyle were talking to J about football at the front of the line. Tyler had no interest in football so he started looking around for Alex again. *Surely, he'd sit with the cabin, even if he'd been helping Charlie, right?* Tyler glanced over to the girls' line to catch Mac and Monica's attention to see if they knew where Alex was. But where were Mac and Monica now? The Elders hadn't arrived yet, so he jogged over to where Dory was holding court with the only three girls of Cabin 8 who really appreciated her important assignment as their feather keeper.

"Where's Mac and Monica?" Tyler asked with no hello or context.

"I dunno," she said, looking surprised. "I guess here in line somewhere." Dory looked around in front and behind and then looked both ways a second time. "Well, they were at the snack bar . . ." she said, now confused.

"They didn't say they were going anywhere?"

"No, they didn't. It's powwow. Where, exactly would they be going?" Dory was not good at thinking on her feet and was getting irritated.

"Did either of them say anything about Alex?"

"No."

"Well, actually they did," Kaitlyn interrupted.

"When?" Dory asked, sounding hurt that there was something she didn't know.

"On the way over to snack bar time. Remember that note after supper—the one everyone was teasing Monica about? Well she said it was from Alex."

"What note?" Tyler asked, confused.

"Mason, the feather keeper from Cabin 7, gave Dory a note after supper to give to Monica." Kaitlyn said.

Tyler looked over at the boys' line and spotted Mason with the boys from Cabin 7 and quickly jogged over to where he was standing. Dory followed him with Kaitlyn right behind.

"Hey, Mason, I need your help," Tyler said quickly and quietly. "Kind of important, okay? You gave Dory a note after supper to give to Monica. Who gave it to you?"

Mason looked at Dory and then back at Tyler. "That guy who cleans the trays at the kitchen window. He said it was from her friend, Alex."

"You didn't tell me that." Dory objected.

"Well, not a big deal, I imagine your friend knew who it was from."

"Thanks, Mason—that's all I need!" Tyler said. "Dory, you guys better get back in line with your cabin. See you later."

Charlie and the Elders were just getting ready to line up but noticed the commotion between the girls' line and the boys' line. The moment was looking a bit confused and certainly not quiet and dignified, which was the camp rule.

Kelley turned to Charlie. "What's going on?"

"Not sure," he said, and then Tyler suddenly appeared out of the twilight darkness with a look of panic on his face.

"Alex," he began, sounding winded, "was he with you just now?" Tyler sounded like it was an urgent question.

"No, why?"

"He's missing, man. And so are Mac and Monica. And it sounds like Monica got a note from Alex after supper, but it wasn't really from Alex, it was from Presley. I think something's wrong!"

Charlie and Kelley looked at each other. As soon as Presley's name was mentioned they knew something serious was up.

"Stall," Charlie said to her and then put a hand on Tyler's shoulder to pull him along with him to run as fast as they could. The two sheriff's deputies were in the corner of the clearing, just out of sight from the kids but standing where they had a good view of things. They'd been briefed on tonight's show and recognized Charlie as one of the four Elders as he ran toward them with a camper in tow.

"Whoa, hold up now," the taller of the two said to Charlie as they got closer. "What's going on?"

"I need you to get on your radio and get Captain Stone on the line." The deputy looked at his partner and back at Charlie and the boy; he could tell there was a sense of urgency so he asked only one question: "You're fully briefed?"

"Yes, sir, and this is critical. We might have a problem developing that no one planned for."

Within moments, the deputy had Captain Stone on his walkie-talkie. He got permission to pass the mic to Charlie. The deputies listened as Charlie explained everything as best as he understood it—which was still pretty sketchy. The bottom line, though was simple: "We've got three campers missing and it looks like Presley might be involved somehow."

Suddenly Tyler's digital watch dinged that he had a text message.

"I thought all watches were supposed to be on silent," Charlie said, reminding Tyler of the camp rules for digital watches.

"Sorry," Tyler said as he looked at his watch face. "Hang on," he said, holding his wrist up for Charlie to see. "It's a text from Alex: he says, 'it's cold in here.'"

"*Cold in here?*" Charlie repeated, then paused as it occurred to him immediately what Alex must be trying to say. "Did you copy that, Captain?" Charlie asked, the mic still in his hand, "I'll bet they're in that big, walk-in fridge in the kitchen!"

"Roger that, Charlie. Lemme have the deputy back on the radio." As Charlie and Tyler stepped back, they could hear Stone ordering one of the two deputies to head over to the camp kitchen but proceed with caution, and then they could hear her on the open channel directing two of her Rangers to meet the deputies there. "Careful, y'all," she added. "We could have a dangerous hostage situation evolving." When she was finished, she asked for Charlie to be put back on the line.

"Charlie, you're a take-charge kind of guy, so go tell your fellow Elders the powwow is off. Got it? Tell all the counselors to move their campers back to their cabins and when they get there go into lockdown mode. Be discrete, though. I don't want a panic; just get the kids secure, understand that? I'll find Murkowski and let him know."

"Got it, I'm on my way!" Charlie passed the mic back to the deputy and quickly jogged over to where the Elders were still waiting on him so they could start the entry procession. "Change of plans," he said quickly and then passed along the captain's instructions. "Show's been cancelled."

49

PROBLEMS EVERYWHERE

S ergeant Smith and Corporal Tran had been stationed near the snack bar plaza on standby. When they saw the sheriff's deputy jogging their way, they dashed over to join him.

Smith got on her radio as they approached the kitchen: "Conner, you still got eyes on Clarke?"

"Did until about two minutes ago. Waters and I are tracking him through the woods right now and Stone's sending backup. Not sure where he's headed but it's not to any of his barrels. Looks like he's headed up to the upper ridge line." He and Waters were moving fast, so he paused to catch his breath, "Suspect's got to know we're following him by now, though."

"Got it. What was his location before he started moving?" Smith and Tran had just caught up with the sheriff's deputy.

"We saw him go into the kitchen about 8:20, then he left about 8:35 and went into the locker room a few minutes after that. We never saw him come out, so we checked the room at 9:05 and he wasn't there. Must have pulled a runner out a window and gotten back into the kitchen because we spotted him coming out the back door of the kitchen at 9:15. He took off at a jog, headed to the ropes course down in the woods. I think he spotted us about 9:25—that's when he took off into the deep woods."

Smith checked her watch—it was 9:37. If the text message was right and the kids were in the fridge or freezer, they could be getting close to hypothermia by now. "Copy that. We're heading to the kitchen . . . you be careful out there, this guy's no good. Out."

As the deputy, Smith, and Tran arrived at the back side of the kitchen they were immediately hit by a powerful smell. "I smell gas," the deputy said. They froze and just before the deputy could open the back door, Tran pulled the officer's hand back.

"Oh, no." Tran said, guiding the deputy quickly back down the steps. "I've only been around this kind of concentration once before and it didn't turn out so well!"

"Slightest spark of anything, and this building, the kids, all of us will blow sky-high!" Smith motioned them all back while she got on her radio. "Captain Stone, we've got a problem, here."

"Go."

"Someone's opened a gas valve here at the kitchen and dining hall. This building could blow any moment. We need back up and a gas plan . . . and fast!"

Stone now had two problems escalating: a prime suspect doing a runner through the woods at night and a fully gassed kitchen that could blow at the slightest spark.

"Smith, you and your team need to stand by. Do not enter, repeat, do not enter! I'll be back to you after I get fire and rescue patched in. Standby."

While Smith was on the radio, Tran spotted the gas meter for the building just around the corner. He tapped the deputy on the shoulder and said, "Quick, follow me!"

"What's the plan?" the deputy asked as he followed the Ranger.

"Gas meter," he replied, pointing to the big silver regulator. It was attached to the building with a large, two-inch pipe. "The main shut-off valve usually needs a crescent wrench, but it also has a lock-hole so you can crank it closed with a screwdriver shaft. We'll need some way to turn it off. Only takes a quarter turn, but if we don't have a wrench then we're gonna need a screwdriver."

The deputy spotted one of the maintenance Gators parked next to the administration building. "Maybe there's something in the Gator." He didn't wait for an answer; he dashed over and spotted a workbox on the back deck. He started searching through the box of odds and ends making a fast sweep with his light, then fished out something. He ran back to where Tran was waiting by the meter.

"How about this?" he asked Tran.

"A screwdriver? Man, that was lucky! Let's give it a try."

The deputy pushed it into the hole Tran was pointing to and then leveraged it to turn the valve. It was tough but suddenly it started to budge and then made its quarter turn and stopped. Tran looked at the meter and saw that none of the spinners on the gauges were turning. The gas was off!

"Good work, you two!" Smith said when they got back. Now we've gotta have help getting the building ventilated safely. Stone said to wait —I'm guessing we'll have some fire and rescue response people here soon!"

Tran and the deputy looked at her skeptically, then the deputy said exactly what they all were thinking. "If I was in town, I'd wait, but we're fifteen miles from the closest station out here. We'll be lucky if anyone gets here in a half hour. At the very least we need to get that door open and start reducing the saturation of the gas."

Tran agreed with his assessment.

"So, act now . . . ask forgiveness later, right?" Smith asked with a grin, knowing this decision could cost her job—but more important, it just might save the kids' lives by buying some time. "Okay, let's do it," she agreed.

Tran reminded them that any spark, any light switch, or the scrape of a rock, even static in their clothes could spell disaster. He pulled out a water bottle and got his hands wet before he carefully turned the doorknob of the kitchen door and very slowly pushed it open. The powerful smell of the gas built up inside almost knocked him over, but he managed to close the screen door without incident and carefully backed down the steps. The smell of the gas outside quickly became thicker.

Just then they spotted the sheriff's department helicopter passing overhead with its powerful search light scanning the ground on its way to assist with the manhunt happening in the woods. The rotor blast stirred up the air as it kicked up dust. *If only we had the whole building open and those rotors stirring up the air, we'd have it cleared in no time,* thought Smith. But as quickly as the copter arrived, it was gone.

Her thoughts were interrupted by Sam and Big Mike who had jogged over from the powwow grounds. They checked in with Smith. "What do you need us to do?"

"If you've got keys and can unlock the front doors of the dining hall and prop them open, we might get some fresh air to start blowing through," Smith said.

"Clear the gas out faster?" Sam looked at the Ranger.

"Done." Big Mike pulled a fat key ring out of his pocket and took off running for the front of the building.

"What about the walk-in fridge and freezer inside?" Smith asked Sam. "What's the set up?"

Sam immediately knew what she was getting at. *Did the kids have fresh air in the walk-in or had they been breathing toxic natural gas for the past 25 minutes?* "The cooling units for both the freezer and the fridge are on the roof. It's a closed-loop air system—it just keeps circulating the same air through the cooling stack. The door seals are tight enough that there shouldn't be any gas getting inside either of them. That's the good news. Bad news is that whatever oxygen they started with when the doors were closed is all there is in there. They might have passed out by now—I have no idea how long it would last for three people."

Smith decided it was time to give Stone an update. She came clean on the decisions she'd taken and told Stone her idea. Stone complimented her for using reasonable initiative and approved her plan. "The chopper and the search team have lost contact with the suspect so I think we can spare a few minutes to try your idea. Fire and rescue are on their way but they're still fifteen minutes out."

Two minutes later, the big helicopter circled back to their part of the compound and began to hover. Its powerful prop wash was moving air, dirt, and debris around like they were standing in the vortex of a tornado. After five minutes of deafening noise the helicopter banked and flew back to continue supporting the search of the woods.

Sam showed up with a paint respirator from his workshop and offered to go in and have a look. Smith shook her head. "Tran, you know what you're doing, you can decline if you like—but if anyone is going in before fire and rescue get here, I'd rather it be you."

"Happy to help!" he said, excited to be asked to do something heroic. He put on the filtered mask that covered his eyes, nose, and mouth, then stepped inside. He worked his way through the kitchen with his flashlight, stepping carefully. At the far side of the kitchen he spotted the big door of the walk-in fridge. His heart sank. It was padlocked.

Outside, Smith got a text update from Stone: *Tyler rec'd txt msg from Alex: sleepy, cold, where r u? —Be advised Rescue team apx 2 miles out. Situation?*

Tran stepped out and reported to Smith what he'd found. Sam was listening and when Tran described the lock, he shook his head. "A padlock as big as you're talking about is gonna take my biggest bolt cutter and more likely is gonna take a grinder. Either way, if there's still gas in there, we've got a problem getting it cut off anytime soon."

The adrenaline was starting to wear off and for the first time in the past hour, Smith felt the weight of what might happen to the kids if the professionals didn't have a solution when they got here. She and the team had given them a head start, but they were at the limit of what they could do.

Hang in there, guys! she said silently. *Just a little bit longer.*

50

TEXAS SUMMERS ARE HOT ... BUT CAMP FRIDGES ARE COLD!

Marc Torre had grown up in a family of firefighters. His dad was a firefighter, his uncle and his cousin were firefighters, and he was proud to carry on the family tradition. True, they were all still in Chicago where he grew up, but when he'd come to live with his grandma in the Hill Country of Texas, he brought his passion with him. He was the driver and a pumper on Truck 12 out of Marble Falls Station Two and proud of it. Torre had done his fair share of big fires, like the bad warehouse fire last fall that burned for almost two days and also the seemingly endless wildfires that went with Texas droughts. But it was the rescue work that excited him the most. If there was someone trapped or in danger, he was always asking his captain to give him a shot. *"Lemme go in, captain!"* seemed to be his mantra.

The phone briefing by the Texas Ranger in charge of a big operation, which had suddenly gone wrong at the summer camp, had him really worried. Natural gas was nothing to mess with. Highly flammable and lighter than air, it rose and it pocketed near ceilings. Just when you thought you'd properly vented a room, your meter could show it had concentrated at the top, again. His uncle had the burn scars to prove its dangers, especially to first responders.

His partner, "Cat," was riding shotgun in the front, scanning the road ahead for Torre. "The hydraulic cutter's not going to do us any good," Cat said, puzzling through the same thing Torre was trying to figure out. He was silent again because a rural road like this at night required a lot of attention. A wild deer could jump out and wreck a truck as badly as if it hit a telephone pole. "The accumulated gas issue is going to really throw us a curve ball."

They turned off the state highway onto the winding, narrow road that led to the camp entry. Cat glanced over at Torre and asked him how long he reckoned it would take them to clear the gas from a room the size of a commercial kitchen.

"Twenty, maybe thirty minutes, I'm thinking. The air would be close to breathable at head height after about fifteen minutes, but we'll need the big fans to pull out that last layer at the top, and it could still flash-fry you if it ignited."

"Not excited to have that ignite on us! We'd be a couple of crispy critters," Cat joked. Everyone on the truck was plugged into the headset channel and a couple of them snickered at his description. Cat was always kidding around about death, dying, and injuries. It was part of their job but that was how he dealt with the darker side of it.

"There's the gate," Cat said, pointing to the turn in and spotting a Burnet County sheriff's car waiting for them.

"Truck 12, this is Burnet one-twenty," crackled the voice of the deputy's mike over Cat's radio.

"Copy that Mr. One-twenty. You going to be our tour guide tonight? Over."

"Ten-four; follow me, kids. Times a-wasting!"

The deputy's car rolled through the gate and Torre followed him around the camp road until they came to a plaza in the middle of the grounds.

"Where's all the campers?" Torre asked to no one in particular as he scanned the grounds and parked the rig.

"On lock-down," Captain White replied over the headset. "Just got that update from Smith, she's the site lead." As they all clambered out of the truck he reminded the crew, "Respirators and extra tanks, everyone!"

Torre strapped on his respirator tank then slung the mask and line across his shoulder before following Captain White. Cat was already heading around to the back of the building for an initial assessment while the captain was checking in with Sergeant Smith with the Rangers.

Torre listened to the quick download of details from Smith. "Good thinking on the chopper," he said, complimenting her original thinking. "That's going to shorten the amount of time it will take us to clear the air."

"Here's the real problem," Smith said, ignoring the quality of air issue. She glanced at her watch. We suspect the three missing kids got padlocked in around nine or nine-o-five. It's been almost an hour now. There's no re-circ fan in there, thank goodness, or they'd be dead by now. Bad news is, they're getting drowsy and probably starting to experience hypothermia." She called Tyler over.

"This is Tyler; he's a camper here and he's good friend of the three kids inside. He's gotten several texts from one of the trapped kids, his friend Alex. Show them the last one, Tyler."

Tyler held up his digital watch for them to read: *super cold man, can't think straight. m'nca sleeping n mac talking crazy. hurry, k?*

"Cold talk and oxygen deprivation, both," Torre said, shaking his head.

Cat jogged over to report on inside. "Nice prelim job on trying to clear some of the gas," he said, "but that's a big building with the dining hall and all. We're still too high on the methane count to bring in any cutting tools. We could try the hand pump bolt cutter but that could still spark when the bolt breaker makes its final snap."

"Same issue if we super-freeze the metal to shatter it . . . I just can't do a fast rescue in a gas-filled room with a lock in the way!" Torre said, his frustration showing. Suddenly something about the building caught his eye. Now he was looking more closely at the building's construction. "It's a cinder block building," he commented, quickly putting together a plan in his head. "Where's the walk-in fridge?"

"Rear corner over there on the back side," Cat replied nodding his head. "I think I like where you're heading."

As soon as they had briefed Captain White on the idea, he simply said, "Do it." White called out to two of the men who were standing by for orders to get the two, big twenty-inch cutters and follow Torre over to the far side of the dining hall-kitchen building. "Cat, bring us a pickax and a couple of shovels."

"What's going on?" Tyler asked, confused.

"Going in the 'back door,' son. But first, we'll have to *make* a back door."

Tyler caught on when he saw the big cutters that looked like a portable chain saw except with giant pizza-sized cutting wheels instead of limb-cutting chains.

"Tyler, is it?" White asked.

"Yes, sir."

"Text your friend in there. Tell him we're coming through the outside wall. Get him excited, tell him to move stuff. He probably can't, but he needs a dose of adrenalin about now and that might help him, okay?"

"Got it."

Tyler went over to a bench where he could watch what they were doing but stay out of the way. Soon, two cutters were revving at a high-pitch whine, cutting through the blocks like they were butter. The two firemen traced a series of deep cuts about four feet wide and four feet high. When the outline was complete, the other two firemen started swinging their pickaxes to break out the wall.

Tyler started texting Alex.

alex, its cool, they're using chainsaws with blades like big pizzas to cut thru the wall

dude, I hear em! Alex texted back.

monica still asleep?

yes. macs tryn to wake her up

theyre breaking up the wall with picks!

yeah. noisy

can u c anythng yet?

o cool, a big chunk just fell in!

hang in there, alex

dude, you did it! oh man, that air smells so sweet

looks like theyre about to crawl thru

monica needs some air, t. shes still asleep

Tyler showed the string to Smith who radioed Captain White of the Rescue Response crew to let him know one of the kids was really out of it and looking non-responsive. She needed air fast!

As the rescue team pulled away the last big chunks of debris and thick insulation board, Tyler could see them shining big work lights into the hole. It was hard to see all the details from where he was, but he did see Torres crawl into the hole carrying an extra portable respirator on his shoulder.

"Stretcher!" Torres called out from the hole. The ambulance that had been trailing them by five minutes had arrived and the EMTs hurried over with a stretcher board which they slid through the opening in the wall. Moments later five workers carefully slid it back out with one of the girls, wrapped in a blanket, strapped to it. She had a respirator over her face and the EMTs quickly hustled her into the ambulance. Tyler couldn't see for sure, but he guessed it was Monica.

Next, Tyler saw someone more like his size crawling out the hole and over the rubble—it was Alex! As he got to where he could stand up, he lifted his arms in the air to celebrate. His enthusiasm was short-lived though because he was dizzy and almost fell over. One of the EMTs and a fireman grabbed him to steady him and handed him a portable oxygen bottle like football players use on the sidelines. When he'd caught his breath, the EMTs walked him over to a waiting ambulance. Tyler tried to wave and get his attention but Alex didn't see him.

The workers from the ambulance brought over another stretcher board to shove through the hole in the wall. It seemed like it took forever, but finally it reemerged with Mac securely belted to it and wrapped in a blanket. She had a mask strapped to her face but she was looking around.

"Mac! Over here!" Tyler shouted. She looked over his direction and spotted him. Even though she couldn't speak or wave, he saw her nod her head before they got her into the ambulance where Alex was being looked at.

Charlie and Kelley had finally been asked to come over to the plaza ASAP and they came running over just as Mac was transferred from the stretcher board to an ambulance gurney. Tyler was glad to see them and fought back some emotions that were building up inside.

Kelley put her arm around his shoulder. "Hey, it's okay. They're safe now. They're going to be all right."

"They're my best friends," Tyler said, on the verge of breaking out in sobs. "They're my best friends and I thought I'd lost 'em!"

"Hey, now. It's okay." Charlie said, sitting on Tyler's other side. "Thanks to you, everyone here was able to get them out in time. I'm thinking they couldn't ask for a better friend than you. And that makes you their hero, too."

"Not sure I like being a hero all the time. It gets a little freaky to do big things like that."

"You mean like flying that plane and landing it earlier this summer?" Charlie said, getting a big smile on his face. "I heard about that."

"Actually, I read about it, too," Kelley said. "Two big saves in one summer is a pretty tall order, I guess."

"Yeah, well, like you say, at least they're safe." He took a deep breath and a drink of water from the bottle they gave him. He was starting to feel some of the emotion lift but he really enjoyed the encouragement.

He heard Sergeant Smith calling his name. "Tyler, I need you over here, please!" Tyler jumped up and walked quickly to the Ranger. "Alex is asking for you," she said. "They're going to take him to the hospital to get fully checked out. EMTs are telling me that all three of your friends are going to be kept overnight for observation. Monica's had it a little worse than the other two, but the paramedics say she's going to be fine. Go say hi to your friends and then we'll have you and your counselor get on the phone with your aunt and uncle. Mr. Murkowski is talking with them right now."

"Thanks," he mumbled and followed her to the back of the second ambulance. The door was open and Alex was sitting on a bench inside with a huge smile on his face. Mac had her oxygen mask off and gave him a smile and a big thumbs-up, too.

"Dude, you were amazing!" Alex said loudly, pulling Tyler over to him and giving him a big bear hug. "I thought we were goners there for a little bit but you came through, man. Just like clockwork."

"Thank you, Tyler. Not sure I'd have lasted much longer, and Monica almost didn't make it." Mac added. She looked at him and smiled but was starting to get drowsy. This time it wasn't from lack of oxygen; she was simply exhausted.

The EMT was ready to get rolling but Alex motioned for him to hang on a second. "Quick question, Tyler—why the wall? What was wrong with the door?"

Tyler shook his head. "Too long of a story for tonight, Alex. I'll fill you in tomorrow." Then he decided to at least give him a hint: "But think natural gas and big explosions and you'll get the picture."

"So *that's* what I'm smelling out here. Whoa!"

Tyler stepped down from the van and went back over to wait with Charlie and Kelley. Together they watched as the two ambulances pulled away to drive Mac, Monica and Alex to the hospital.

They really are going to be okay, he realized. But as the emotion began to subside, he decided he was pretty much ready for camp to be done. Ready to get back home and spend time at the neighborhood pool and cruise on his skateboard. *I'm ready to sleep in my own bed. And I'm really ready to not be anyone's super-hero!* That last thought brought a smile to his face. *Well, then again, at least maybe not until next summer.*

51

SOMETIMES, THE BAD GUYS TRY TO GET AWAY . . .

Presley Clarke had watched enough movies to know how things fall apart—badly, when someone tries to escape on foot. Eventually it's the hound dogs or the choppers or the drones or some helpful convenience store clerk—just as the escapee thinks they're home free. That was *not* going to be his story, not tonight! *Nope, he was a genius and the cops chasing him were amateurs.*

He'd sensed something was falling apart when Derrick called yesterday. There was that odd digital pause the call made when they'd hung up that worried him. Plus, all the questions and interest in what exactly he was up to . . . questions that Derrick never asked and never wanted to know. Somebody might have been listening in or maybe he was being set up.

And then there was his stuff. That kid Monica and her two pals, they'd been too nosy. And the kicker was last night when he'd gone to get his big firecrackers out of the boat shed. He could tell his bike tarp had been messed with. That was his final warning. Sure, he'd gone ahead and set up the firecracker barrels. *And why not?* If they hadn't called off the show, it would have been a big, spectacular event! And those big booms would surely have ignited his grand finale: "the Gas Leak Accident!"

None of that mattered, now. He'd played a double "stay-out-of-jail" card with Derrick instead. It took some doing, but he'd managed to call Derrick on his direct office line instead of his cell. And he knew people like Derrick and what made them tick. If the cops were after Derrick to get him to flip, well, a simple counter-deal could save him all the terrible headaches and aggravation of an investigation, testifying at a trial, some sort of prosecution, loss of reputation . . . blah, blah, blah.

And me? I walk away with a cool million. Maybe not the 65 million I'd hoped for, but a million bucks all the same!

But as Presley rehearsed his success in his head, he also recognized that he still had to make it to the old hay shed on the far side of FM 2135. He had a pic on his phone, texted two hours ago, of the pickup truck at the shed: a black RAM 4WD, all topped off and waiting for him—courtesy of Derrick Ball.

He kept his eye focused on his trail. He'd prepared it early this afternoon, spilling bits of white flour along the way that now popped out like a neon highway in the beam of his ultraviolet flashlight. The cops could struggle with their searchlights and flashlights and trails trying to navigate the woods in the dark while he took an off-trail shortcut they'd never find.

For now at least, there hadn't been enough time to call in the hound dogs, thank goodness! The helicopter that had arrived on the scene ten minutes ago was sweeping the floor of the woods in the ravine with their big searchlight. They were using a methodical pattern, but it would take time for them to make their way to the far eastern edge of the woods.

Presley stopped long enough to get a quick drink of water, then continued on up the last hill that led to the ridge line, and then beyond to the road. He looked back from the height. Through the breaks in the tree canopy he could see high-powered flashlights at work. He counted at least a dozen trackers now looking for him. He smiled, knowing they were all headed in the wrong direction. He looked both ways before crossing the narrow country road, which was clear. No cops parked up here. Of course not. They were all over on the north side of the ranch. He felt so good about how all this was going that he could feel a giggle welling up inside. He stifled it.

There was a quarter-moon in the sky tonight and in its partial light he spotted the hay shed in the field beyond, the one he'd told Derrick about. He jogged along the side of the road until he got to a cattle gate. It was unchained. Derrick had followed all the instructions!

Presley swung the gate open and then set out at a jogger's pace on the gravel road up to the truck. He wanted to get this over with. He figured if he could make it to Georgetown tonight, he could find a motel and then take his time making his way north back to Canada tomorrow. There was still the challenge of getting into Canada as a fugitive, but he had plenty of time to sort that out!

A million dollars, though! He smiled at the thought. That was chump change—nothing, really to a guy like Derrick. And look what it bought him: no Presley, no trial, no questionable involvement with attempted fraud. It was all so clean and simple. All Derrick had to do was wire the money to Presley's bank in Canada and buy him a decent pickup truck.

He pulled out his phone to look at his screen capture of the bank page once more: *$1,014,293.63 CD.* The $14,293 was his own money, *but just look at that!* Maybe he'd print the page and frame it some day!

The truck was exactly what he'd been promised. Black and relatively new, but not so shiny new as to attract attention. He felt on top of the back tire on the passenger side and found the remote control for the starter. *Perfect.* He started to push the unlock button but wondered how loud it was going to be, then looked around and reminded himself there was no one out here tonight—just him. Well, at least for another twenty or thirty minutes. *Then they'll realize they need to widen their search. But I'll be long gone.*

The truck made a small chirping sound as the doors unlocked and he got in and started it up. *This was so sweet!* He'd always wanted a pickup truck when he grew up. *No more twenty-year-old, cast-off minivan!* He shifted it into gear and started to roll down the gravel road to the gate. He'd left it open so he wouldn't have to stop. Presley did pause to double check that there were no headlights coming from around the bend on the road beyond him. Nothing. He accelerated and headed south. Presley gave a slight nudge to the steering wheel as he began to make the curve and suddenly found himself slamming on his brakes.

Two sets of headlights lit up from the two cars blocking the road in front of him. The headlights were immediately followed by red and blue police lights. Presley quickly looked over his shoulder, ready to shift into reverse and try to get away, but it was no use. There were already two more cars that had pulled up behind him when he'd skidded to a stop. He was blocked in.

Two sheriffs' officers and a Texas Ranger appeared on foot approaching his truck. All three wore a standard issue, cream white, working cowboy hat and had their weapons in hand, pointed his way. Behind his truck, several more officers had their shotguns in hand as backup. The officers ordered him to put his hands on his head and he decided that was probably an excellent suggestion, so he did as he was told.

One officer opened the door while the other two continued to cover him. "Mr. Clarke," the Ranger said, "please step out of the truck and keep your hands in plain sight. You're under arrest."

52

LABOR DAY

"Dang . . . it's hot out here!"

Tyler twisted his head to look at Alex who was stretched out on a sun lounger beside Monica's pool. "Dude, you told me you were never going to say that again."

"Yeah?" Alex asked with an air of innocence. He lifted his Ray Bans for a moment to glance at Tyler then set them back in place to block the sun. "When?"

"In the ambulance. After the EMT had given you that warming blanket and a hot water bottle."

"Really? Hmmm." He continued to lay motionless in his lounger with his face observing the cloudless west Texas sky. "Must have lied."

That got a laugh out of Tyler. He knew better than to imagine *anyone* could actually love the Texas heat enough to *never* say it was too hot. You had to say that at least once a day, every day, all summer long.

Sandra Morrison-Parker walked over carrying a tall iced tea glass with a lemon and a festive party umbrella resting in a straw.

"Mind if I join you two?" she asked, before having a seat in the armchair beside them.

"Please do!" Alex said, sitting up and raising the lounge chair to its upright position.

"Are you enjoying Monica's cookout?" Tyler asked, taking a big slug of his ginger ale.

"Yes, as a matter of fact, I am. It was very kind of Monica's parents to put this little soiree together and to invite me and Mike and Chuck. I'm sorry Charlie couldn't make it, but I did spot Kelley and Zoe to say hi. Where's Mac, by the way?"

"My cousin Kyle had to run Leslie to the airport to catch her flight to Boston. Mac and Monica decided to ride along to say goodbye."

"They should be back pretty soon," Alex said, "it's only fifteen minutes from here."

"I was proud of her for getting the journalism scholarship for this fall," Sandra observed. "She's a very impressive young woman."

"Uh huh," Tyler said, trying to sound interested but not really sure he knew what else to say.

She glanced at Alex and then Tyler and then back towards the swimming pool. "Certainly is hot out here, isn't it?" Sandra said, took a sip of her tea then set it down. "But enough college chit-chat. Can I count on the two of you to join us again at Camp Tonkawa next summer? Maybe give it another go without all the drama found in a major motion picture?"

"You can count me in!" Tyler said enthusiastically. "Apart from the Crazy Presley stuff it was a lot of fun."

"For sure," Alex, said, toying with the earpiece of his Ray Bans. "Any update on all that? Monica said there had been a conference call between all our parents and the Burnet County prosecutor last week— something about some kind of a plea deal."

"Well, yes. I think you'll be getting a formal notification soon, but if you'd like an early read out, I trust the two of you to wait until you see it in print to discuss it with anyone else."

"No problem-o," Alex winked.

"You did your research on the Hoffmeier Compact which established the land trust for the camp, so you're generally familiar with its terms, correct?" she asked.

"Yeah. The clause about it going back to direct blood relatives if the camp ever closed . . . that was Presley's motive for trying to wreck the camp's reputation and cause an impossible to forget incident that scared off campers and parents," Alex summarized.

"He planned to file for possession and then sell it to that real estate developer in Austin, right?" Tyler added.

"Exactly, gentlemen. A reasonable precaution on the part of Mr. Hoffmeier at the time the grant was written, to create a fall back to avoid an unscrupulous board from selling the ranch, but not exactly helpful almost a century later when a greedy great-great-grandson decides to exploit the clause."

"So what now? I know you had to shorten the final summer session when they sent us all home."

"The camp will survive just fine." Her voice was quite confident. "In fact, my lawyer has been working out an arrangement that will fix some of the loose ends of the Hoffmeier grant. I suspect it will make the popular news in the next week or two once it is all official and complete."

"And . . ." Alex teased, hopefully, "you're going to give us an idea of *what* that arrangement's going to look like?"

"Indeed, I will. You two are quite endearing so I'd love to share my little secret with someone." She winked at Alex and took a long sip of her iced tea, then looked at them as if sharing a covert secret between spies. She touched her finger to her lips and then began by raising her pointer finger like she was counting.

"Problem number one was the old compact itself. It has that terrible dangling clause about blood relatives. The purpose was simply to ensure the camp's board could never profit by selling the land, but the major certainly never intended to incent a hostile takeover by a future great-great-grandson."

She added a second finger to her count. "Problem number two was that the old man simply wanted to honor the memory and legacy of the Tonkawa Tribe. So much has changed over the years, but in his day, he never involved them directly as one would, today." She shook her head with a pause. "That was a sad oversight on his part, but understandable."

"And problem three?" Tyler asked expectantly.

She grinned and added a third finger to her count. "Problem three is more pragmatic. That is, even though there is only one true blood heir left, without his consent to change the grant, he is still a potential legal obstacle."

"Hmm," Alex nodded, thinking through all these pieces.

"And the solution?" Tyler asked, cutting to the chase.

Sandra laughed. "Why, to tear up the old agreement, of course! And then build a better, modern agreement which addresses each of those problems."

"That's what lawyers are for," Tyler said, having learned a lot about lawyers after their lost silver mine adventure earlier in the summer.

"Yes, that's what makes them worth the dollars you pay them— and I pay Travis very well for his services, I might add."

Alex and Tyler laughed. They both remembered meeting Sandra's lawyer, Travis Maguire, back in July in his fancy downtown office with the cool views from his top-of-the-skyscraper windows.

"Travis had a conversation with the Burnet County prosecutor. Based on the prosecutor's favorable point of view, he had a chat with the current president of the Tonkawa tribe to discuss the framework of a new arrangement. Then, with those bits in place, he called one of his law school alums who works in the governor's office these days to see if there were any theoretical objections the State of Texas might have to his plan."

"And . . .?" Tyler prompted.

"They had none."

"Okay, it's complicated, I get that," Alex said, almost pleading, "but you're killing me, what's the actual plan?"

"Oh. Well, simple enough," Sandra said after another drink of tea. "Presley's attorney and the prosecutor have come to an understanding on a proposed plea agreement. Presley will still be charged with a number of felonies and do some serious prison time—but rather than the three counts of kidnapping and attempted murder he'll instead be charged with three counts each of imprisonment and reckless endangerment."

"For locking Mac and Monica and Alex in the fridge?"

"Yes, plus another fourteen counts of reckless endangerment for the bridge incident."

"Wow!" Tyler said.

"So, he's agreed to plead guilty to all those charges?" Alex asked, double checking he understood the plan.

"Yes, but he and his attorney understand the only reason he's being offered the deal at all is that he must agree—and has agreed, to waive any objections to the proposed restructuring of the original Hoffmeier agreement and to forever vacate any claimed rights."

"But he's still going to jail, right?" Tyler asked, just to be certain he was tracking the details right.

"Absolutely, dear. He's pleading guilty to a total of twenty felony counts. Why, he'll likely be in his late forties or early fifties when he finally makes parole. But then, of course, the other charges would likely have carried three life sentences if he'd been convicted by a jury."

"And so you tear up the Hoffmeier Compact and what replaces it?" Tyler asked. He was starting to think he might want to study law someday.

"Well, now, here's how that works. The State of Texas, on behalf of the camp board and in keeping with the *spirit of intent* of the original grant, will recommend to a state district judge that the original grant be vacated in favor of a new grant."

"Okay, and that means . . . ?"

"The new grant will transfer the ranch property to the Tonkawa tribe as a gift that comes with a pre-agreement between the Tonkawa tribal government and the camp's board to grant the camp board a ninety-nine year concession to manage the land as the summer camp on their behalf, just as Major Hoffmeier originally intended. And, of course, the board will be restructured to include members of the tribe to provide leadership to the camp's programming and strategic direction." She relaxed and sat back in her chair before taking another long sip of her iced tea.

"Wow." Alex said, nodding his head. "That's an arrangement that Charlie will be proud of. I know he's a big fan of the Tonkawa tribe and their heritage."

"I'll let you in on a secret—but don't tell Travis," Sandra said with a secretive smile. "It was partly Charlie's idea that took us in this direction."

"No way!" Tyler said, totally surprised.

"Yes, way!" Sandra said with a laugh that caught both Tyler and Alex off guard.

"So, like, it's really all a done deal?" Alex asked.

"As done as the nuts and bolts of a deal ever are until the ink is dry. Presley's plea deal has been agreed to by his attorney, and your mom as well as Monica's and Mac's parents have signed off on the prosecutor's recommendation, too. Only thing left is for Presley to appear in court on Wednesday and plead guilty to the slightly reduced charges."

"Okay,"

"Once that hearing is closed, Travis tells me he's got a slot reserved on the district court docket for September 20. If the judge approves it —and, since the State of Texas is endorsing it, he likely will, the new grant to the Tonkawa tribal council can be completed before the end of the month."

"Sounds complicated." Tyler shook his head and looked over at Alex who was distracted by something, but he couldn't tell what.

"It is complicated, Tyler, but in the end, it will be worth it," she said. Sandra gazed at the pool and they each sat in silence for a moment before she suddenly added, "Oh, and Elsa, my 'PR Meister' called me this morning to say she has been in contact with a reporter from a major *Texas magazine* about a feature story describing the unique land deal we've put together with the Tonkawa tribe. They sound pretty excited!"

"Hopefully they leave out the part about the kids locked in the meat locker!" Tyler said to Sandra with a grin.

"Stop it, Tyler," Alex corrected him for the fourth time this week, "it was a walk-in fridge—not a meat locker!"

"No, dear." Sandra laughed. "There'll be no dirty laundry or distraction from the really important story. The point will be all about the Tonkawa tribe's heritage here in Texas being honored and the history they had in Texas before the Comanche and the Apache tribes arrived—"

"And before the Tonkawa people got moved to Oklahoma—twice, by the way!" Alex added quickly.

"Yes, that too," agreed Sandra.

"Well, I'm happy for Charlie," Tyler said, satisfied. "Maybe after we graduate from high school, Alex and I can be counselors at the camp like him."

"And maybe Mac and Monica too?" Sandra asked. She glanced over to the patio doors and noticed the two girls stepping outside onto the pool deck. "And speaking of the two, here they are," she added.

The two spotted Sandra and waved, then walked over to join her and the boys. Sandra stood to offer a French *bisou-bisou* kiss on both cheeks to the girls as they walked up.

"Did you get Leslie safely delivered to her plane?" Sandra asked.

"Yes, but she's got a long trip ahead of her today!" Mac replied.

"El Paso to Dallas, then Dallas to Boston," Monica added. "I think she said she'd land there about 11:40 tonight, Boston time."

"Still, very exciting for her to be stepping into a special scholarship for her junior year. That should help her land a wonderful internship next summer."

"You mean—no Leslie at camp next summer?" Monica asked, just realizing what *getting an internship next summer* meant for next summer's camp.

"I'll miss her!" Mac said.

"She's very sharp and she'll be missed by all of us next summer," Sandra agreed, then changed the subject. "So, the two of you will be back next summer, too? In spite of such an unusual end to camp this year?"

"That's not the camp's fault!" Monica said. "That Presley guy is just totally whacko!"

"Well, I'm pleased we'll be keeping one of our legacy campers and gained three returning second-year alums!" Sandra smiled. She picked up her almost empty glass of iced tea and then glanced across the pool to spot Big Mike, who gave her a friendly wave.

"Are you leaving, so soon?" Monica asked.

"Indeed, I think it's time," Sandra said. "The brisket taco spread was amazing. Your dad is quite the grill master, Monica! And Alex, I loved your guacamole. It was seasoned perfectly." She took the final sip of her tea. "Still, it's getting to be late afternoon, so it's time for me to get home and review my schedule for next week."

Turning back she added, "We'll be in touch, soon."

"Bye," they all said in unison.

"Cool lady," Alex observed when Sandra had stepped inside the house.

"Yeah, hope I'm that classy when I'm her age," Mac said.

"Pretty smart deal her lawyer put together," Tyler said.

"What deal?" Monica asked.

Tyler and Alex spent the next ten minutes explaining the big plan to Monica and Mac. Finally Monica leaned back in her chair and acted exhausted. "My brain hurts from all your legal junk, Alex, please just stop!" She feigned the distraught diva with perfect drama and then added: "It's just . . . well, it's just so dang hot!"

Tyler and Alex laughed, looked at each other and nodded. Each knew what the other was thinking. Before Monica could figure what was up, Tyler grabbed her legs and Alex got hold of her arms and the two of them tossed her into the pool with a big, messy, wet splash! Then, to add insult to injury—they both ran and jumped in, holding their knees to make the biggest splash possible to swamp her. Not willing to be left out, Mac slipped off her flip-flops and ran in after them, adding yet another splash.

After a lot of dunking, splashing, and pool-play, Tyler swam over to the edge of the pool to watch his cousin and friends. He glanced up at the bright Texas sky and felt the warm sun on his wet skin. *Summer might be over,* he realized, *but the fun was only just beginning!*

ACKNOWLEDGMENTS

As an author, I'm constantly reminded of the awkward balance between having good fun with my fictional characters while staying relatively credible in settings and detail. So, as in my first two books in this series, let me say that all of the characters in this book are fictional and none are intended to be mistaken for any actual person, living or dead.

Second, as you might imagine, there is no actual Camp Tonkawa near Marble Falls or anywhere else in Burnet County Texas. However, the Balcones region of the Texas Hill Country along Texas State Highway 1431 between Marble Falls and Round Rock, Texas near Austin is a beautiful part of the State of Texas. It is in this beautiful area that I have set the story. Sitting along the Colorado River, this location would be within the general, expansive boundaries where Texas historians place the Tonkawa Tribe prior to the arrival of the Apache and then the Comanche tribes.

With the arrival of European settlers, the Tonkawa territory continued to shrink to an area roughly between the Colorado and Brazos River watersheds here in Texas. After the Republic of Texas joined the United States, federal agencies relocated the tribe to other parts of Texas and twice moved them to Oklahoma, once before the Civil War and a second and final time after the Civil War. The tribal headquarters today are near Tonkawa, Oklahoma, a town named in their honor—over 450 miles north of the Colorado River Valley where this story is set.

I want to thank the Tonkawa Tribe's President and Executive Committee for allowing me permission to use their name in association with a fictional Texas summer camp in this adventure story.

It is my hope that in some small way, this exposure—even if fictional, will create an opportunity for young readers to learn about, and to honor, the memory of the Tonkawa Tribe's legacy here in the State of Texas. Many thanks also to Bob O'Dell of Austin who provided invaluable assistance in vetting my historical and cultural references related to the Tonkawa Tribe and offered helpful insights in the preparation of my final manuscript.

Next, I note that I've once again created a number of professional characterizations herein of deputies, EMT's, Texas Rangers and other first responders whose actions play key roles in the telling of this story. Please know that I hold the men and women represented by these characters in the highest regard. As an author, I love the potential for these characters to serve as role models for a generation of young readers.

That said, as I've deployed these fictional characters from the Burnet County Sheriff's Department and the Texas State Rangers, I suspect I may have made errors in protocol or tactics or possibly in professional approaches. If so, please have a smile at my expense and know that any mistakes made were without malice or intent.

Next, I want to thank my daughter, Stacey Marx, and her life-long best friend—Leslie Roddy Clancy for their incredibly helpful insights into the traditional Texas summer camp experience. Both served as summer camp counselors during college. The fun stories they shared with me helped to credibly shape the experiences that Tyler, Alex, Mac, and Monica have at camp in this story.

Professionally, my sincere appreciation and gratitude to Sandy Chapman, who has edited all three books in this series and along the way taught me so much as a newbie author. Thank you for investing in me and in these stories! I'm also indebted to my brother Chris, who received the graphic creativity gene in our family and has time and again stepped up to help in art and design. Brenda Elsbury, one of my early readers suggested I provide a map of the camp to accompany the story—thanks for encouraging me to include that!

And finally, as always, my thanks to the resident muse of our household—Anita, who listens to chapters as they come hot off the laptop and encourages me at every turn. It is such a blessing that she enjoys helping me sort through the sundry dilemmas of storytelling that authors regularly encounter. Writing is fun only if someone enjoys it, and Anita is my first reader and biggest cheerleader.

Dave Owen, May 2024

NOTE: As of the publication date for the first edition of this book, the website for *Texas Highways* magazine offered archive access to an article they published in December 2023 titled: "The Original Texans." This article includes comments from Bob O'Dell (who was a tremendous help to me as I prepared my manuscript for this book), and is a great resource for a brief history of the Tonkawa history in Texas.

https://texashighways.com/culture/recoginzing-local-history-tonkawa-tribe-the-original-texans/

Members of the Tonkawa tribe in 1898 as reproduced from Tonkawa tribal archives and published in the December 2023 edition of Texas Highways.

ABOUT THE AUTHOR

Dave Owen is the author of two previous adventure fiction stories in the El Paso Summer series—*Sky High Danger* and *Desert Danger*, and a short novella titled *Ready or Not, Christmas Comes*. Before retiring, he was a digital marketing professional with a Fortune 500 company. These days—when he's not writing, he spends his time pursuing hobbies, passions, projects and enjoying life's adventures with his wife, Anita. They have three adult children and five grandkids nearby in the Dallas area.